I0557239

Other Books by David Lee Summers

The Solar Sea
The Astronomer's Crypt

The Space Pirates' Legacy Series
Firebrandt's Legacy
The Pirates of Sufiro
Children of the Old Stars
Heirs of the New Earth

The Clockwork Legion Series
Owl Dance
Lightning Wolves
The Brazen Shark
Owl Riders

The Scarlet Order Vampires Series
Dragon's Fall: Rise of the Scarlet Order Vampires
Vampires of the Scarlet Order

Heirs of the New Earth

David Lee Summers

Hadrosaur Productions, Mesilla Park, NM

Heirs of the New Earth
Hadrosaur Productions
Second Edition: February 2022.

First date of publication: February 2007
Copyright © 2022 David Lee Summers
Cover Art Copyright © 2022 Laura Givens

ISBN-13: 979-8-9851120-1-6

Hadrosaur Productions
P.O. Box 2194
Mesilla Park, NM 88047-2194
www.hadrosaur.com

This is a work of fiction. Names, characters, places, and incidents are either the product of the author's imagination or are used fictitiously, and any resemblance to any person or persons, living or dead, events or locales is entirely coincidental.

To Kenneth and Shirley Summers
– Dad and Mom –
for teaching me to care about the world and its people,
for teaching me to dream,
for being there,
for everything.

Acknowledgments

I started the "Space Pirates' Legacy" in 1988 as an exercise for a writer's group in Socorro, New Mexico. It began as a humble short story – less than 2000 words – entitled, "The Privateer's License." The story ultimately grew into "The Smoldering Ember" – the first chapter of *The Pirates of Sufiro*, which was published as an audio book in 1994 and a mass-market paperback in 1997. The first edition of this novel, *Heirs of the New Earth*, appeared on the tenth anniversary of *Pirates'* first publication. Now this second edition appears on the fifteenth anniversary of its own first publication.

Thirty-four years is a long time and many people deserve thanks for helping with this novel and this series. However, two people have been there for the whole ride and they deserve thanks above all for their help and support over all these years: Kumie Wise and William Grother. I couldn't have done it without you two.

I started *Heirs of the New Earth* soon after the first publication of *Pirates'* sequel, *Children of the Old Stars*. In that book, Commander John Mark Ellis was booted out of the military when he failed to save a spaceship from an alien intelligence called the Cluster. The story told how Ellis came to terms with what happened to him. As the story ended, the Cluster took control of the Earth. This novel describes what happens next.

Over the course of writing the novel, there were many false starts. More than with any other novel, I wrote myself into corners that seemed insoluble. However, each time that happened, someone would come along and ask about the sequel to *Children of the Old Stars*. The list of people who asked would be a long one – and it amazes me to think about it. I want to say thanks to each and every one of them. That said, two people stand out in my mind and have given the most encouragement and have been asking for this book almost since *Children* first appeared: Bret Badgett and Gary Every. You guys are the greatest.

Many thanks go to Jacqueline Druga-Johnston, editor-in-chief of LBF Books when *Heirs* was first published. Not only did she believe in this series since she first discovered it in 2004, but she provided insight and structure to the series and made it better than it would have been otherwise.

A very special thanks goes to Laura Givens, who has been the cover artist for all four novels of the series. Not only has she given these books a uniform and dynamic appearance, but she's breathed new life into the locations and characters that have been populating my consciousness for the last thirty-four years. Scenes in this book are directly influenced by Laura's vision of this universe and I'm proud that she's been part of the team that's made this book possible.

This book was also created with the generous support of my Patreon supporters. Among them are Robert E. Vardeman, John D. Payne, Anthony D. Cardno and the Creative Play and Podcast Network. I'm pleased to have received their support and comments through the process of revisiting the Space Pirates' Legacy Series.

Heirs of the
New Earth

Prologue

THE CLUSTER

It has been over thirty million years since I last felt anything. I have no arms to lift, nor legs to run. I have no mouth to take in nourishment, no tongue to savor it. I have no skin or hair to feel a soft, cool breeze. While I have the urge to replicate, I have no vagina to accept the loving gift of genetic material from another of my kind, nor do I possess a uterus to cultivate another living being. I am intelligence without appendage, but not without body.

What body I have floats through the void. It evolved somewhere near time's beginning and took the primordial form of a cluster of spheres, mirroring the star cluster whose plasma and gravity conspired to give me life. I was like an island universe, all to myself, drifting from star to star. The electromagnetic energies coursing their way through my body of encased plasma assumed an order and I began to sense the wider universe. I came to understand that no woman is an island and I made a conscious effort to explore. I found purpose in trying to understand stellar orbits around the cluster's core, understanding the stellar cluster's place in the universe, and trying to determine whether or not other sentient things existed.

I discovered I could replicate myself with sufficient energy. My progeny share my memories. As a result, each of us sees ourselves as the original of our kind. We all remember our origin as though we had experienced it. None of us knows who is the original. Likewise none is certain the original still exists. Because the memory lives within us all, it doesn't matter to us who was the original.

I discovered planets – rocky and gaseous bodies that orbited stars. On some planets, I found entities who moved about and replicated much as my sisters and I had. However, some

1

entities did not replicate by duplication. Rather they came together in various combinations and shared components of themselves to make new and different versions. With time, these organisms evolved into new organisms.

We observed a difference between evolving organisms and ourselves. Instead of simply recording the universe, they reacted to it in ways we had not considered. While they had much shorter lives than we did, they possessed qualities that enhanced their purpose. On one particular carbon dioxide and nitrogen shrouded planet, we observed living organisms for over a hundred thousand years. They walked upright and hair covered their bodies. Despite possessing larger teeth than many evolving organisms we had observed, these organisms were not carnivores, rather they consumed their world's methane ice. They retained these characteristics even after they began to make tools that made their fur coats and their teeth unnecessary. When they began to perceive our existence, we communed with them.

During our communion, the organisms learned more about the universe than they had ever known before. Their minds could travel to every star system we had visited. Likewise, while communing, we could feel their emotions. We shared the organisms' delight in their expanded knowledge. We had the ability to help the organisms order their existence and improve it.

When we broke communion with the organisms, we found them diminished. They had better tools, better lives, but not the experience to improve upon what we had given them. In the same way, we remembered feelings, but could not experience new emotion without the organisms.

Thus, we formed a symbiosis with these sensual organisms that lasted for many centuries. The organisms learned to build vessels with which to explore the universe on their own. We gained imagination that enabled us to interpret all we had observed in new and unique ways. While communing with these organisms we felt as though we had appendages. Cool wind blew through the fur of our faces. We shared intimate relations. We experienced birth and holding a beautiful child – like us, but different – in our arms. For the first time in our existence, we could express ourselves. We knew what it was to leave a legacy.

Thirty million years ago, the stellar cluster in which I make my home passed through a larger body of stars shaped like a whirlpool. Our appendages broke their communion with us in the alien galaxy. Without them, we Clusters wandered lost and alone, with only our memories of emotion and sensuality.

Though there are others of my kind, we are so alike that communion with one another is pointless. Without the appendages, some of my kind lost their will to continue and threw themselves into the hearts of stars. I do not know whether that would kill my kind or not, as we were formed from stellar matter. However, our outer shell would likely vaporize and our plasma cores would merge with the star. I do not know whether that is the same as what the appendages call death or not.

As time passed, our stellar cluster's orbit allowed us to jump to the point where our appendages abandoned us. However, a galaxy is a daunting and huge place – much larger than our star cluster. We pondered the odds of finding our appendages again. Despite the low odds, the benefits of having our appendages back spurred us to look for them.

As my sisters and I searched, we encountered many star vessels, which resembled the ones our appendages had built. Examining the vessels, we found no evidence of the appendages but we continued to explore anyway. As the search continued, an emotional disturbance shook the void. Terrible violence overwhelmed me. Only organisms as sensual as the appendages could have caused emotions so great. I went to investigate, but did not find the appendages. Instead, I found strange beings that combined intelligence with an ability to order their own lives using appendages. Sensuality governed their intelligence. I wondered whether the old appendages had evolved, but suspected these organisms were not related to them.

I reached out to two of the beings, I discovered these organisms called the planet they occupied Sufiro and they had just concluded a conflict among themselves. Conflict perplexed me, because my appendages never fought among themselves and I did not fight with my sisters. These new organisms proved quite interesting. They bore watching. They called themselves humans.

In short order, I learned these beings traversed much of the galaxy. Later, I found one I had met at the world called Sufiro aboard a spaceship at a strange new place where two stars orbited one another. One star spewed its gaseous plasma toward the other in an act of almost loving violence. These two stars orbited one another, locked in a gravitational and magnetic dance. It reminded me of the humans themselves.

I brought the human, who called himself John Mark Ellis, to my bosom. His sensuality breathed new life into me. These humans showed more promise than the old appendages. The human's emotion stirred my long-suppressed imagination and I decided to give up my quest for the old appendages. Upon communing with this John Mark Ellis, I realized I wanted new appendages.

The gravity tides carried me away from the whirlpool galaxy. However, tides ebb and flow. I knew I would be back to learn more about these humans.

Upon my return home, I meditated. Ellis and others of his kind demonstrated much variation – like my three sisters and I experienced after our contact with the original appendages. As I knew they would, the gravitational tides allowed me to return to the whirlpool galaxy and somehow John Mark Ellis and another human named Clyde McClintlock, who I had also communed with, had located me. They followed me back to my home in the globular cluster. The one called McClintlock had the audacity to attempt to initiate communion. This McClintlock thought we had created the universe. Correcting him destroyed his fragile mind. A non-human named G'Liat, who accompanied Ellis and McClintlock, put an end to McClintlock's suffering.

We appreciated McClintlock's audacity, but Ellis surprised and delighted us when he initiated communion and entered our minds. Most of my appendages had been female and it felt good to have this man inside me. He was primitive and brutal, but smart. We liked him better than the old appendages. When Ellis and his ship returned to the whirlpool galaxy, we were once again diminished.

We have decided to adopt these humans. They will become one with us. We will benefit from them and they will benefit from us. Together we will build a legacy.

The humans would call it a "win-win" proposition.

Part I: Silence of the Old Earth

Thus with violence shall that great city of Babylon be thrown down, and shall be found no more at all. And the voice of harpers, and musicians, and of pipers, and trumpeters, shall be heard no more at all in thee; and no craftsman, of whatsoever craft he be, shall be found any more in thee; and the sound of a millstone shall be heard no more at all in thee.

Revelation 18: 21-22

Chapter One

CRAFTSMAN

In a one-room apartment in Southern Arizona, two flies buzzed and spiraled in the thick, torrid atmosphere. Dirty plates filled the sink while uneaten remnants of food littered a small table. Unwashed socks and underwear had been draped over the room's two chairs. An alcove, containing a rust-stained toilet, reeked of those odors generated in the human body's deep, dark recesses. The flies were in paradise.

Attracted to the lone human inhabitant's salty sweat, the two flies lit and cavorted near his nose until his hand swept by and they flew away. The man lay on a small cot that creaked each time he swung his arm. A clock on a nightstand counted its way inexorably toward the time its alarm would sound. Undaunted, the flies returned time and time again. If flies had emotions, they might have found taking moisture from the man's nose a fun challenge.

"Goddamn flies," grumbled the man as he swatted at the insects again. This time he sat up on the small cot and blinked at the zebra-stripe pattern on the floor made by sunlight streaming through the window's half-closed blinds. The man, Timothy Gibbs, reached out, grabbed the alarm clock, and stared at it for several seconds while he worked to interpret the numbers he read: five minutes before seven o'clock. Five minutes before the alarm was to sound. "Goddamn it," grumbled Gibbs, as he returned the clock to the nightstand. He rubbed his rough hand across a stubble-covered chin, annoyed because he wanted to go back to sleep but he didn't have enough time.

Gibbs padded over to the kitchen counter. The computer unit recognized its owner and a finger-greased touch pad came to life. Bleary-eyed, he examined the choices from the small inventory of frozen meals-in-one. With a sigh, he chose the omelet, then listened as outdated motors carried the meal from the freezer to the internal cooking unit. For a moment, he thought he smelled acrid, electrical smoke. With a frown, he thought perhaps he should open the unit and take a look, but decided against it as he realized the smell came from some left-over plastic still clinging to the pre-fabricated meal.

With a stretch and a yawn, Gibbs padded to the toilet alcove. He swatted at the swirling flies, which buzzed around his hair while he relieved himself. Leaving the alcove, he looked over at a hologram of his mother, which sat on the nightstand. He hadn't seen his mother since she had lost her job at the paper cup factory almost twenty years ago. Unable to pay her taxes and with Gibbs barely able to pay his own, much less help her, social workers took her to a housing complex. The government didn't bother to tell Gibbs where they had taken her. Without an income, his mother couldn't afford a teleholo call to her son. Timothy Gibbs couldn't know whether his mother still lived, or had already died.

A chime alerted Gibbs that his breakfast was done. He opened the unit's door and retrieved the steaming food. He sipped rancid coffee while picking blackened plastic out of the eggs. He wondered about his father – a man he'd never known. Poking at the over-cooked omelet, Gibbs wondered if he had fathered anyone. Like most men in the thirtieth century, including his own father, he sometimes left sperm at the local Depository. Women who liked his genetic make-up and wanted children could go to the Depository to be impregnated. This meant Gibbs didn't have to risk the diseases and emotional upheaval that came from a sexual relationship. At the same time, he didn't know whether he had fathered a hundred children or none at all.

Not bothering to clean the plate and coffee cup after breakfast, Gibbs removed his sweaty underclothes and stepped into the sanitizer. Water remained a precious commodity in Southern Arizona, even though ice was mined in the asteroid belt. He closed his eyes and enjoyed the hypersonic waves tingling against his skin, removing dirt and sweat, leaving the sanitizer's floor slimy. Stepping out, and wiping his feet on the mat, Gibbs dressed in his work uniform and went out the door pausing long enough to hear the door lock automatically behind him.

Not able to afford a hover-car, Timothy Gibbs walked the mile and a half to Tanque Verde Teleholo, where he worked as a repair technician. He earned a small stipend and a commission on each expensive teleholo he refurbished. In the thirtieth century, most people considered teleholos indispensable. People used them to communicate, transmit holograms, play games and transact finances. A teleholo served as an essential portal to entertainment and communication.

Despite his low pay, many earned less than Timothy Gibbs. While walking to work, he stepped over an old man, sleeping on the sidewalk. Even the old man – too poor to afford a permanent place to sleep – clutched a portable teleholo to his chest.

Stepping through the shop's door, Gibbs forced himself to smile and wave at a fellow sales associate, Louise Sinclair. Sinclair gestured for Gibbs to come see what she watched on a teleholo.

"More news about the Cluster?" asked Gibbs with a weary sigh. A large assembly of iridescent spheres hovered over the teleholo dais. The Earth belonged to the Confederation of Homeworlds, which fought a one-sided war with the Cluster. Whenever the Cluster appeared, it destroyed the ship it encountered. No one knew of a single Cluster ship lost to a Homeworlds' ship. "When will they stop bugging us about the Cluster?" Gibbs grumbled. "It's all so far away from Earth."

"This is different." Louise Sinclair had been following the Cluster story since day one and insisted on conveying what she learned to her co-workers. "A mapping ship followed the Cluster home. They think they have some idea what it is."

"Whatever." Gibbs reached out as if to turn off the teleholo unit, but she batted his hand away.

"Aren't you the least bit interested in the Cluster?" She cocked her head and examined the technician. "They've been destroying ships left and right. They even threatened a colony for God's sake."

Gibbs shook his head. "Sufiro's on the other side of the galaxy. I can't waste my time worrying about stuff in space. I've got enough problems right here on Earth." He shrugged mock apology then strode to the employee lounge.

Sinclair followed right behind him. "I can't believe what I'm hearing," she said, incredulous. "In the thousand years humans have been in space, the Cluster is the first intelligent life we've ever discovered that seems bent on destroying us. How can you ignore that?"

"It's not just us humans." He poured coffee into a paper cup. "We're not in this alone. The Titans will figure out something. They always have before."

"They haven't yet," she retorted. "The only thing the Cluster hasn't destroyed is that colony – Sufiro. They *survived* their encounter with the Cluster."

"Okay, so, now someone's figured out where the Cluster's from, is that it?" he asked, resigned. She wouldn't leave him alone until after she'd given him her update.

"They think it's from outside our galaxy. It's from a globular cluster." She flashed a proud smile.

"Seems a bit redundant, doesn't it?"

"What's redundant?"

"That the Cluster's from a cluster." Gibbs smirked, impressed by his own clever remark. "What is a globular cluster, anyway?"

"They're balls of stars in orbit around the Milky Way Galaxy," she explained. "They're like little mini-galaxies, except the stars are older."

Gibbs nodded, then sipped his coffee. He held the cup out at arm's length and realized it had been manufactured at the factory where his mother had worked. He sighed and took another sip, then poured out the leftover coffee and crushed the cup. He looked up into Louise Sinclair's soft brown eyes. For just a moment, he imagined himself asking her out to dinner, but soon threw the notion aside, knowing he didn't have the money for such an extravagance. "So, tell me." His tone softened. "Who made this discovery?"

It warmed him when she smiled. "A mapping ship called the *Nicholas Sanson*." She reached over and issued a few commands on the telehólo's console. A moment later, a statuesque woman sat across a bare metal desk from a clean-shaven, auburn-haired man. Captions identified the woman as a reporter named Deana Dean and the man as Captain John Mark Ellis.

Ellis leaned forward, brow creased as he recounted a tale. "An associate of mine from Rd'dyggia named G'Liat had an interest in deep space nodes. He also had been corresponding with the Transgalactic Mapping Corporation and exchanging theories. Through him, we obtained our posting on the *Sanson*. As the ship conducted its routine mapping mission, we gathered data on the nodes. We soon came to an especially strong node on our voyage to Alpha Coma Berenices."

"And when you arrived in our system you encountered the Cluster," pressed Dean.

Ellis nodded. "We did and it soon moved away. At that point, we faced a hard choice. We could either stay put or attempt to escape. Just then, I realized no one had ever attempted a third option. We could attempt to follow. I suspected it might have been heading back to the strong deep space node we'd detected. The Cluster soon jumped. We followed."

Dean leaned forward. "And that's how you ended up in a globular cluster outside our galaxy?"

Ellis took a deep breath and blew it out. "That's right."

The reporter's eyes widened. "How in the world did you make it back to our galaxy?"

"We're a mapping vessel. Once we came through the jump point, we could follow its motion. We sustained damage though, and had to conduct repairs to our jump engines. We couldn't jump back until those repairs had been executed."

"It's amazing you made it back to the galaxy in one piece!" Dean flashed a smile at the camera.

"I had every confidence in our crew," said Ellis.

With that, Sinclair turned off the teleholo. "Have you ever seen such a space opera?"

Gibbs opened his mouth to answer, but a voice from the break room door interrupted him. "Hey Gibbs, we've got thirteen teleholos lined up in the back." Gibbs' supervisor, Jerry Lawrence, stood in the doorway wearing a rumpled uniform shirt. He looked at his watch. "We need to get them out by five."

"Sorry, Mr. Lawrence, I'll be right there," he said. Lawrence turned on his heel and left. Gibbs looked up at Sinclair and flashed a sheepish grin. "I guess I need to get to work."

"Me too." She shrugged. "Sorry I kept you. I didn't mean to get you into trouble."

He resisted the urge to reach out and touch her shoulder. "No problem."

"I need to get back on the floor. Customers, you know." With that, they left the break room. She resumed her narrative, though the enthusiasm had left her voice. "Did you know that McClintlock guy who started the wacky Cluster religion up in the New England Sector ran the *Sanson's* galley?"

They stopped at the workshop door. He tried to think of something witty or charming to say. Instead, he noticed two people browsing the displays. "I think you've got some customers." He shuffled his feet. "I need to get to work."

"I know." She turned away.

Pursing his lips, Gibbs entered the workshop, glad to spend the day with computer chips and electronic components that only spoke when he hit the on switch and if he didn't like what they said, he could always change the channel.

After a long day, Timothy Gibbs trudged home. As he pondered what he would have for dinner, he looked to the sky. The sight made him pause. On most nights, the pollution reflected the city lights and the night sky was a deep rusty orange. On this night, Gibbs noticed a few of the brighter stars overhead. He traced out the Big Dipper then the stars Vega, Altair, and Deneb which formed the Summer Triangle. Four lights, brighter than those stars, leisurely moved across the sky. His forehead creased. They didn't blink like aircraft and they seemed too bright for Confederation spacecraft, which were constructed of black erdonium. However, the four lights resembled spacecraft moving in a diamond formation.

Gibbs shrugged, then shook his head, as he stepped up his pace through the unsafe city streets. He soon entered his apartment building and frowned at the new graffiti on the walls. The local gang once again had marked their territory. Timothy Gibbs sighed relief after he used his palm imprint reader to enter the apartment and the door locked behind him.

Gibbs removed his uniform shirt, then turned on the teleholo with the volume down low providing a simple background noise. The hologram showed four Clusters. A red light flashed under the three-dimensional image indicating a news alert. Gibbs was too hungry to pay much attention. Newsflashes had become a routine occurrence during the Cluster War. As Gibbs had mentioned to Sinclair, the events all happened so far away they didn't matter to him.

After selecting a meal of roast beef and potatoes, he stepped over to the dresser and frowned when he could find no underwear. While dinner cooked, he made his weekly round of the apartment, picked up the dirty clothes and tossed them into the washer-dryer unit. The dinner-ready chime sounded. Gibbs retrieved his meal from the preparation unit and shoved plates aside on the table, upsetting the flies. He sat down and reached for a Dairtox bottle. The drug kept the pollutants in Earth's atmosphere from building up to toxic levels in people's lungs.

The teleholo flickered and the image blurred as Gibbs began to eat. He slumped, a forkful of beef smothered in gravy halfway to his mouth. It seemed he would need to take his own unit into the shop the next day so he could fix it. The Clusters morphed into an indistinct shape and a single syllable began repeating from the speakers: "da … da … da…"

Annoyed, Gibbs put his fork on the plate, stepped over to the table, and slammed his fist down next to the teleholo. The image solidified into a young man with haunted eyes. Gibbs appraised the image wondering if a call had interrupted the broadcast. That seemed to be it – the teleholo's interrupt function had failed. It should have chimed and placed the news broadcast into its own corner of the teleholo dais. Instead, it tried to play over the broadcast, causing interference. Irritated, Gibbs fingered the volume stud. He assumed it must be a sales call. It would be quickest to answer and be done with it. "Hello, this is Tim Gibbs."

"Dad?" said the figure on the teleholo.

Gibbs fell into the chair facing the unit. "Uh, I think you have the wrong number."

"Are you Timothy Allen Gibbs?" asked the figure as Gibbs reached out to disconnect the call.

Gibbs blinked a few times, then looked at the young man's eyes again. He glanced over to the hologram of his mother – they were identical. No wonder the eyes haunted him.

"Are you Timothy Gibbs?" asked the young man again.

"I am," Gibbs responded. "Who are you?"

"I'm Jeremy Williams," said the young man. "I'm pretty sure I'm your son."

"Pretty sure?" Gibbs leaned forward and examined the young man. "How did you find out? How *could* you find out?" Fatherhood anonymity laws prevented Gibbs from reporting his name at the Depository. The only information they had came from the DNA he'd left behind. Sure, someone could use that to trace his identity, but it would be a difficult chore.

"I didn't find out." Williams' brow creased. "I was just thinking about my father and the name Timothy Gibbs came to my mind. A moment later, I found myself dialing your teleholo. I live in the Los Angeles sector." Williams looked down, as though seeing the number he'd input for the first time. "You're in Southern Arizona, aren't you? I don't know anyone in Southern Arizona."

"I don't know if you're my son." Gibbs shook his head. "How could I know?"

Williams held out his arms, imploring. "You must be. I feel it. I've never felt anything so strongly in my life! Don't you feel it?"

Gibbs shook his head, desperate to believe and know a child he had never been allowed to know, but finding the possibility just too much to process. Perhaps he had more unknown children. "I don't know…" Gibbs hugged himself, guarding against the holographic arms reaching toward him even though the hologram was just empty air – an illusion.

Williams' arms dropped to his side and he looked toward the ground. The young man gathered resolve, then looked up again. He typed on his console. "I'm a computer programmer in the L.A. Sector. I'm transmitting my number. You can call me anytime." He paused. "Do you want me to give you a location where you can check my DNA? You could find out if I really am your son?"

Again, Gibbs shook his head. "No, that won't be necessary. Give me some time. I'll try to call in a few days, once I've sorted out my feelings."

Williams nodded, accepting the verdict – saddened, but

understanding. "I know you're my dad," he said. "I don't know how, but I know. My emotions have never been so strong about anything before." Williams sighed, then terminated the call.

The Clusters reappeared over the dais and Gibbs focused on the announcer's words. "Four Cluster ships entered Earth space today. There has been no evidence of personnel from the ships trying to land. Based on the Cluster's appearance at the planet Sufiro, we believe they are just here to observe. There is no cause for panic or alarm. We will keep you updated. In the meantime, we advise Earth's citizens to go about their business."

Timothy Gibbs hugged himself as he continued watching the teleholo. First, a son he never knew called. Now the distant, mysterious Cluster had appeared around Earth. Military ships had gone to full alert. As he watched Clusters on the teleholo, Timothy Gibbs – a man who had never loved, never been loved, a man who didn't have strong feelings about much of anything aside from his own survival – began to feel regret for the lost opportunities in his life. A tear eased its way down Gibbs' cheek followed by another. His emotions turned from regret to anger as he scrubbed the tears from his face.

"What do I have to feel bad about?" growled Gibbs to the empty room. "I'm no different than most people on this miserable planet. Just a guy trying to make ends meet." He stood and returned to his tepid meal.

After he finished dinner, Gibbs gathered the old plates from the table and placed them in the recycler. He puttered around the apartment, cleaning. He couldn't say why he'd been spurred into activity. He just wanted to put his life in some order.

A while later, Gibbs dropped onto his cot, exhausted. The teleholo continued to play news updates about the Cluster. In the meantime, he dreamed he had married Louise Sinclair. Their grown son, Jeremy Williams – no Jeremy Sinclair-Gibbs – had come home for a visit. They sat down to a dinner that resembled one from the twentieth century more than the thirtieth. Bowls filled with potatoes, green beans and cranberry sauce surrounded a turkey, which steamed in the middle of the table. Gibbs's subconscious had pulled the meal's image from stories of the first Thanksgiving when colonists had come from England to the United States. Certainly, Gibbs had never experienced food set out as it appeared in the dream.

Someone banged at the door. Gibbs excused himself from the table and answered. His jaw dropped open when he answered. His mother pointed an accusatory finger at her son. Charlotte Gibbs' skin began to dry and decay on her skeleton. Her jaw, no longer attached by muscle, fell open in a silent scream.

"Mom," called Gibbs. "You're still alive?"

A voice croaked from the open mouth. "No. I died ten years ago." The mummified vision of Timothy Gibbs' mother moved past her son and turned. "I've come to ask why you never tried to contact me. Why didn't you try to find me? Didn't you love your mother?"

Gibbs gasped for air. "Of course I loved you, Mom. The government took you to a retirement home. They didn't tell me where."

"Why didn't you ask?"

"It wouldn't have done any good. You owed too many taxes. I couldn't help. I wanted to, but there was nothing I could do." Gibbs hugged himself, trying to rein in his emotions and keep from being overwhelmed.

"You could have fought the government," said Gibbs' mother. As she spoke, Charlotte Gibbs desiccated further, becoming little more than a skeleton.

"No one can fight the government. I would have been destroyed!" Gibbs chewed on his finger.

"Your body might have been destroyed, but you would have proven you had a soul. You would have proven your worth as a human being. You would have proven you cared about something besides yourself."

Timothy Gibbs awoke in a cold sweat, clutching his sheet to himself. He stood and rushed over to the table with his mother's hologram, picked it up and hurled it to the floor, smashing its micro-circuitry. His mother's image vanished forever. "Leave me alone!" he shouted to the smashed holographic display. "I'm just a guy doing his best to make it in this world! Leave me alone!"

Chapter Two

DOOMSDAY

In his quarters, the warrior G'Liat watched on a monitor as space ships from Alpha Coma Berenices met the *Nicholas Sanson* and began to deploy repair crews. The eight-foot-tall, orange warrior sat in a chair that seemed too small for his large frame. John Mark Ellis had come to him on his home planet, Rd'dyggia, seeking to understand the alien known as the Cluster. He had been on a similar quest. He had communicated with many beings around the galaxy and prided himself on understanding them. The Cluster had proven to be an enigma and he did not like enigmas.

G'Liat listened to the chatter from the repair crews. When John Mark Ellis followed the Cluster through a jump point to a globular cluster, which orbited the Milky Way Galaxy, it had damaged the *Sanson's* sensitive jump engines. After consulting with Chief Engineer Mahuk, Ellis had rerouted conduits on the ship's hull to give it power to jump back to the galaxy. The repair crews hurled jibes to each other about the amateurish repair job. Yet, G'Liat detected a certain admiration behind their words.

The workers also shared estimates with one another about repair times. Based on their numbers, G'Liat estimated it would take nearly two weeks to return the *Sanson* to operation. It pleased G'Liat to know *Sanson* had not been damaged beyond repair. Even he found it an elegant and beautiful ship. Most human-built star ships in the thirtieth century were simple and functional black cylinders with engines at the stern, which glowed blue when active. Like arrows in the night, those ships shot through the fourth dimension. The *Sanson*, on the other hand, had been designed to map the fourth dimension, feeling its way along, charting gravity's subtle and ever-changing

19

pathways, which allowed all other ships to thrust their way through the void faster than light speed.

Like the other ships, her hull was erdonium: the sole material known that could withstand the fourth dimension's ravages. She was also cylindrical overall, but she bulged in places Navy ships did not. Attached to the hull were eight fan-like sensor arrays, which swept back toward the vessel's stern and resembled sails. They pivoted, sensing the gravitational interactions of many stars. Each array controlled an engine, petite compared to one on a freighter or a warship. The glow from each engine surrounded the ship like a halo.

After returning to the Milky Way from the globular cluster, Captain John Mark Ellis had visited G'Liat in his quarters. The warrior had displeased his human companions. Ellis and G'Liat had been accompanied by Clyde McClintlock, an evangelist who had come to believe the Cluster was God made manifest. When the Cluster shattered McClintlock's illusion, the evangelist's mind snapped and he planned to kill Ellis. G'Liat had killed the evangelist to stop him. He hadn't wanted to, but it seemed a bitter, necessary act, like a human killing a rabid animal. When Ellis had visited G'Liat, he had informed the warrior that the ship's manager, Kirsten Smart, had told him to leave the ship to avoid facing charges. G'Liat agreed to the terms.

After Ellis had left the warrior's cabin, G'Liat activated the computer interface and searched for companies that chartered spacecraft. While he could take a commercial flight back to Rd'dyggia, he wanted solitude and quiet so he could decide his next move. He limited his search to those companies with Rd'dyggian names. The warrior had grown weary of acting like a human. He wanted to be among his own kind for a time.

He had called the first company on the list and had been pleased when a Rd'dyggian answered. "Money I have," G'Liat had spoken the words in his native language. "Ships you have. I will return to Rd'dyggia. I require retrieval from a human ship in orbit, the *Nicholas Sanson*."

The Rd'dyggian on the other end had bowed. "Understood, my Lord G'Liat. A ship will be dispatched from our docks when we start business tomorrow morning. Be ready."

The Rd'dyggian had terminated the call and included the time he should expect the transport to arrive.

G'Liat looked at the time, then stood and knocked the end from some incense he burned. He packed his few belongings in a small, metal case, and then sat down to await the transport's arrival. The warrior continued to reflect on John Mark Ellis and what he relayed about the Cluster's communications.

G'Liat wished to understand the Cluster so he could destroy it. Even so, he began to wonder if the Cluster could be used to eliminate other barriers to Rd'dyggian dominance of the galaxy. If so, perhaps the Cluster's elimination could be delayed.

On Earth, Timothy Gibbs awoke in his apartment with red-rimmed eyes. Not bothering with breakfast, he approached the holographic display he'd smashed the night before, swept up the unit's remains, and put them in the garbage incinerator. He dressed, grabbed his own malfunctioning teleholo unit, and then went into work.

He stifled a squawk when he encountered Louise Sinclair. Her normally impeccable store uniform was rumpled as though she had slept in it. Her eyes were bloodshot and she wore no makeup. She flashed a brave smile at him. "I see you didn't get much sleep either."

"Bad dreams." He moved past her to the employee's lounge and grabbed the coffee pot. A few minutes later, he blinked as she took his hand and helped him put the pot back on the warmer. The cup had overflowed and coffee dripped from the counter.

Gibbs looked into Sinclair's eyes and sighed. "If I asked, would you go out to dinner with me?"

Sinclair staggered back, away from him. Conflicted emotions played across her face before she straightened her jacket and forced a certain resolve. "Mr. Gibbs, you realize I could report you for making such a suggestion at work."

Timothy Gibbs looked down at his feet. "I know," he whispered. He picked up the over-full coffee cup and took a sip.

Some coffee splashed onto his uniform. Louise Sinclair made as if to reach for a towel – as if to help clean it up. Instead, years of training had kicked in and overrode human instinct. She strode from the break room, indignant shock on her features.

Gibbs dropped into a chair and sipped the coffee. Twenty minutes later, it dawned on him that Jerry Lawrence hadn't appeared to shuffle him off to the repair shop. He crumpled the paper cup and threw it into the trash, picked up his teleholo dais, then left the break room. Louise Sinclair stared at the street through the shop's large window. He couldn't quite tell from where he stood, but it looked as though tears glistened on her cheeks. Taking a deep breath, he pushed open the workshop's door and entered.

Jerry Lawrence sat silent and examined a teleholo's control chip. He held a test probe listlessly in his hand.

Gibbs cleared his throat, but Lawrence didn't respond. "Mr. Lawrence?" he ventured.

At last, Lawrence looked up. "Sorry, Gibbs ... I guess I was lost in thought. What do you need?"

"What did you want me to work on today?"

Lawrence set the test probe down and looked up into Gibbs' eyes. "It almost seems pointless, doesn't it? I'll be surprised if we have a single customer come in today, even to pick up things they expect to be ready."

Gibbs stepped over to the workbench and sat his malfunctioning teleholo unit down. "Sir, do you have any kids?"

"I don't know." Lawrence flashed a wan smile, "but I had a dream about a daughter last night."

Gibbs snorted. "I had a ... a dream, too ... at least I guess it was a dream ... about my son. Then I dreamed about my mother."

Lawrence nodded. "My daughter was a prostitute in Central Texas. She looked at me with drug-clouded eyes and accused me of being a bad father; of leaving her to an abusive mother instead of raising her myself." Lawrence looked down at his hands. "I didn't even know I had a daughter. I have no idea who her mother is." He took a deep breath then blew it out before he looked up at Gibbs. "I hope you had a better dream than mine."

Gibbs stood and moved over to the storage shelf and stared at it. After a moment, he grabbed a teleholo dais at random. He took it back to the workbench. "I think I need to work, whether or not we have any customers today," he said. "It'll help take my mind off bad dreams."

Lawrence nodded. "You're right." He looked at the teleholo dais Gibbs had taken from the shelf. "That one's got a tricky problem. I had planned to assign it to you. Judging from the symptoms, I'd say the central processor malfunctioned. However, I replaced the processor and the problem didn't go away."

"Sounds like fun," said Gibbs with a genuine smile. He set the teleholo dais on the workbench, glad for anything that would distract him from his dreams. He retrieved his tools and turned on the diagnostic computer then let his mind escape into the puzzle.

When the workday ended, Timothy Gibbs dreaded the return home. He feared another dream about his mother or something worse. With unaccustomed sadness, he downloaded his end-of-the-week pay and stepped out into the showroom, just remembering to retrieve his own teleholo dais that he'd stayed late to repair. As it turned out, he hadn't found anything wrong with the unit.

Louise Sinclair prepared to step outside. Their eyes met, but she flushed red and averted her gaze a moment later, then ducked outside. His brow creased when he realized she should have turned right to go home. Instead, she turned left. Gibbs shook his head to stop the pointless conjecture, and then strode across the showroom and out the door himself.

As he walked toward his apartment, dark thoughts entered his mind. He wondered if he had abandoned his son and his mother. He wondered how many children he had, in fact, abandoned. Gritting his teeth, he tried to tell himself he hadn't abandoned anyone. He lived his life the way most people in the thirtieth century did. However, that caused his mind to take an even darker turn and he questioned the very point of human existence. *If humans are so horrible to one another*, he thought, *do we even deserve to live?*

Gibbs gasped and shook his head, then remembered his success with the problematic teleholo earlier in the day – the one with the broken central processor. He'd managed to solve the problem and even received accolades from Jerry Lawrence. For a moment, Gibbs' lungs expanded to their fullest, through deep, satisfied breaths. Then he looked across the street where two teenage boys played a game on a portable teleholo; both sets of eyes glazed over. Holographic guns blazed, sending up all-too-realistic sprays of blood. Gibbs tightened his grip on his own teleholo dais and walked on, feeling as though he was in part responsible for the simulated killing spree.

A few minutes later, he realized he had passed his apartment complex and faced a weapons' shop. He licked his lips and considered turning around but, instead, entered the shop. The clerk behind the counter didn't look much better than Gibbs felt.

Numb, Gibbs stared at the heplers, laz-rifles, and stunners on display. "I'm going hunting," he lied.

The clerk nodded. "Seems a lot of people are going hunting this weekend," he said. "I don't have much left that's good for taking down animals." The clerk brought out some street heplers – the types the gangs around the city used. Pointing to a Hepler 220-K, he continued. "I'm taking one of those hunting this weekend myself. You have to be careful though. You can remove the head from just about anything with a 220-K."

"I'll take it." Gibbs entered the payment codes onto a touch pad then took the weapon and continued down the street to a liquor store. After making the purchase, he returned to his apartment.

There were no signs the gangs had returned. In his experience, the gangs put up a few tags on Thursday night then returned in force on Friday. Going out on Saturday was taking one's life in one's hands. Gibbs thanked the powers-that-be for small favors.

Entering the apartment, Gibbs took the hepler from its case and set it on the table. Then he opened the whiskey bottle and took a drink. Wiping his lips, his gaze settled on the gun. He blinked several times and backed away from the table. "I need to get a grip on myself," he said aloud. "It's not like the world's coming to an end."

Forcing himself to act, Gibbs retrieved his teleholo dais and sat it in the dust-free circle on its accustomed table, then turned it on. A Cluster hovered over the dais. Without turning up the volume, he stared at the image, spellbound. He remembered what Louise Sinclair had told him about the Cluster. She'd mentioned the colony, Sufiro. Something about the planet was significant. Looking back at the hologram of the Cluster, he remembered a childhood friend named Ed Swan who wanted to be a police officer. Somehow, Gibbs knew Swan had moved to Sufiro. Shutting his eyes, he tried to think how he could possibly know. He'd last seen Swan in high school. Still, he reached out and took the teleholo controls, shut off the news, and entered a directory search. Within five minutes, he found a listing for an Edmund Ray Swan, Deputy Sheriff of New Granada, a continent on the planet Sufiro.

Without questioning his actions further, Gibbs commanded the unit to connect to his old friend.

A handsome, clean-shaven face with a square jaw and mismatched eyes appeared over Gibbs' teleholo unit. "Ed Swan." The man spoke in a booming baritone. "May I help you?"

"It is you," said Gibbs. "I doubt you remember me. My name is Tim Gibbs. We went to school together in Southern Arizona."

Swan's steel-gray eye dilated while his brown eye narrowed. Gibbs realized his old friend had a cybernetic eye implant. "It's been a long time," said Swan after a moment. "Did you ever build that … what was it? That computer memory circuit you used to talk about in high school?"

"What? The plasma quantum computer idea I did a report on way back then?" Gibbs smiled despite his dark mood. "I went to college and found out it was impossible. You'd need to build it in almost absolute vacuum and it would need a large quantity of highly charged particles like you'd find around a neutron star or better yet a black hole. I don't know anyone who's interested in building a computer around a black hole."

"Lost dreams, eh?" said Swan.

"So, what about you?" asked Gibbs. "Did you ever get your law enforcement degree?"

"I did and after twenty years, I'm glad to say I now live in a place where I don't have to use it often. Sufiro's a quiet place;

almost a paradise – at least now." Swan looked down at the floor, then back up at Gibbs. "So, what can I do for you, Tim?"

"I'm…" Gibbs struggled to find the words. "I'm not quite sure. I've just been feeling kind of down. You know there are four Clusters orbiting Earth right now, don't you?"

"What?" Swan's mouth fell open. "There are four of them?"

"Four," repeated Gibbs. "I don't know why, but I can't seem to stay focused. My mind just keeps drifting … thinking hopeless thoughts. I'd go see a psychologist if I could afford one."

"One Cluster orbited Sufiro just a couple months ago." Swan chewed his lower lip. "It made everyone…" The holographic image of Swan's head began to break up. Gibbs slammed his fist down on the table next to the teleholo dais, but the image didn't clear. Instead, static filled the display.

"Ed, can you hear me?" Gibbs waited a moment for a reply. "Ed?" Swearing, Gibbs tried to reach Swan again.

Red letters appeared above the dais: "No EQ Carrier."

Gibbs shook his head as he realized the problem wasn't in the unit. He turned back to the news where a floating head said, "We have just lost contact with planets outside the Solar System. Authorities are trying to resume contact. Be calm and…" Gibbs turned off the unit.

"Damn," he hissed. He stepped back to the table, retrieved the whiskey bottle, and took a shot, then another. He stripped naked and sat down on the cot. After his fourth shot, his head swam. He began to think about his mother's words from the dream. He wondered if she had, in fact, died or if he should seek her out. Gibbs took another sip of whiskey, realizing he was too much a coward to act, even if he could locate her. Four more drinks and thoughts of his mother faded, replaced by a fantasy about Louise Sinclair. He imagined touching her smooth skin and wondered what her breasts felt like. Was there a way he could have a relationship with a woman? Though rare, it did happen. Still, some women's groups had begun to argue that men weren't necessary for reproduction. Because DNA could be engineered, it didn't have to come from men at all. Two more drinks and Gibbs had driven the image's coldness away. His thoughts turned toward Jeremy Williams. Was

Williams his son? He wanted it to be true. Two more drinks and Gibbs' thoughts went dark again. He imagined that he had the DNA tested – and the test turned out negative. Instead of wanting to be close, Jeremy Williams turned from Gibbs much as Sinclair had earlier in the afternoon.

Timothy Gibbs stood and paced the apartment. After several turns, he reached for the bottle again. This time, he raised the hepler instead of the bottle. He leaned his head back, as though to take a drink.

The hepler flew from his hands just as he started to squeeze the trigger. "Oh my God." He followed the gun's motion with his eyes. It clattered into the corner. Looking forward, he faced a nude woman with black hair, but he couldn't quite focus on any part of her except for her penetrating green eyes.

"Do not give up hope, Timothy Gibbs," said the woman. "You have a legacy."

The room swirled and he dropped to his knees then fell over sideways.

The next morning, Timothy Gibbs awoke with a hangover and stared at the hepler in the room's corner, where it had landed. He wondered if the woman he had seen had been real or an alcohol-induced hallucination. Putting on clean clothes, he stepped outside into a quiet morning.

A rank odor like an outhouse assailed his nostrils. He looked down at his feet where a man had lost half his head. The man's dead fist clenched a hepler similar to the one he had purchased the day before. The man's bowels had released upon death. Bile rose in Gibbs' mouth and he struggled not to vomit. He looked up and stepped around the corner where a hover had crashed into the building's first floor. The driver had been smashed to a pulpy mess. Gibbs couldn't control his stomach any longer. He fell to his knees and vomited onto the sidewalk. His abdominal muscles kept contracting and releasing well after his stomach was empty and he had to struggle to stop the dry heaves.

When he did stop, he stood up and forced himself to look up and down the silent street. Bodies were strewn everywhere, as though there had been a plague, except it looked as though everyone had taken their own life.

In a daze, he walked the familiar path to work. Once there, he found the doors locked. He sat down in front of the doors and put his face in his hands. He didn't know how long he sat there before Jerry Lawrence appeared and knelt down to face him. "How are you doing?"

"What the hell happened?" asked Gibbs, looking up with tear-stained cheeks.

"I don't know." Jerry spoke in a hollow, haunted voice. "They say the Cluster did this."

"How?" Gibbs snorted, then wiped his nose on his uniform sleeve, not caring about the mucous trail he left behind.

"I don't know." Lawrence took a long, deep breath. "When no one showed up to work this morning, I looked for some of the people. I found Louise Sinclair drowned in her bath-tub. When the cops arrived they said she overdosed on Dracan Love Crystals."

"What is this, the end of the world?" asked Gibbs. "Is this doomsday?"

"I don't know, Tim." Jerry stood and held out his hand. "All I know is that I'm still alive and I'm not going down without a fight."

Timothy Gibbs reached out and took Jerry's hand.

Chapter Three

POLITICIANS

A small, egg-shaped craft accelerated from Alpha Coma Berenices toward the jump point for the planet Rd'dyggia. G'Liat reclined against the control cabin's rounded back wall and stared at the holographic projection of space, which hovered over the central console. Unlike most human vessels, Rd'dyggian ships did not waste energy by simulating gravity. Then again, Rd'dyggian skeletons did not deteriorate in null gravity as human skeletons did. Even so, G'Liat took advantage of the ship's acceleration to recline without restraint, inhaling the comforting aromas of sulfur and ammonia. Though Rd'dyggians could survive in the same atmosphere as humans, they did not enjoy it. To G'Liat, the air aboard the *Nicholas Sanson* had been dry and foul, like a tomb deep underneath a desert where no life could flourish.

A young Rd'dyggian named Rizonex remained strapped in at the central control console. Like G'Liat, he had orange skin, no hair, a purple mustache-like growth over his mouth, and large, black eyes. At seven-feet tall, he was shorter than G'Liat. His six-fingered hands rested on the console and he controlled the ship with his mind. Rizonex lifted his hands from the control console, and then turned to look at G'Liat. "My Lord, we have intercepted a broadcast from Alpha Coma Berenices. You may find it interesting."

G'Liat pushed himself off the back wall and grabbed the control console. With feline-like grace, the eight-foot tall warrior contorted then settled into the empty chair and belted himself in. "What is this broadcast's nature?" he asked.

"It's what the humans call a news broadcast. They have lost contact with Gaea, their mother world," reported Rizonex.

"Display the broadcast," ordered G'Liat.

Rizonex returned his hands to the console. The image of a human woman with long blond hair appeared over the console. "We have not been able to contact our sister stations on Earth or Titan for over twelve hours. Senator Herbert Firebrandt's office has confirmed the loss of all communications and says the government is trying to reestablish contact." The woman's image faded from view, replaced by the Cluster. "However, the government has declined to comment about whether the Clusters reported to be in Earth orbit are responsible for the communications blackout."

G'Liat placed his hands on the console and searched the network archives for more information. He learned about the four Clusters' arrival in Earth orbit and that the Gaean Navy had sent ships to monitor them. However, those ships dared not attack the Clusters for fear they would retaliate.

G'Liat reached out with his mind and touched Rizonex's thoughts. "Alter course," commanded the warrior. "We go to Gaea."

"The ship's owners protest," replied the pilot through the interface. "The charter was from Alpha Coma Berenices to Rd'dyggia. No course change is stipulated in the contract."

"The owners know contracts do not apply to me," said G'Liat. "We will change course despite their protest. My operatives are instructed to compensate the owners in the event this ship is lost due to my actions."

G'Liat sensed the pilot's compliance, but the pilot's fear disgusted him. The warrior pulled his mind back from the pilot and continued to monitor human broadcasts. Though he longed to return to Rd'dyggia, G'Liat realized he must determine what the Clusters wanted at Earth. As he searched the broadcast, Rizonex carried out his orders. The ship changed course for the nearest jump point to Earth.

Jenna Walker, President of the Gaean Alliance – Earth and its colonies – rode into Arlington Cemetery in a black limo-hover. Instead of clamoring for attention, her aides sat in grim silence. Many governmental staff members had taken their own lives during the previous twenty-four hours. Everyone in the president's inner circle knew someone who had died. President Walker looked from one person to another. "Is there any way the Cluster can be responsible for all these deaths across the planet?"

Several black-suited figures shrugged. Others stared at the floor without speaking. One aide looked as though he might nod off. The president and her aides had been awake all night, trying to decide what to do about the Cluster and the epidemic of death happening around the planet. Before the Clusters arrived at Earth, almost every ship that had approached one had been destroyed. No one could prove the Cluster had caused the deaths on Earth, so the Gaean Military's Chiefs of Staff hesitated to attack the intruders. Some even suggested the Clusters might be able to help understand why so many deaths had occurred. If so, they needed to figure out how to approach the Clusters without being destroyed.

Walker looked to the surgeon general, a normally high-energy woman, whose red-rimmed eyes betrayed exhaustion from reading reports all night. The president decided she needed to reassess the information she had. "So, the deaths are not a disease? There's no doubt whatsoever that clinical depression is responsible?"

Dr. Cooper nodded. "Nothing seems to contradict that."

"Doctor, I'm tired of you pussyfooting around this issue. Did clinical depression cause all these deaths or are there other factors?" Walker slammed her fist on the car's door.

Dr. Cooper glared at the president and bared her teeth. "Every single one of the billions dead would have to be examined for me to know for certain, Madame President. Unless you really are the idiot the press makes you out to be, you know such a task would be impossible!"

President Walker sat back stunned. The aide who had been dozing off snapped awake. The president's mouth twitched into a humble smile. "We're all tired, Dr. Cooper. I just want to find some answers." She paused and took a deep breath. "Is there any way the Cluster could cause the depression?"

Dr. Cooper rubbed the bridge of her nose. "I'm sorry I snapped, Madame President." The president waved the apology aside and glanced out the window. The limo approached the stage where she would make a speech commemorating the so-called Doomsday Dead. "I wish we'd had a chance to review the *Sanson's* official report. The press reports suggest the Cluster must broadcast some kind of emotional energy, but without the official report, I don't know how it works."

"And," said the president, as the limo came to a stop, "I presume you don't give much credence to press reports – especially those that say I'm an idiot."

"There's a difference between editorializing and factual reporting." Cooper shrugged.

"Are you so sure?" asked the president as she exited the limo.

Behind her, the planetary minister, Gordon "Dick" Richards, leaned over to the surgeon general. "I'd be careful which press reports I relay to the president. She would be a bad enemy to have."

The president smiled as she caught the surgeon general's reply. "She watches late night telehelo just like we all do." The surgeon general huffed a weary sigh. "I'm not out to offend her, but she needs to know I don't have all the answers."

Walker, followed by her aides, strode to the podium and waited while a stylist checked to make sure her hair and suit were presentable for the cameras. Once they finished, the president stepped up to the podium where she put on her best solemn expression. "I grieve for all of the Earth's people. We have all lost loved ones in the last twenty-four hours. Rest assured that I will work day and night to find out why this has happened. Some say the four Clusters orbiting Earth caused the deaths. Let us not allow supposition to force us into hasty action. My staff and I are working to determine whether the Clusters are responsible in any way. If so, we will demand retribution. If not, we will determine the real reason for these deaths."

The president paused while her brain implant relayed her speech's next lines. "Let us take a minute to remember our loved ones who have passed before us. Today is the time to celebrate their lives and what they mean to us. Let's have a moment of silence." During the silence, President Walker wondered if any friends had died. She knew a janitor at the capitol had died with no explanation and a Secret Service agent who guarded her had committed suicide. They were acquaintances, not friends. As leader of the Earth and its colonies, she wondered if she still had any friends or just political allies. She shot an almost indiscernible glance at Surgeon General Cooper – the one member of her cabinet who spoke openly and without fear. Was she a friend or an enemy? Certainly, Dr. Cooper was more a friend than those cabinet members who remained silent to avoid aggravating her.

The clock in the president's brain implant told her the moment of silence had extended long enough to be proper. If she waited any longer, people would get nervous. The president continued her speech.

A man with long, white hair tied back into a ponytail stood on a ladder mounted to a hover tractor and leaned over the power unit. He cursed as he removed the burned out transfer coupling and set it next to the open compartment. He leapt to the ground and surveyed the field around him, shaking his head in dismay. The man's name was Ellison Firebrandt and at one time, he had captained the privateer vessel *Legacy*. Now, at 84-years-old, Firebrandt was a farmer on the planet Sufiro – a colony he founded with his lover, Suki, and his first mate, Carter Roberts. Suki had died just a year after their crash, but Roberts lived on. Even though arthritis confined him to a hover chair, Roberts still possessed a sharp mind.

Roberts guided his chair over the field and stopped next to his one-time captain. "Transfer coupling?" he asked.

"Couldn't happen at a worse time," growled Firebrandt. "We need to get the harvest in before the first snowfall. I don't think we can get a replacement from Earth before two weeks."

"Let me have a look at it," suggested Roberts. "Maybe I can repair it."

"You've already repaired the damned thing five times," said Firebrandt.

"If I can make it six, we'll save the harvest," said Roberts.

Firebrandt reached for the coupling, but Roberts stopped him.

"You'll hurt your back. Let me." He activated the chair's controls and it floated over the tractor. He reached out and grabbed the transfer coupling then placed it into a compartment in the hover chair. Just as Roberts drifted back toward the ground, an alarm sounded on the chair's console. "We've got a call up at the house."

"Who from?" Firebrandt looked toward the homestead he had built from the *Legacy*.

"I don't have an ID, but the call is from Alpha Coma Berenices."

Firebrandt shot a glance at his long-time friend. Sufiro had been founded when Firebrandt's mother – an admiral from Alpha Coma Berenices – attacked the *Legacy* and exiled Firebrandt to a world where he could survive but would be unable to commit piracy. "Signal for them to hold. I'll answer as soon as I get up to the house."

Roberts did as he'd been instructed while Firebrandt strode ahead and pondered his life on Sufiro. His daughter had been born and his lover had died on the planet. Colonists seeking to escape an overcrowded Earth settled. Some settlers discovered the galaxy's most precious metal, erdonium. The desire to maximize profits led the claimholders on the continent of Tejo to kidnap their fellow homesteaders from the continent of New Granada to work the mines. This sparked a war, but the New Granadans won. Those abducted had returned home and peace now prevailed. Firebrandt hoped nothing would shatter that peace.

Reaching the house, he strode through the adobe section he built with his own hands and through an airlock into the old pirate ship. The ship's teleholographic booth still served as the primary means of contact with the outside universe. The one-time pirate captain activated the control unit and the forward wall extended into an expansive office. A tall man with angular features, steel-gray eyes and red hair streaked white sat behind a desk, working at a computer. He looked up when Firebrandt answered.

"You must be Ellison." The man stood.

"I'm afraid you have me at a disadvantage." Firebrandt evaluated the unfamiliar room. His eyes fell on a portrait hanging on the wall. It was his mother, Admiral Barbara Firebrandt. "I see you admire my mother."

The man looked back at the wall, then turned with a smile as he stepped toward Firebrandt. "Our mother," he corrected. "I'm Senator Herbert Firebrandt of Alpha Coma. I'm your half-brother."

The pirate captain's jaw fell open. "I had no idea…"

"Neither did I … not until four hours ago."

"What happened four hours ago?" The captain's eyes narrowed.

"I responded to an alarm at mother's tomb. I discovered your daughter and grandson," explained the senator. "They went to pay their respects."

"I'd heard that John Mark's ship, the *Sanson* had gone to Alpha Coma for repairs after they'd jumped to the Cluster's home, but what the devil was Fire doing there?"

"I gather the Titans sent her here." The senator grabbed a chair and sat down facing his half-brother.

"Perhaps you'd better explain." Ellison placed his hands on his knees.

Herbert nodded. "Your daughter and a companion – a man named Manuel Raton – went to Titan to investigate whether or not the Titans and the Cluster had a connection. I gather they found one. Fire and Manuel discovered the Cluster and the Titans used to be symbiotic organisms. The Cluster called itself 'the intelligence' and the Titans were 'the appendages.' The Titans caught Fire and Manuel and imprisoned them until after Captain Ellis followed the Cluster to its home system."

The captain nodded. "The bit about John Mark and the *Sanson* was on the news. Thank God he survived."

"Indeed," agreed the senator, who had already grown fond of his niece and grandnephew. "The Titans transported Fire and Manuel here to Alpha Coma."

"So, are they available?" asked the captain. "Could I talk to them?"

"I'm afraid not." The senator sighed. "I don't know if news has reached you out there on Sufiro or not, but we've lost all contact with Earth and Titan. According to reports, four Clusters entered Earth orbit just before the blackout."

Ellison Firebrandt looked down at his feet as the news settled in. "I gather the Cluster has gone to reclaim their former symbionts, the Titans."

"That's one possibility," said the senator. "Or, John Mark thinks the situation could be worse. He thinks the Clusters may have identified an even better symbiotic partner – humans."

"Damn." The captain met Herbert Firebrandt's steel-gray gaze. "So, where is John Mark? Where's Fire?"

"I made John Mark a captain in the Alpha Coma Navy. He will take the *Nicholas Sanson* to Earth to find out what's happened and report back to us. Fire and Manuel volunteered to go with him."

Ellison Firebrandt noticed some dirt on his coveralls and swiped at it, then looked up. "I wish I could help them."

"As do I." The senator flashed a reassuring smile. "More than anything else, I suspect they need our prayers."

"They have them," said the captain, with resolve.

Herbert Firebrandt stood from the chair. "I'm glad we finally met," he said. "If we survive this crisis. I'd like to come to Sufiro and meet you in person."

Ellison Firebrandt stood and smiled. "I'd enjoy that."

Earth's government had offices around the planet and at least one office building on each colony world. Geneva was Earth's capital, but most senators did not live or work there. Instead, they worked from the regional capitals closest to their homes – using teleholos to project their images to important meetings in Geneva. The president maintained an office in every regional capital so she would have a base of operations when she traveled.

After the speech at Arlington Cemetery, President Walker and her aides went to the capitol building in the District of Columbia. The president had been there meeting with American continental senators when Doomsday struck. From the capitol, the president went to the old White House complex, dropped into her chair, and rubbed her eyes while the aides made a show of consulting handcomps. The president looked around the room, and then shook her head. Rolling her chair up to the desk and sitting up straight, she cleared her throat.

"You're all exhausted and I need some time to think. Go grab some shut-eye and let's meet back here, in say, four hours." Most in the group nodded groggy relief and stood to leave the room. "Dick," she called to the planetary minister. "Would you mind keeping an eye on things for the next two hours? I'll take over then."

Dick Richards, looking the most alert, except for maybe Dr. Eva Cooper, nodded while folding up his teleholo unit. "I'll talk to you in two hours."

Surgeon General Eva Cooper lingered behind as everyone else departed the room. "Madame President, I respectfully submit that you need more than two hours' sleep," she said once she and the president were alone.

"Now you're respectful." The president's mouth turned up. She motioned to a chair across the desk. "Have a seat. Care for a glass of wine?"

"Wine?" Dr. Cooper's brow furrowed. "You need sleep, and I can't advise alcohol right now."

The president stood and walked to a cabinet. Despite the surgeon general's objections, she retrieved two glasses and a wine decanter. "What I need is someone to talk to … for just a bit." The president set down the glasses.

"I'm a medical doctor, not a psychiatrist. I'm not even your personal physician."

The president sighed. "I don't need a medical or psychological opinion. I want someone I can confide in … as a friend." Jenna Walker filled both glasses with a deep red Merlot and sat in the chair next to Eva Cooper.

"You're the president. You must have friends to confide in," said Cooper, wary.

"Political allies and trusted advisors, yes. Friends…" Jenna Walker looked at the floor and allowed the word to trail off. She couldn't think of anyone she could call a friend. She remembered having friends. However, as she entered politics, she had limited her confidences. Walker sipped the wine and began to brood. "Have you ever been married?"

The question caught Cooper off guard. She picked up her wine glass but didn't take a drink. "Yes, but I'm divorced now."

"What was it like to have someone so close? So intimate?" Walker sat forward, elbows on her knees, and peered into the wine glass.

"It was wonderful at first. He was handsome and we could talk about anything. Then something changed. His ego grew, or something. He cared less for me than for himself. We grew apart." Dr. Cooper inclined her head and examined the president. After a moment, she took a small sip and smiled. "Haven't you been close to anyone? Been intimate?"

The president sighed and continued to look into the wine glass. "No. Like most people these days, I'm afraid. I fear disease and dishonesty. I'm afraid of being hurt." Jenna Walker sat up and sipped the wine. "The thing is, my fear never bothered me or seemed unusual. I'm not even sure I knew I was afraid. So many studies have demonstrated the harmfulness of human relationships that I deluded myself into believing them. Now I'm tired of the fear."

Eva Cooper pursed her lips and seemed uncomfortable with the conversation's direction. She took a more academic approach. "I think the fear started in the nineteenth and twentieth centuries as people better understood sexually transmitted diseases. Fear of disease made some people fear intimacy. Also, there have always been certain men who think being masculine means being an asshole. Feminists back then demanded laws to protect themselves from the assholes. They weren't necessarily wrong, but it started a cycle of regulating courtship and sexual behavior by law rather than tradition."

Jenna Walker snorted. "I know my history and I'm not sure they had any better options. Still, history created a set of circumstances where I could delude myself into believing I didn't need intimacy." Walker sipped her wine again and then placed the glass on the desk. "For some reason, that's changed in the last twenty-four hours."

"You're scared." Dr. Cooper leaned forward, studying the president. "Between the Cluster and the Doomsday Dead, who wouldn't be?"

"There's more," said Walker. "It's as though some deep-seated part of my psyche has been triggered, running me through a gamut of emotions. It's like I've returned to my hormone-laden teen years."

Eva Cooper set her wine glass aside, then looked at her watch. "Sleep will help. As I said before, you're exhausted."

Jenna Walker retrieved her wine glass from the desk, and remained silent for some time. As she sipped the wine, she stole glances of the doctor over the glass's rim. Like herself, the doctor was a middle-aged woman. Eva Cooper's nose was a little beakish and her lips were a little thin, but her wide, curious eyes entranced the president. Likewise, the doctor kept in good shape. "Are you scared, Eva?"

"Terrified." The doctor allowed her barriers to drop somewhat.

The President of the Gaean Alliance took another drink. A woman who had ordered people to their deaths, who routinely made decisions that affected the entire galaxy, worked up courage to ask a simple question. "There's a sleeping chamber next door. Would you come with me? I need someone to hold me and help me ward off the fear."

Doctor Cooper released a deep breath. "I'm not interested in a sexual relationship, Madame President."

"I want comfort from another human being – for closeness more than sex. Would you deny your president that? Or, do you think she's just an idiot?"

Eva Cooper shook her head. "I think you are a brilliant, beautiful woman and it's a tragedy no one says so."

The president stood and held her hand out to the surgeon general. Eva took the hand, but didn't meet Jenna's gaze. Jenna led the way through a back, unguarded door and turned into a room with a comfortable-looking, but simple double bed. Each woman removed her jacket and shoes.

Jenna gazed at Eva with longing. She reached out and the surgeon general trembled and backed away. Jenna looked down, and a tear ran down her cheek. Compassion seemed to overcome fear and Eva folded the president into her arms. They sat down on the bed and Jenna laid her head against Eva's soft breasts. Jenna breathed harder – from exhaustion, from fear, from lust. The two lay down, side-by-side and Eva allowed Jenna's hands to roam, to pull her blouse from her slacks, and move up against her naked skin. Rigid at first, Eva began to relax and stroke Jenna's shoulders. Jenna's sleepy eyes looked into Eva's. Drawn by some force – perhaps the simple desire to be as close as possible to another human, Jenna kissed the doctor. Eva's eyes went wide, but the president's firm hand on her back soon calmed her. Jenna's strong gaze compelled Eva to return the deep, passionate kiss. Jenna moaned as Eva's tongue probed her mouth, then she responded in kind. Her own tongue circled Eva's then pushed into the doctor's mouth. An unfamiliar heat rose in Jenna's groin and abdomen. They broke the kiss, panting for air.

For the first time in her life, Jenna Walker understood the closeness humans could feel for one another. She longed for Eva's touch to go lower, to help release the building fire in her body, but exhaustion overwhelmed her and it was just so nice to be held, to feel close to another human. Her explorations of Eva's body slowed. Her eyelids fluttered, unable to stay open any longer. Her breathing deepened, not from passion now – simply from exhaustion. Jenna Walker, President of the Gaean Alliance, fell asleep and dreamed.

Chapter Four

REVELATION

alling asleep in Eva Cooper's comfortable arms, Jenna Walker dreamed she was in the most peaceful place of all – her mother's uterus. She floated, content to take nourishment from her mother. As president, her mind seemed to work all the time, even while she slept. Now, her mind floated free, without a care in the world. Too soon, though, Jenna found her head wedged in a tight place, being pushed, shoved, moved through by any means possible. Ahead, she could sense a dreadful light. Somehow, she knew it was the light of knowledge. When it swept over her, she would never be the same again. She didn't want to go any farther, but the pushing and the shoving continued against her best efforts. Her home in the uterus had grown too small. Hours of pain and terror passed before she broke free from the vice-like grip of bone and found herself moving through translucent, crystalline yet fleshy folds and gushed out into the terrifying light in a burst of clear moisture and dew reminiscent of blood, but infinitely older – as though the color had been washed away.

Like Athena, Jenna Walker found herself born fully formed. However, while Athena had sprung from the head of the male god, Zeus, Jenna Walker came from a god-like female's uterus and vagina. Whereas Athena had been born armed with spear, helm, and mail, Jenna was armed only with those things that had prompted Eva Cooper to call her beautiful: deep brown eyes, an easy smile, long, muscled legs, well-proportioned hips and breasts. Jenna Walker took a moment to admire her body as more than just so much anatomy put together, but as a deliciously sensuous whole.

The light of knowledge washed over Jenna and she realized she had entered the presence of a Cluster in orbit around the Earth, but she wanted more information. The woman who had given birth to Jenna reached down and gathered her into her arms, bringing Jenna to her breast. Jenna brushed the woman's long, black hair from a rigid and unyielding nipple, more like a sculpture of Venus's breast than a human's tender flesh. Instinct told Jenna to disregard the breast's cold rigidity and latch on. As she suckled, the woman who held her seemed to become warmer, more tender, more human. At the same time, Jenna's mind filled with images of an Earth she'd never dreamed of before.

Jenna had always known the Earth as a planet overrun by people. However, Earth's governments had been able to utilize resources from outside to keep people fed. Ice mined from the asteroid belt provided fresh water. Farms and mines on Mars supplied the Earth with crops and minerals. Maintaining all those outside resources required a delicate dance of politics, money and technology. Jenna had joined the dance when she had been elected a senator, then named a minister and ultimately elected president of the Alliance. Many believed Earth's tax structure had grown too steep. It made housing a challenge for many people. During her presidential campaign, she'd vowed to meet the challenge, even though it appeared to be insurmountable.

Then came the Clusters.

Then came Doomsday.

Jenna knew both occurrences could spell disaster for her presidency. She hadn't been responsible for either occurance, but people wouldn't see it that way. As Jenna drank in the Cluster's sweet milk, she understood Doomsday in a new light, which both frightened and compelled her. Fewer people on the Earth meant fewer people to feed and house. Jenna looked into Mother-Cluster's green eyes and somehow conveyed her sadness for all the lives lost.

Mother-Cluster smiled, "It is sweet of you to care for those who died." She spoke in a gentle voice, not the booming or resounding voice one might expect from a godlike entity. "They were invited to be born again. However, the images my sisters and I presented proved too intense for them and they did not understand. Birth is a dangerous process – rebirth even more so. Some are stillborn; others miscarry. Those who survive are the strongest. Grieve for those who died, for they will not know the wonders you and the other survivors are about to experience."

Looking into Mother-Cluster's eyes, Jenna glimpsed billions of years of experience. The Cluster could take humanity into the future. Jenna began to understand ways machines could be more productive on Mars and in the asteroids. She saw ways the Earth could be cleaned up and made beautiful without giving up the comforts she had grown to love. Humans with little vision or drive had been swept asunder. She would work with the remaining humans to rebuild the planet; humans, with a drive to serve their fellow man, had imagination, and wanted to explore.

"Yes, my little one," said Mother-Cluster, "grieve for those who have died. But also celebrate with those who live. You are the heirs of a new Earth that you will build. You will be remembered forever."

Jenna released Mother-Cluster's breast – now softer, almost human – and swallowed the milk. A tear ran down her cheek and she woke up to find herself in Eva Cooper's arms. Jenna eased herself from Eva's arms and kissed the doctor on the forehead. The President of the Gaean Alliance tucked in her blouse, threw on her jacket and slipped into her shoes. With a deep breath, she knew she had work to do.

Arriving aboard the *Nicholas Sanson*, John Mark Ellis, Kirsten Smart, Suki Ellis and Manuel Raton went to the ship's command deck. Navigator Laura Peters turned as they entered and flashed a relieved smile. The ship's first mate, Simon Yermakov – a man whose round face and puffy cheeks caused him to resemble a squirrel – turned in his chair. "Top of the morning, Skipper," he said. "We've been trying to reach you all night."

"We've heard the news," said Ellis. "It seems the Cluster ships went to Earth."

"So much for this week's pay." Yermakov grimaced.

"We might just be able to save your check, Simon." Kirsten

winked. "I have volunteered *Sanson* for a special reconnaissance mission."

"Recon mission?" asked Laura – who served in the Confederation Reserves in addition to being the *Sanson's* navigator.

"We're a mapping vessel." Simon's brow furrowed. "What's this all about?"

Ellis motioned for Yermakov and Peters to approach. He introduced his mother and Manuel. "Has G'Liat left the ship yet?"

Simon Yermakov nodded ascent. "He left yesterday. A Rd'dyggian charter vessel picked him up."

"Good." Ellis nodded. "Please ask someone to fix up his quarters for my mother and Mr. Raton."

Simon examined the two new arrivals. Just short of six-feet tall, Manuel Raton had salt-and-pepper hair, a long, droopy mustache, and sleepy-looking eyes that hid keen observational skills. Somehow, he seemed as though he would be more at home with hepler pistols in each hand than accompanying the captain's mother. Fire Ellis was tall and rail thin, except for an expansive bosom, which made her look top-heavy. Hands on hips, she admired the *Nicholas Sanson's* command deck. Her almost battle-ready stance made Simon re-evaluate his first impression – Manuel Raton *was* at home with this woman.

"Will do, Skipper," said Simon. "Now what's this about recon work? The *Sanson* won't even be ready to leave orbit for another two weeks."

Ellis looked around for the ship's communicator, but didn't see her. "Where's Natalie?"

Laura Peters let out a slow breath. "In the infirmary. When Earth went silent, it overwhelmed her and she collapsed."

"The Emergency Med Tech gave her some Proxom to calm her nerves," explained Simon.

Kirsten frowned. "Proxom interferes with the communication's implant. Are you sure that's wise?"

Simon Yermakov shrugged. "It seemed better than having her hysterical. The Med Tech suggested it for a dose or two, then we'd see if we can bring her off."

Ellis nodded approval. "Good. We'll need her back to duty as soon as she's able. In the meantime, I want to talk to you two," he nodded to Peters and Yermakov in turn. "I have been appointed a captain in the Alpha Coma Space Fleet. My mission is to determine just what happened on Earth. Kirsten has volunteered the *Sanson* to serve as my command." Ellis chewed his lower lip for a moment and Simon looked as though he might interrupt, but seemed to change his mind. Ellis continued. "I want to make it crystal clear that no one aboard the *Sanson* is obligated to come on this mission. You are civilians and this is military service. However, the *Sanson* has a good crew that works well together. I do not want to break this crew up if I don't have to. If you two stick with me, I'm sure most of the crew will come along. We all want to find out what's happened to our friends and family back on Earth. I need you. Are you with me?"

"You can count on me, sir," piped Laura Peters.

Simon Yermakov looked down at his feet, then looked back up into Laura's beaming face. He turned to Kirsten, who smiled. He swallowed as his eyes roved over to Fire and Manuel. He shook his head. Lower lip trembling, Simon stepped over to the command deck's holographic viewer and looked off into the image of space.

Captain Ellis lifted his hand, indicating that everyone else should stay put. He alone approached Simon and put his hand on the first mate's shoulder. "Simon, is there anything I can say to persuade you?"

Simon took a deep, shuddering breath. "Skipper, I have a talent for geography. As a kid, I could name every major planet's capital and tell you its precise location before most kids could recite the ABC's. I'm a good mathematician and a decent physicist. Those same talents brought me to the TransGalactic Corporation's cartography division. I like maps and equations better than people – that's why I shipped out. What do I owe Earth's people?"

Ellis responded in soft tones. "What about your parents? Siblings?"

"I never knew my father," said Yermakov. "But, what else is new? My mom left Earth after I went to work for TransGalactic. She lives on New Earth. My sister followed her."

"The Cluster is a threat to humans everywhere," explained Ellis.

Simon slammed his palm against the wall then took a few deep breaths and nodded. "I'm a good map maker. I should have commanded this ship. Not you."

Ellis took a deep breath, then looked up at the ceiling. Simon Yermakov had been up for promotion to *Sanson's* captaincy when he, G'Liat, and McClintlock had sought a ship they could use to search for the Cluster. G'Liat had called in favors with the TransGalactic Corporation and landed them jobs on the *Sanson*. Kirsten Smart had confessed to Ellis that she had not wanted Yermakov as captain. The reason Yermakov shipped out to begin with – the fact that he didn't enjoy working with people – kept him from the captaincy. Kirsten had considered it a blessing when Ellis had been named the new captain. Ellis blinked and looked at Yermakov's back. "What would you do if you were the *Sanson's* captain?"

Yermakov's back stiffened. "My first order of business would be to repair the ship."

"What would happen after the ship was repaired? What would you do?" Ellis stepped up to Yermakov and whispered in his ear. "TransGalactic isn't responding. There are no instructions."

"You know damned well what I'd do," growled Yermakov. "I'd consult Kirsten. She's the corporate officer. It would be her decision."

"And you know damned well what she wants to do," Ellis growled back. "She's back there, ready to take this ship into Hell to find out what's happened."

Yermakov whirled around and looked Ellis in the eye. "Only because of you, Captain, sir," he spat. "She loves you."

Ellis put his hands behind his back. "This is the critical question, Mr. Yermakov. Has that love changed her in any way? Would her decision to go back to Earth – resources permitting – be any different? Or, are you just using my presence as an excuse?"

Yermakov looked down at his feet. "Damn you."

Ellis risked putting his hand on Yermakov's shoulder. "Will you come with us to Earth? You're more than a good mapmaker. You know this ship better than me – better even than Kirsten."

"Mahuk knows the ship. He has family on Earth – he'll go with you."

"But, Mahuk isn't the first officer. You are." Ellis squeezed Simon's shoulder. "I need you. Kirsten needs you. Mahuk needs you."

"I have to think about it, Skipper," said Yermakov. "If you're sincere that we're not obligated to follow, you'll at least allow me time to decide whether or not I'm going to Earth, won't you?"

Ellis nodded. "Will you, at least, agree to stay on for the next day or so and oversee the repairs to the ship?"

Yermakov looked into Ellis's eyes again. This time, the gaze softened. "I'll do that much for you, sir. I have to consider the rest."

The captain stepped into the hologram of space and looked around at the distant stars. "Alpha Coma Berenices's government has put all of their resources at our disposal. Given that, how long do you think it'll be before the ship can be ready to proceed toward Earth?"

"I'd have to consult Mr. Mahuk," said Yermakov. "But I can't imagine it'll take more than three to four days with unlimited manpower and no wait time for parts."

"Then meet with Mr. Mahuk and speed up your repairs, Mr. Yermakov. You have two days to make up your mind." The captain stepped back to the command deck's rear wall where Suki and Manuel waited. Laura had returned to her post at navigation and Kirsten had stepped into her office. "Shall I show you to your quarters?"

"Please do." Fire nodded to her son.

"Then find us some food," said Manuel. "I'm starving."

Eva Cooper awoke several hours later. Her head swam as she tried to remember what had happened before she fell asleep. The memories came back to her in a rush. She bit her lower lip, feeling both liberated and frightened. Thighs sticky and hair mussed, she sat up, realizing she would have to exit through the Oval Office. Looking at her watch, she gasped at the time.

Anyone could be there. Peeking into the hall, she noticed a restroom across the way. She did her best with the sink and washcloth to make herself look presentable. Returning to the bedchamber, she finished dressing, then went to the president's office door. Eva eased the door open and looked in to see the president meeting with the holographic images of numerous senators from around the planet. Their discussion had an eerie, almost philosophic tone. They discussed diseases the doctor knew to be incurable. However, as she listened, she realized the president and the senators discussed cures – and the cures sounded both plausible and obvious. It sounded as though incurable diseases didn't exist.

Jenna Walker looked up, smiled and waved, then returned her attention to the meeting.

Eva Cooper stepped into the room, moved through, but lingered near the main door. As she did, she caught snippets of conversation about humanity moving into the future and cleaning up the Earth. No one seemed worried about the Doomsday Dead except for the logistics of dealing with the bodies. It seemed as though they knew the answers to Doomsday and it no longer concerned them. Neither did the Clusters concern them nor how the Earth had lost touch with the remainder of the galaxy. Eva swallowed hard, knowing she had some research to do. She looked at her watch and noticed it was time to take her next dose of Proxom. With the emotion-stabilizing drug in her system, she'd be better able to deal with whatever she learned.

Samuel "Old Man" Coffin swore as he dug through his sea chest, searching for a tobacco pouch. Although Coffin had a nicotine addiction, he smoked his pipe less from being an addict than from a sense of history. Nantucket Island was his home and legend said God created Nantucket when he dumped his gray pipe ash into the Atlantic Ocean. In the late 25th century, many people in old Nantucket families took up smoking as a way to set themselves apart from off-islanders and to retain a sense of island history. The drug Dairtox, introduced to reduce toxins in the lungs from air-borne pollutants, made smoking a relatively safe pastime. After several minutes, Coffin still could not find the tobacco. He sat down on the floor and stroked his snow-white beard – eyes searching a room that was at once familiar, yet not his own.

Old Man Coffin sat in a guest room of the Ellis house – one of the last homes on Nantucket still owned by one of the island's old families. While Suki and John Mark Ellis searched for the Cluster, Coffin stayed at their home – a sentinel guarding the old house against off-islanders, tax collectors, and vandals. Coffin stood, joints complaining, and left the guest room. The night before, he'd watched the teleholo and learned that four Clusters had appeared in Earth's orbit. He had shut off the teleholo and spent a restless night huddled under the covers, wishing the Ellises would return from their sojourn in space. In the morning, Coffin awoke. Not used to owning a teleholo, he hadn't bothered to turn it on. Instead, he sought the comfort of his familiar pipe. Though he'd found the pipe, he couldn't find the tobacco.

Coffin descended the creaking, wooden staircase and searched the living room to see if John Mark Ellis or his late father had left any tobacco behind. A pipe rack stood on the fireplace mantle – but he ignored them. More promising was a wooden box with a sailing ship's image on the lid sitting on a table beside an old couch. Coffin opened the box and discovered it to be a small humidor containing a few cigars, but no pipe tobacco. Coffin almost took a cigar, but decided he would prefer the comfort of his old pipe. Sighing, he realized he had no choice but to ride out to his shack in the nearby village of Madaket.

Coffin pulled himself upstairs and found a backpack and shoes. As he prepared for the short trip, he grew light-hearted. It had been too long since he had been out to his own home. While it may have only been a shack, it contained the last vestiges of his life: his own books as well as books his ancestors had left behind, memorabilia from old whaling days and from the days when the Coffins turned their attention to studying, rather than killing, whales. Coffin realized he'd been inside too much. He needed fresh air.

Samuel Coffin went back down the stairs and locked the Ellis house's front door. Stepping into the backyard, he retrieved a bicycle from the shed and peddled toward his home, five miles away. For his age, he was in good shape and refused to buy a hover car. While his joints groaned and complained, riding the bicycle kept them from seizing up. "The day I have to buy a goddamned hover is the day they'll bury me in the island's sand," he'd said once. Off-islanders loved hovers and used them to speed around looking for souvenirs or admiring the island's "quaint" charm. "The island's charm can't be seen at 200 kilometers per hour," complained Coffin another time. "You have to take your time and savor it."

On his way through the village of Nantucket, Old Man Coffin rode past a red brick building with white columns – an impressive example of Greek revival architecture. It was the Coffin School, named for one of the old man's ancestors, Tristram Coffin. He had been one of the island's original English settlers and by the mid-nineteenth century, most people on the island claimed to be Tristram Coffin's descendants. Now, in the late 30th century, Samuel Coffin was the last living descendant who bore Tristram's surname. As he rode through the village of Nantucket, Coffin did notice how quiet the streets had become. Again, he remembered news stories describing the Clusters in orbit around the Earth. "People must be inside, noses stuck in the holos," said Coffin to himself, unaware of the Doomsday Dead.

Samuel Coffin sped past the school and left town, then followed a plascrete roadway to the village of Madaket. As with Nantucket, both the road and the village had fallen silent. Twisting and turning his bike through the tiny village's streets, Coffin waved to a few old friends – like him, descendants of the old families. He grumbled the word "off-islanders" at a few people whose families had moved to the island within the last century or two.

Leaving the village behind, Coffin followed a decayed asphalt roadway out into the moors. At last, even the ancient asphalt disappeared and Coffin dismounted and pushed his bicycle over the sandy road rather than try to peddle. At last, he arrived at a small, dilapidated shack sitting alone in the sand save for some scrubby green plants. He leaned the bike against a gray, wooden wall and licked his lips.

Old Man Coffin sighed as he faced his shack and stared at a carving of a whale's spout, which hung outside the door. The shack's electrical power generator had failed since his last visit, and the force field that protected the sign had also failed. Without protection, the sign would rot away in the island's wet weather.

Entering the shack to look for a step-stool, he recalled words from Herman Melville's novel, *Moby-Dick*: "Moving on, I at last came to a dim sort of out-hanging light not far from the docks, and heard a forlorn creaking in the air; and looking up, saw a swinging sign over the door with a white painting upon it, faintly representing a tall straight jet of misty spray, and these words underneath – 'The Spouter Inn: – Peter Coffin.'"

Most people didn't realize that Peter Coffin of New Bedford had been a historical figure. Like Samuel, he had been Tristram Coffin's descendant. Melville probably stayed at Coffin's inn, and then described it in the novel, *Moby-Dick*. Finding a stool, Coffin pulled the Spouter-Inn's sign from its hooks and brought it inside.

Gaunt, white-bearded and back-bent, the moniker "Old Man" fit Samuel Coffin well. However, he'd earned the nickname when he had been in his thirties. The young Samuel Coffin, a marine biologist, bought a large ocean-going boat and took Nantucket's young people – including John Mark Ellis, at one time – out on cruises to instruct them in ocean science and the whaling industry's history along with its connection to Nantucket. Coffin told students how ship captains had been known as "the old man." The students, who loved their captain and teacher, teased him by calling him the old man of Nantucket. Soon, they shortened the moniker and referred to Samuel as Old Man Coffin. Samuel Coffin's career as an ocean-going teacher had been a natural choice given his love of family history. His ancestor, Admiral Sir Isaac Coffin, purchased the first training ship in the old United States – the *Clio* – that took Nantucket students to far-off lands in the mid-nineteenth century.

Old Man Coffin ambled through the shack, pausing to look at a nineteenth century sextant. A few steps further on, he picked up a copy of the "Nautical Handbook" from the twentieth. Shaking his head, Coffin thought he should take some of these things to Ellis's house and considered packing them into his backpack. He snorted disappointment when he realized he didn't have the room.

At last, he found what he sought – a pouch of Navy Flake pipe tobacco. Coffin crumbled some tobacco into the pipe he'd brought with him and smoked while he continued to contemplate his collection of antiques. Old Man Coffin's eyes fell on a polished round of whale baleen. A black etching of a sperm whale adorned the bone. Coffin sucked in warm, soothing smoke – drinking it in like mother's milk – as he contemplated the scrimshaw. He shouldn't possess bone from a murdered whale. However, the scrimshaw had been in Coffin's family for centuries. Either way, he realized he should not leave it in the shack where anyone could get it. It would be safer in Ellis's home.

Coffin packed his tobacco pouch, the scrimshaw and a few other odds and ends into his backpack. He exited the shack and locked the door. A futile gesture he knew, looking at the ancient, rotted wood. Still, he didn't feel he could leave his shack open to just anyone. The tourists would never come out this far – Coffin's shack was too far from the plascrete roadway.

Coffin looked out toward the sea and smoked his pipe a little while longer. Black-accented gray clouds met white-accented gray ocean at the horizon. The old man longed to be on a ship, sailing the waves. The ocean was the Nantucketer's true domain. The pipe smoldered to a finish. With reverence, Coffin dumped the pipe, adding his ash to God's own. He climbed on the bike and rode back to Nantucket Village.

Night fell as Coffin took his bike to the storage shed behind the Ellis house. He stowed the bicycle, went inside and turned on the teleholo while he ordered the food preparation unit to produce quohog chowder and ale. As he slurped the chowder, he watched a rerun of Gaean President Jenna Walker's speech at Arlington Cemetery. Turning up the volume, the newscaster described the deaths around the Earth. Coffin picked up the glass of ale and swallowed a large gulp. "Where's John Mark when we need him?" Coffin took a deep breath.

A newscaster interrupted President Walker's rerun speech – a literal talking head that floated over the teleholo dais said the president would soon make a live announcement. Coffin grinned at the notion of the president interrupting the president.

"People of Gaea – Mother Earth," began the president as her miniature image faded into view: a doll standing on the teleholo dais in front of the Gaean flag, "for all of human history, we have been a people in crisis. We have fought wars with one another to determine which group would have the right to rape Gaea – our own mother. Many times, we have raped her to get at her breast's milk: the fuel to run factories, the land to raise crops and animals. Other times, we have raped her for pleasure: energy to run our teleholos and games. We humans are like depraved sex addicts, who have stopped seeing the Earth as mother…"

Samuel Coffin shook his head as he listened to the speech. Hadn't the president just been describing the dead all around the Earth? Didn't she suspect the Cluster had caused those deaths? What was all this talk about "rape of the Earth?" What did it have to do with the crisis at hand?

The president went on to say she had been in contact with the Cluster and explained that each Cluster was a life form in itself. "Again, I come before you to mourn the Doomsday Dead. However, I also come before you to tell you with absolute certainty the Cluster did not kill them. The Cluster is ancient and vastly experienced. The Cluster is even older than Mother Gaea. Like Gaea, the Cluster has much to offer Earth's people. Earth has tornadoes, earthquakes, and floods. Still, Earth produces the bounty that allows humans to survive. In much the same way, the Cluster produces a flood of emotional energy. While the Cluster's emotional flood can be devastating, the lessons it can teach are profound."

Horrified, Coffin turned off the teleholo. Unable to finish his chowder and beer, he let the dishes sit and went upstairs to his room where he undressed and pushed back the covers on his bed, then opened his backpack and retrieved the scrimshaw.

Sitting down on the bed, Coffin held the scrimshaw and

looked at the whale's image. He considered the deaths happening around the globe and the president's glib words. In Coffin's mind, the Cluster was killing people just as his ancestors once hunted whales. He placed the scrimshaw on the nightstand next to the bed, lay down and fell into a deep sleep.

He awoke the next morning to a swaying followed by a lurch. He found himself bathed in filtered twilight, but not the twilight of his room in the Ellis house. The odors of wet wood mingled with humanity invaded his nose along with a pungent undertone. "Whale oil?" he half whispered. Wood creaked and he lurched again. He looked at his hands. They appeared to be the hands of a man thirty years his junior.

Coffin climbed out of bed and looked around in the dim half-light. Shutters covered the window over the bed. He threw the shutters open and gaped at the open ocean. He had to grab onto a beam in the wall to keep from stumbling during another lurch. He looked around the room and realized he stood in an old wooden sailing vessel's after cabin. Charts were laid out on a table. A black coat and white pants hung over a chair. He scratched himself and noticed he wore wool. Someone pounded on the door.

"Come in," whispered Coffin. The pounding came again. "Come in," he growled.

A young teenager opened the creaky wooden door. "The mate's compliments, sir," said the boy. "He wants to know what course to make."

Coffin rubbed his thin, white beard. He stepped over to a table and noticed both antique charts of Earth's oceans and star charts heaped one atop the other. The universe had opened up to Coffin. He could see anything he wanted to see; go anywhere he wanted to go. "My God. What's happened? Have I gone crazy?"

A soft feminine voice reassured him. The voice spoke directly to his mind but not quite. He seemed to hear an echo from outside. The sense was strong enough for him to know he was not imagining this. "This galaxy is new to us. Take us to any place, any time."

"Sir?" asked the boy standing in the doorway.

"Damn it, boy! The mate can wait while I get my bearings.

Get me some coffee and let me review these charts!" The boy
ran from the room, slamming the door as he hastened to leave.
Coffin took a deep breath and smiled. Not only the oceans of
the Earth, but the entire galaxy, were his to explore. "Where do
we begin?"

Chapter Five

SAILORS

"Man, it stinks in here," complained Manuel Raton as he entered the Rd'dyggian warrior G'Liat's former quarters.

Ellis shrugged. "G'Liat burned incense. I think it reminded him of Rd'dyggia."

"Rd'dyggia has a high concentration of ammonia in the soil, doesn't it?" Fire wrinkled her nose.

Raton nodded. "That explains why it smells like cat piss in here."

Ellis moved across to a chair and fell into it. He held up his hands in appology. "The air scrubbers will freshen the room within a few hours." The captain retrieved a cigar from his jacket. "I could cover up the smell."

Raton shook his head. "No, that's fine. We like it just the way it is."

Fire sat down at the white table, next to her son. "Mark, I hope you don't mind that Manuel and I invited ourselves along."

Ellis grinned at his mother. "Mind? If Simon's reaction is any indication of what I'll face from the rest of the crew, it may be you, Manuel, Kirsten, Laura and I flying the ship back to Earth."

"You're right to give the crew a choice, Mark." Fire took her son's hand. "You can't force them to go. But, I think you underestimate them. Most people will want to go because they're human and they want to help."

Ellis nodded. He looked up at Manuel. "Do you want me to order some breakfast? You said you were hungry." Ellis's voice held a bitter note.

Manuel moved over to the window and looked out at the

stars and the planet below. "The lingering incense has caused me to lose my appetite." He shrugged. Looking around at Ellis, Manuel flashed a brief grin. "Maybe we'll have some breakfast in a little bit."

Fire squeezed her son's hand. Ellis looked down, refusing to meet her gaze. "What's wrong?" asked Fire.

Ellis shook his head. "I want to talk to you." He looked up at Manuel. "In private."

Manuel shrugged. "I think I'm a little hungry after all." He patted his stomach. "No need to order anything on my account, I'll go see if I can find the galley." Manuel turned and left the cabin.

Before the door closed, Ellis noticed Manuel had turned the wrong way. "Galley's aft," called the captain.

Manuel turned on his heel just as the door closed.

"What is it, Mark?" asked Fire.

Mark Ellis looked into his mother's eyes and sighed. "I like Manuel Raton. We fought side-by-side on Sufiro. But, are you...?"

"...sleeping with him?" Fire finished when Mark couldn't complete the thought. She stood and moved to the window. "Yes, I am."

"Doesn't it seem a little soon after dad..." Again, Ellis let the words trail off. He thought about his father who the Cluster had killed almost a year earlier.

Fire let out a long breath as she continued to look out the window. "I loved your father a lot. However, in thirty years of marriage, we spent maybe ten years together. He had been away well over two years before the Cluster killed him. Don't get me wrong. We loved each other a great deal, but we were independent people with our own goals." Mark Ellis looked at the deck and frowned. "I don't say that to upset you. Manuel and I have been close for a long time. He's helped me heal wounds that would have taken a long time if I'd been alone."

"It may take some time for me to adjust to this element of our relationship." Ellis looked down at his feet.

Fire leaned across the table, lifted Mark's chin, and met his gaze. "Relationships are always in flux, kiddo. I meant it when

I said I loved your father. His loss hurt us both. But just because
he died doesn't mean I can't go on living."

Ellis nodded, but didn't say anything.

"How are you and Kirsten getting along?" asked Fire.

"Pretty well. But our relationship is still pretty new – still
changing."

"It always will." Fire's eye twinkled. "It makes life exciting."

Ellis looked back to the cabin door. "Do you suppose Manuel found the galley?"

"We'd better go see. Besides I'm hungry, too." Suki Ellis
grinned. He stood up from the table, took his mother's hand
and led her to the galley.

Edmund Swan stood at Ellison Firebrandt's door on Sufiro. He
remembered the first time he had come to Firebrandt's homestead, less than a year before. At the time, the one-time pirate
had summoned him, asking him to lead an army to defend the
continent of New Granada from invaders from Sufiro's other
major continent, Tejo. At the time, Swan had been afraid, in-
timidated by the man who had tamed a planet. Now, like many
on Sufiro, Swan regarded Firebrandt more as a grandfather figure than a planetary leader.

The door slid open and Roberts greeted Swan. More than
eighty years old and bald, Roberts reminded Swan of a pirate
flag's skull and even the warm smile managed to send shivers
up the deputy sheriff's spine. "Hello, old friend," said Swan. "Is
the captain in?"

"He is. We're just finishing breakfast." Roberts maneu-
vered the hover chair back away from the door, then led the
way through the house and up a staircase to the second floor.
He drifted through double doors into a glassed-in room, where
he could look out and see Firebrandt's farm and the great river
beyond – the Nuevo Rio Grande. Upriver stood a small village
called Succor. Pushed by the river's current, a great wooden
wheel creaked as it turned slow circles. Manuel Raton once
told Swan how Firebrandt and Roberts had built the wheel
by hand during their first year on the planet. It turned an old

auxiliary electrical generator from the *Legacy*. The generator supplied power to the village and the homestead.

Firebrandt turned his head as Roberts and Swan entered the room. The captain sat at a glass table holding a porcelain cup in strong, callused hands. "Ah, Edmund!" he exclaimed. "How good to see you." He set the cup down on the table. "May I offer you some coffee?"

"That would be nice, thanks," said Swan.

Roberts indicated a chair and Swan sat down. Firebrandt passed a cup.

"So, have you heard what's happened at Earth?" Roberts glided around the table and came to a stop. He grabbed the carafe and warmed up his coffee.

"Yes," said Swan. "I suppose that's why I'm here. An old friend from Earth called. A short time later, the channel went silent. I hadn't spoken to this friend in years. For some reason he felt compelled to call me. I'm worried."

"You're not alone," said Firebrandt. "I just learned that John Mark and Fire will be on their way to Earth soon. They want to find out what's happened."

Swan sipped his coffee and then set the cup down on the saucer. "So do I." New Granada's deputy sheriff stood, stepped around the table and looked out the window, arms behind his back.

"Tell me about this friend who called," said Firebrandt.

"I haven't talked to him since we were teenagers." Swan sighed. "Back then, he was a computer genius. He thought he could use a black hole to build a vast data storage system."

Roberts shot a glance at Firebrandt then looked up at Swan. "What has your friend done since then?"

"I have no idea." Swan shrugged.

Firebrandt stroked his long white mustache for a moment then stood and joined Swan at the window. "The reason Roberts asks is that John Mark thinks the Clusters may want to form a symbiotic link with humans."

"Humans might not find your friend's dream practical." Roberts picked up his coffee cup. "But the Cluster…"

Firebrandt put his hand on Swan's shoulder. "I begin to think you should go to Earth and see what happened to your friend."

Swan nodded. "That's what I want to do, but with Manuel gone…"

"There are other deputy sheriffs here in New Granada. I think we can spare you." Firebrandt gave Swan's shoulder a squeeze. "Besides, you might be able to help John Mark and Fire."

The doorbell chimed. Roberts activated his hover chair, lifted off the ground, and went through the breakfast room's double doors. Swan snorted and returned to the table. "John Mark Ellis and your daughter can take care of themselves."

The one-time pirate captain grinned. "They can also get into a lot of trouble. I suspect they'll need all the help they can get."

The deputy sheriff sat down and sipped his coffee. "We have one last problem. How do I get to Earth? I don't have much money and I suspect most transports aren't in a hurry to go to Earth and find out if the Cluster will destroy them."

Roberts drifted back into the breakfast room. A seven-foot tall, orange being with an eye patch and flowing robes followed him. "Arepno managed to find us parts for our transfer coupling." Roberts flashed a self-satisfied grin. "I should have it up and running this afternoon."

"Hallelujah! The harvest may not go to waste after all." Firebrandt inclined his head toward the Rd'dyggian pirate captain. "Thank you, my friend. Once again you have saved us."

Arepno turned his black eye on Swan. "Brother Swan," he said using a translator unit. "It is agreeable to see you again."

"And you," said Swan. The two had defended New Granada side-by-side.

Firebrandt stepped forward. "Arepno, if you would care to earn more gold, I'd be happy to pay you to transport Edmund here to Earth so he can find out what's happened to his friend."

"It would mean facing the Cluster again." Arepno moved around the table. The purple mustache-like appendages in front of his mouth wriggled in agitation. He sat down and remained silent for several moments. "Learning what the Cluster is doing could be valuable information," mused the Rd'dyggian, at last. "Sounds exhilarating."

"Sounds like you have your ride." Firebrandt forced a

brave smile. "I'll pay your fare. All I ask is that you check on John Mark and Fire."

"I will, sir." The deputy sheriff stood and shook Firebrandt's hand. Turning, he left with the Rd'dyggian warrior.

Ellison Firebrandt picked up his coffee cup and looked out the window, not out toward the river and the fields, but back toward the sleek, black hull of the old privateer vessel he and Roberts had used as their home's core. "How many years have we been here?" mused the captain.

Roberts moved the hover chair next to Firebrandt and looked out at the ship. Few people had noticed how broken gun ports had been replaced with new weapons over the years or how the doorways that led from the ship to the house's adobe sections were now equipped with space-worthy airlocks. "We've been on Sufiro for almost fifty years, sir," said Roberts with a gleam in his eye.

"That's a long time," said Firebrandt. "Time enough to repair almost all the damage done to a crash-landed vessel, isn't it?"

"Almost?" Roberts lifted an eyebrow. "I'd say the man who couldn't make a vessel spaceworthy in forty-nine years should be shoved out the nearest airlock rather than serve on your crew, sir."

Firebrandt sipped his coffee, then smiled. "I think it may be time to get some fuel and a minimal crew assembled." He examined the clean thrusters surrounding the EQ generator at the ship's stern.

"You know, launching the ship will destroy the homestead," said Roberts.

Firebrandt nodded. "If we don't launch the ship, the homestead may be destroyed anyway."

"We'll miss the harvest," said Roberts.

Firebrandt looked at his friend and winked. "I don't think you'll miss it at all."

Eva Cooper sat in her office in the old White House building in the Columbia District. Holographic charts floated above the desk, showing the president's brain-wave patterns. An implant monitored the president's brain activity around the clock for health reasons as well as planetary security. Cooper had sample scans from the past three years along with a scan taken within the past day.

A sharp rapping sounded at the door. "Come in," said Cooper.

Dick Richards strode into the office and sighed when he noticed the charts. "You're supposed to have me here if you call up the president's brain scans."

Cooper looked up at Richards. "How did you know I'd accessed the president's brain scans?"

"The White House protocol sensors alerted me." Richards sat down in a plush chair facing Cooper's desk. "No one person is supposed to access that information. It would be a security breech."

Cooper shook her head. "I'm not planning a coup. I just wanted to see if the president's okay."

"In what sense?" Richards' eyebrows came together. His fingers danced on the chair's wooden armrest.

"Before I answer that … tell me how the Cluster contacted the president? I reviewed the White House communication's logs. There's no record of the Cluster sending a signal."

"I won't ask how you got access to those logs," said Richards. "Why do you want to know about the Cluster's communication methods?"

Eva stood and moved around the desk, blocking Richards' view of the three-dimensional brain-scan charts. "I'm concerned about planetary security and concerned the president may be compromised."

Richards held out his hands. "In that event, you should have contacted me before accessing the brain scan records."

Cooper shook her head. "I can't be sure you haven't been compromised as well."

Richards leaned forward. "Now that sounds a little paranoid."

"Just how did the Cluster communicate with the president? Why has the president implemented all these new directives?

Why is she no longer concerned about the Doomsday Dead? Doesn't any of this bother you?"

Dick Richards sat back in his chair, as though the questions pummeled him. "No. It doesn't bother us, because we've all spoken to the Cluster at this point. More than anything, I'm surprised it hasn't spoken to you."

Eva Cooper's mouth dropped open. "You've communicated with it?"

Richards nodded.

"What's going on?" Cooper asked in a whisper.

"The Cluster finds humans fascinating. It wants to help us," said Richards. "The Earth has been dirty and overpopulated for centuries. The Cluster has shown us how to fix our planet."

Cooper folded her arms across her stomach. "Well, the Cluster seems to have solved the overpopulation part of the problem. Over a third of Earth's people dead on Doomsday … People continue to die because they're depressed … At the rate things are going, we may lose half the planet's population – maybe more." She stepped away from the president's brain scan, allowing Richards to see. She chewed her lower lip, wondering if she suffered from paranoia. Dick Richards was an old and trusted friend. The man facing her had not changed in any way she could detect. His sharp blue eyes were the same as they'd always been – commanding, questioning, and compassionate. Dick Richards was not the enemy, though he might be a friend in trouble.

"You're right." Cooper sighed. "I've been looking at the president's brain activity. Brain waves are like a fingerprint. They're unique to each individual. Unlike a fingerprint they do evolve." Cooper pointed to three charts and indicated similar dips and valleys in each graph. "Here we see three different scans of the president over the last three years. Several features are the same despite the progression." Cooper highlighted the fourth scan. "Notice how this one is completely different. It's as though the president has become a completely different person overnight"

"You said yourself that brain scans evolve and change." Richards shrugged.

"Not this much," said Cooper. "Is the Cluster doing this?

If the Cluster is doing this to everyone, it would explain what's happening."

Richards stood and paced the room. "I understand your concern and it seems valid. However, I think you should give it time – see what happens. The Earth is evolving and improving. I think you'll like the new Earth." Richards stopped pacing and looked Eva in the eye. "What bothers me most is why you don't know this already. Why hasn't the Cluster communicated with you?"

Eva sat down in her chair and turned off the displays. "That's an excellent question. Why hasn't the Cluster talked to me?"

Samuel Coffin decided the first order of business was to test his new ship's capabilities. While he could travel anywhere in the galaxy, there was one place he knew no human, Rd'dyggian, or even Titan-built ship could go. However, if he could go anywhere he wanted, he would go to a forbidden ocean: the galactic core, where stars were so massive and numerous, where gravity was so intense, humans would not survive. At the galactic core, he would find a super-massive black hole. Humans had observed the galactic center from afar using radio and x-ray telescopes, but no one had ever viewed it with the naked eye, even in the 30th century. Coffin summoned the cabin boy. "My compliments to the mate. Set course for the galactic bulge."

"Aye aye, sir." The boy ran off.

Coffin finished sipping his coffee, then went to the deck. The second and third mates shouted orders and myriad people scuttled up the rigging. Others scattered around the deck, securing hatches and a crew hoisted the anchor. The first mate paced the deck, observing the crew's work, and shouting an occasional admonition. Coffin took a good look at the first mate and blinked several times. The robust, vigorous man marching about the afterdeck shouting orders should not have been able to do so. "Elisha Folger?" asked Coffin.

"Samuel Coffin!" called the mate. "You old sea dog, I should have known you'd be behind this!"

Coffin climbed up the ladder and shook hands with his old

friend. "How are you here? Last I knew, you were in the hospital on Nantucket, hooked up to machines." Coffin remembered how Folger had looked on their last visit. He'd been over 120 years old, a frail ghost of the man he once had been – a living brain trapped in a worn-out, dead body. As he had no living family, Folger had no one who could order the life-support shut down.

"I don't know how I'm here," said Folger, perplexed. "All I know is that I've been given freedom again. I'm back in my old body." Folger lifted his arms in the air to feel the breeze. "Have we died and gone to heaven?"

"If I died, I died in my sleep," said Coffin. "But somehow I know we're very much alive, my friend. Somehow, I know this ship can take us places no human has ever been. We'll get to see things with our eyes that no one has ever seen."

"That's why you ordered us to the galaxy's center, eh?" Folger winked.

"Do you think I'm crazy?"

"You're asking a man who has been living in a dream world for the past decade. For all I know, I'm still in a damned hospital bed and this is all a hallucination." Folger's eyes swept the deck, making sure preparations to depart continued.

"I hate to say this, but I'm not sure you aren't still in bed – but I don't think you're hallucinating. Somehow this is real – a reality that's somehow physical and not physical. Don't ask me how I know, or even how it works." Coffin turned around and surveyed the deck himself. He stood on a whaling ship, like the type that used to call Nantucket home. He noted three masts, with square sails on the fore and main masts, and fore-and-aft-rigged sails on the mizzenmast. Five whaleboats were secured to the ship. He guessed the ship was around 125-feet long: a whale bark with thirty to forty people in the crew. With a deep breath, Coffin looked at the first mate. "So, how do we know we'll get where we want to go?"

Folger smiled and looked over his shoulder, indicating a woman talking to a man at the helm. "You see that – our navigator is Kumiko Meiji. Remember? She came to Nantucket just to sail with you on the *Clio II*."

"That's right." Coffin nodded. "I haven't seen her since she was a teenager. She was one of the few kids I'd let steer the old ship. She wanted to be a cartographer. She went off to work for TransGalactic Corporation, didn't she?" Coffin looked at Folger. "Are we all Islanders, or associated with the Island?"

Folger shook his head. "I don't think so. It's just the three of us, as far as I can tell."

"Strange, though. How do you suppose we all ended up commanding this ship?"

Folger shrugged. "You of all people questioning why Nantucketers are the most qualified sailors? I'm surprised at you, Samuel."

Samuel Coffin straightened with mock indignation. "I'll remind you to address me as Captain Coffin."

"Aye aye, sir," boomed Folger. The two men laughed. Looking around, Folger nodded satisfaction. The anchor had been raised and the ship moved, as though the wind propelled it. Folger and Coffin stepped to the deck rail and watched as the wind lifted the ship up and out of the water. They moved skyward. "So," said Folger. "What do we name the ship? *Clio III?*"

Coffin's eyebrows came together as he considered the question. "No, I think *Pequod* would be more appropriate." He watched water flow from the ship's sides. He could see Nantucket in the distance, growing smaller. The ship passed through a misty veil of clouds and the island disappeared from view.

"You aren't seeking revenge, are you?" asked Folger.

"No, but I think our souls may be at stake on this voyage, Mr. Folger. Somehow, I think we may be just as doomed as Ahab's crew." The sky darkened as the atmosphere around the ship thinned. There was still plenty of air to breathe on the ship's deck as stars appeared. The Earth curved below the ship. As they continued, he began to make out cloud-shrouded continents and blue oceans. The Earth receded into the distance. Coffin faced the galaxy's central bulge, bright and sparkling on the edges, obscured by black dust clouds in the center. He nodded satisfaction. "Steady as she goes, Mr. Folger."

"Steady as she goes," echoed the mate.

Part II: Tribulation

"And every shipmaster, and all the company in ships, and sailors, and as many as trade by sea, stood afar off, and cried when they saw the smoke of her burning, saying, 'What city is like unto this great city?'"

Revelation 18: 17-18

Chapter Six

ASCENSION

After breakfast and a nap, John Mark Ellis rode the lift to the *Nicholas Sanson's* command deck and surveyed the situation. The shipyard staff supervised most of the repair activities. With little damage to the command deck itself, the ship's nerve center was quiet.

A sophisticated holographic tank, which could show different views of space in three dimensions, occupied the command deck's forward section. It served as a chart room and presented a way to see space around the vessel. Two unmanned consoles, which met in a V-shape, faced the holographic tank. One console controlled navigation and recorded the pathways the ship traversed through fourth dimensional space. The other was communications, which oversaw internal and external comm traffic and disseminated mapping data to the galactic networks. Each station had a holographic control panel that could be customized to suit the user's needs. Some users preferred black pads with colorful buttons. More eccentric users might choose levers and knobs set in a simulated wooden panel. Behind the control stations, stood the command chairs – captain's to the left, mate's to the right. Each command chair had a holographic console similar to the forward stations, but somewhat smaller. The holographic controls allowed for different jobs to be performed at different locations. On *Sanson*, the first mate maintained the mapping instrumentation while the captain oversaw all other ship functions. Behind the command chairs were offices for the corporate officer and the captain.

An image of the *Sanson* filled much of the holographic tank. When Ellis had approached the *Sanson* earlier in the day aboard the launch, the repair crew had resembled a large swarm. Now, so many people worked on the ship that Ellis feared they might get in each other's way. Below the hologram of the *Sanson*, Ellis could discern two booted feet.

"Mr. Yermakov?" asked Ellis.

Yermakov looked around from behind the holographic *Sanson*. His features were set in a grim scowl, but his eye gleamed in a way Ellis hadn't noticed before. "Yes, Skipper."

"How go the repairs?" Ellis inspected the ship's image as he strolled toward the holographic display.

"Very well," said Yermakov as he came out from behind the image. "The burned-out Erdon-Quinn Engine has been repaired. New conduits are being installed." Yermakov shook his head. "I've never seen this many people come together to get a ship ready for a mission. I'd never have guessed the work could be completed in such a short time."

Ellis nodded. "They all want to know what's going on back at Earth. All humans came from there, after all. They want to do their part for the mother world."

Simon Yermakov's eyes rolled skyward. "Don't push your luck, Captain. I've already decided to go back to Earth with you. But, if you start in on speeches about why I should do my part for king and country, forget it."

Ellis inclined his head. "Do you mind me asking why you're going?"

Simon looked at the ship's image, then back to Ellis. "Some of it is how many people are helping us to get going. Some of it is a conversation I had with Mahuk while you were in your quarters. I have to admit, selfishness plays a role. I don't want the Cluster to take over my mind. If I'm not willing to do the work to make sure that doesn't happen, I can't ask anyone else to do it for me."

"Fair enough. How long before we'll be ready to depart for Earth?"

Yermakov looked at numbers scrawled in mid-air in the holographic chamber. "I'd say we'll be ready to leave orbit within thirty-six hours."

"I need to make an announcement to the crew, to let them know what we're about to do and to ask them to decide whether they want to come along or not," said Ellis.

"That's another reason I decided to go. Ms. Smart could

have declared this mission a job requirement. I appreciate the fact that you asked, sir." Yermakov stepped over to the communications station and activated the interface. "You're on ship-wide speakers."

Ellis put his hands behind his back and made the announcement to the crew. He detailed what little data they had about the Cluster's appearance at Earth. "I'm acting in an official capacity as a captain in the Alpha Coma Fleet. Ms. Smart has volunteered her services and the services of the *Nicholas Sanson*. First Mate Simon Yermakov, Chief Engineer Mahuk, and Pilot Laura Peters have all volunteered their service as well. I'm asking all of you to serve with us, to determine what has happened at the Earth. If anyone is staying behind at Alpha Coma, I need to know in twelve hours so I can determine which positions need to be filled." Ellis paused and considered whether he needed to add anything else. "I won't pretend this will be an easy or safe voyage. You are not a military crew and, as such, you are not required to sacrifice yourselves for Earth. I ask you to come along because you all know this ship better than anyone I can find on Alpha Coma in short notice. Many of you have family and friends back on Earth. We're all humans and, as such, the Cluster poses a threat to us all. Our job will be to find out what can be done to stop the Cluster at Earth and get back here to Alpha Coma so I can help formulate a strategy to stop the Cluster. I sincerely hope you will help us in this mission." Ellis reached out and turned off the inter-ship speakers. The captain released a deep sigh.

Yermakov put his hand on Ellis's shoulder. "Let's hope no one does have to be sacrificed."

"Amen to that, Simon." Ellis gave a curt nod, then turned and went to his office to review the latest reports from the repair crews for himself.

It took two days for Captain Samuel Coffin and his crew aboard the whaling bark *Pequod* to reach the galaxy's center. To them, it appeared that a wind billowed their sails, pushing them through the Milky Way galaxy's arms. They sailed through a black fog, like wafting coal dust and came out in a day-lit world filled with billions of stars – the galactic bulge. The ship proceeded through stars closer together than they had seen before. Elisha Folger stood at the deck rail with Coffin and the navigator, Kumiko Meiji.

"I've heard the phrase, it looks like you can reach out and touch the stars." Folger glanced from Coffin to Meiji. "This looks like I could reach out, touch one star and put my hand on another."

"You know," said Meiji, "the gravity from all these stars should tear us apart. There's no way any vessel could traverse this region of the galaxy."

Coffin looked down his nose at the petite mathematician. "That's what bothers you? Not how we're standing on the deck of a ship over a thousand years old with an atmosphere and no obvious force field, flying through vacuum? Not how we crossed vast distances of space without making an EQ jump?"

Meiji looked up at Coffin and shrugged. "It seems pretty clear we're experiencing an illusion. I just don't know whether the illusion is technological, like holograms, or hallucinogenic in nature. Either way, it's extremely realistic."

Folger put his hands behind his back. "Okay, so why worry about whether or not a ship could really be here? If this is just a hallucination, why couldn't it be a kind of theater of the mind?"

"Because it's too realistic." The mathematician held her hands out to the stars. "I've spent years pouring over galactic charts built up from images TransGalactic ships took while traversing the galaxy. I've walked through chart tanks filled with holographic images. I've never seen the galaxy's center with my own eyes, but I can say with some authority, this is what it would look like." Meiji paused and admired the starscape. "Somewhere, somehow, a ship is traveling through the center of the galaxy, taking these images. Somehow, that ship is not being torn apart in the gravitational tides here."

Coffin looked out over the railing. The stars were getting closer together. He pulled a pipe from his coat pocket, packed and lit it. "Are we aboard that ship?"

"Maybe, or maybe the ship is taking these images and

feeding them back to us on Earth," said Meiji.

Folger rubbed his chin. "Still, what about the jumps? There's no way a ship could cross the distances we've traveled without making EQ jumps."

"True." Meiji pondered the question for a moment. "Still, it's theoretically possible for a ship making those jumps to image the normal space it's passing through. We haven't managed it, but it's possible. It could be presented to us as though we traveled through normal space."

Coffin snorted, blowing smoke through his nose. "Not even the Titans have managed that trick."

As the three watched, the stars around the ship began to thin again, as though a vast wind had swept the stars away. The ship listed to one side, as though a powerful current caught it and carried it toward the stellar clearing. "Straighten your helm!" called Folger over his shoulder. A deep black void – blacker somehow than space itself – sat at the heart of the stellar clearing. The black mass resembled an oblate spheroid surrounded by a whirlpool of glowing matter. The blackness seemed wrapped in a crystal ball, warping and twisting the light from stars behind it into rainbow swirls. Folger, Meiji and Coffin all gasped at the sight.

"The galactic core," said Meiji in a hoarse whisper. "We've made it."

"You're saying that's for real?" asked Coffin.

"Take a good look, gentlemen, that's as real as you're ever going to see the black hole at the center of the galaxy."

Later that day, John Mark Ellis sat at his desk and reviewed the *Sanson's* manifest, confirming the ship had sufficient provisions for the return journey to Earth. Kirsten Smart sat across from him, reviewing a list of potential crewmembers, in the event that anyone decided to leave the ship. Herbert Firebrandt had provided the list, which contained names of Alpha Coman sailors who had some experience with mapping vessels.

Both looked up at a rapping on the door. "Come in," called Ellis.

Natalie Papadraxis entered the office wearing a bright, flower-print sundress. She held her hands and her eyes were wide. "I came to say that I'm sorry I passed out while on duty."

Kirsten stood and took Natalie's hands, then led her to the chair next to the one she had been seated in. "Natalie, how are you doing? We've been worried about you."

"It shocked me to lose contact with the Earth. I still don't feel myself," said Natalie, her voice faraway, almost dreamy.

Ellis flashed a reassuring grin. "I know what it's like to have a shock and pass out on the bridge. That happened to me when I commanded the *Barbara Firebrandt*. It's why the Gaean Navy requested my resignation. No one understood." Captain Ellis stood and moved around the desk. He sat down on the edge and looked into Natalie's eyes. "I understand what it's like to have the Cluster hurt you."

"Thank you, sir." Natalie looked from Ellis to Kirsten and back to the captain. "Sir, I heard you address the crew. I know the twelve hours are almost up, but I wanted to let you know that I would like to stay with the ship."

Ellis looked at his watch, and then rubbed his eyes. He hadn't realized how long he'd been working.

"Are you sure?" asked Kirsten. "You've had quite a shock. No one would hold it against you if you stayed behind."

"I know." Natalie shuffled her feet. "But, I want to find out what's happened. I want to help if I can. Will you let me?"

"Of course," said Ellis. "You're a valuable member of this crew."

Natalie smiled. "That means a lot to me. Thank you." Natalie tapped her head to indicate the communication's implant. "The Proxom they gave me hasn't interfered with my implant as much as I thought it would. I've been getting messages from around the ship. The entire crew wants to stay on as well. A lot of them are scared, but they can't let the ship go home without them."

Kirsten nodded. "We're all scared, Natalie."

Ellis put his hands behind his back. "The Cluster is intelligent and it likes humans. I don't think we can overestimate the danger."

Natalie sighed. "I can't help but wonder, though, why it

cut off communication with the home system. If it wants to help humans, why won't it let us talk to those people it's helped."

Ellis swallowed hard. "That's why we need to go." The captain stood and moved to the wall. "Have you been in touch with the ship yard? How are repairs progressing?"

"They say we're on schedule. We should be able to leave orbit in just a little over twenty-four hours," reported Natalie.

Ellis nodded, satisfied. He looked to Kirsten. "That should be enough time to get the provisions on board. If you'll approve the list – I'd say it's time for us all to go and get a good night's sleep, so we can be ready to leave tomorrow night."

Kirsten gave a thumbs-up. "Sounds like a plan to me."

Edmund Swan felt like a nine-year-old child strapped into a seat that was too big for him. He faced a central dais, which projected a hologram that resembled a transparent honeycomb. Each cell of the honeycomb-like display held its own three-dimensional projection. Some cells showed space as it appeared around the ship. Others showed exterior and interior views of the ship itself. Still others flashed Rd'dyggian words so rapidly Swan suspected he couldn't have read them even if they had been Terro-Generic. Six Rd'dyggians occupied chairs in each corner of the command center. Their massive six-fingered hands rested on smooth consoles standing before them. Swan knew Arepno acted as a privateer, raiding ships the Rd'dyggians considered enemies. The deputy sheriff had never imagined a more serene pirate ship.

On human ships, there was a constant buzz as humans moved around and various machines performed their tasks. The only sound in the Rd'dyggian command center was the Rd'dyggian warriors' gentle breathing. On human ships, care had been taken to add design elements and artwork to catch the eye. The Rd'dyggian ship's command center reminded Swan of sitting inside a smooth six-sided jewelry box. The walls flowed into the ceiling, floor, and each other. Swan had fallen asleep, but he'd awaken a few hours later to an unchanged tableau.

At last, Arepno lifted his hands from the console and looked at Swan. "We are nearing Saturn and executing a scan of the system." He touched the control plate and one honeycomb cell expanded to show the great, golden planet Saturn and its glistening rings. As Arepno held his thumb on the control plate, the view zoomed in and showed the rust-red moon, Titan. "There are no Clusters out here near Titan."

As Swan watched, the view shifted through different wavelengths. On the red end of the spectrum, a halo of glowing dots surrounded the moon, which served as the known galaxy's capital. Each dot represented a space vessel. "You would think the Clusters would be interested in reuniting with the Titans based on what Firebrandt told us," mused Swan.

"Indeed," said Arepno. "However, this does lend credence to Ellis's hypothesis that the Clusters are no longer interested in the Titans." The Rd'dyggian captain turned back toward the console, lifted his thumb from the control plate, and pointed to the display. "Ship activity appears normal, which is also interesting. I see no evidence that ships have been damaged or are being interfered with. A ship from Zahar has just arrived and the Titans have launched a probe."

"Meaning the Cluster is not afraid of what ships will do." Swan narrowed his gaze. "So, why would the Cluster block communication, but not ship transport?"

"That is a good question, Brother Swan." Arepno's mustache wriggled.

Swan smiled as he remembered how Arepno had started calling him "brother" on Sufiro when they fought the Tejan forces that threatened New Granada.

Arepno placed his thumb on the control plate again and the honeycomb cell showed the Earth. "I detect only two Clusters in orbit at this time. It would seem two are elsewhere."

"Or they're hiding," mused the deputy sheriff.

"It would be impossible for them to hide from Rd'dyggian sensors," said Arepno. Swan thought he detected slight indignation from the large warrior. "We will land on Earth in about thirty of your minutes presuming the Clusters don't challenge us."

Swan swallowed hard, wishing for something to drink.

Just then, he had an urge to get up and find the restroom, but he didn't know how or even if Rd'dyggians needed to relieve themselves. With a deep breath, he sat back and did his best to enjoy the ride. Arepno placed both hands on the control console and fell back into silence. The honeycomb cell that showed Earth shrank and morphed back into its place in the larger structure.

The deputy sheriff attempted to follow the ship's progress on the displays. In two, the Earth seemed to remain the same size. In three others, the Earth grew larger until its light filled the displays. A moment later, the displays flashed white, and the strange Rd'dyggian letters appeared. Judging from the displays, Swan guessed they had entered Earth's atmosphere even though he didn't feel the telltale rocking and bumping that usually accompanied a ship during re-entry. A few moments later, Arepno startled Swan when he lifted his hands from the control console and announced, "We have landed."

This time, he placed one finger on the console and a hole appeared in one wall as a tunnel congealed and extruded itself toward the ground. Swan unbuckled the harness, stretched and stood. "I presume the Cluster didn't challenge us."

"Indeed it did not," said Arepno. "Most odd."

The deputy sheriff started toward the tunnel but looked around when he realized that Arepno hadn't followed. "Aren't you coming along … to get information about the Cluster and its activities?"

"We are accumulating information."

"Where are we?" asked Swan.

"Southern Arizona spaceport," explained Arepno. "Do you require transport to your friend's domicile?"

Swan considered the question for a moment. "No." He shook his head. "I'll just catch a cab."

"Very good." With that, Arepno turned and faced his console again.

With a shrug, Swan stepped into the tunnel extending toward the ground. He found his luggage waiting at the tunnel's end. He grabbed it and stepped out onto the spaceport's tarmac. Right away, he noticed the deep blue sky. Growing up in Tucson sector, the sky had always been hazy. Next, he noticed the near-silence. At a busy spaceport, ships should take off and land at regular intervals. Swan looked around and counted ten ships in port, including Arepno's.

He shook his head, then strode to the main terminal so he could go through customs and locate Tim Gibbs' home.

Chapter Seven

MISSION TO EARTH

The next afternoon, John Mark Ellis sat on the *Nicholas Sanson's* command deck watching as the work crews departed the ship's surface. Shuttles and launches that had brought provisions left for the planet below. Natalie Papadraxis sat at her station, coordinating with the shipyard crews, making sure no pods, shuttles or space-suited workers collided. Ellis and Yermakov each consulted their displays and talked with each other in hushed tones. There were sufficient provisions aboard the ship for a three-year voyage. Captain and first mate alike hoped the voyage would take days rather than years – however, neither knew what they would find when they reached Earth. Along with the engineering crew, Ellis and Yermakov ran simulations, checking how well the four engines were tuned. At her station, Laura plotted a course to Earth using an unobtrusive jump point to enter the solar system.

Kirsten stepped onto the command deck from her office and placed her hand on Ellis's shoulder. "Looks as though we're almost ready to go. I never dreamed we'd be heading back out this soon."

"We maybe heading out, but we aren't ready for a mapping voyage." Yermakov shrugged. "We can jump from here to Earth like any other EQ ship, but the engines aren't calibrated for charting jumps. We'll need more time for that."

As Yermakov spoke, the lift doors opened. Fire and Manuel emerged. "Do you mind if we watch as we leave orbit?" asked Fire. "The view up here is better than the one in our quarters."

Ellis looked to Kirsten, whose features remained neutral. "I have no problem," said Ellis, with a smile. "But don't get too used to special privileges, mom."

"Incoming transmission from the planet," announced

Natalie. "Senator Herbert Firebrandt."

"Put him in the holo," ordered Ellis.

The holographic tank metamorphosed into Herbert Fire-brandt's planet-side office. He stood next to his desk. The setting sun could be seen through the senator's windows. "I understand the *Sanson* is preparing to depart for Earth. I wanted to check that you have everything you need and to wish you a successful voyage."

Ellis stood and entered the hologram. To Firebrandt, it would have looked as though the captain had strode from a viewscreen into his office. "Thank you, sir. The ship is provisioned and repairs are complete. I'm certain TransGalactic will request some calibration and simulation time in the ship yard upon our return." Ellis phrased his statement less to actually request time than to convey to the bridge crew his certainty that the ship would be back soon.

Firebrandt nodded approval and seemed to understand the impression the captain wanted to convey. "Very good. Likewise, I hope we'll have some time to talk when you return. I'd like to learn more about my distant relatives." Firebrandt's image stepped close to Ellis. "Godspeed Captain." The senator looked out to the command deck. "Godspeed to you all and good luck."

"Thank you, Senator." Ellis left the simulated office before the holographic tank once again displayed the planet below. A miniature image of the *Sanson* hung over the planet. In the distance hung a flashing red sphere marking the jump point for Earth.

"Orbital control says we are clear to depart," reported Natalie. "All service vessels are clear."

"Take us home," ordered Ellis.

Laura pushed several simulated buttons and then gave a signal to Yermakov. The first mate wiped sweat from his brow, then pushed a lever forward on his console. "Thrusters responding normally," he reported. "Proceeding to jump point at one-quarter speed, Skipper."

Ellis clasped his hands behind his back and joined Kirsten, Manuel and Fire at the command deck's rear wall. "Natalie, would you please give us the bow camera?"

"My pleasure." Natalie touched a control and the view shifted to show the planet rolling away below the ship. The stars ahead seemed fixed as though one stood on a planet looking up at a crystal-clear night sky. Manuel caught his breath at the stunning view. Fire took his hand and squeezed it.

Ellis grinned, then returned to the command chair where he prepared the EQ engines for the imminent jump. "Please overlay the course projection on the standard view," asked Ellis.

Again, Natalie complied and a broad yellow line with tick marks shot out in the holographic display to the flashing point in space. While the distant stars remained fixed, the moving tick marks showed their forward progress.

"Follow the yellow brick road," quipped Fire.

"Lions and Tigers and Clusters, oh my," replied Kirsten with a giggle.

Ellis and Manuel each shot a glance at the women. Kirsten shrugged while Fire smiled and shook her head.

"Approaching jump point, sir," reported Laura as Yermakov slowed the ship. Laura doublechecked the jump trajectory and nodded to the captain. "We're ready to jump on your command."

Yermakov sounded the jump alert and Ellis looked at Manuel, Fire, and Kirsten. "Time to get to your positions. Next stop, Earth."

Kirsten passed his chair and gave his shoulder a slight squeeze, then departed into her office. Fire and Manuel each nodded to the captain and entered the lift.

After a moment, Natalie looked around. "All decks report ready for jump to Earth. The lift tubes are all clear."

Ellis looked at Yermakov. Sweat beaded on the first mate's brow, but otherwise he appeared calm. Ellis turned his gaze to the holographic viewer. "Okay, let's get moving. Ms. Peters – Jump!"

The navigator entered a command and the *Nicholas Sanson* jumped out of three-dimensional reality, en route to Earth.

Edmund Swan breezed through customs and had no problem finding a public teleholo where he called Timothy Gibbs. His friend appeared, looking more relaxed than the last time Swan had seen him. "How are you doing?" asked Swan.

Gibbs smiled. "Surprisingly well … though things have been happening … things that are hard to explain."

"Tim, I'm on Earth," explained Swan. "I'd like to come by and see you."

"What a pleasant surprise," said Gibbs. He gave directions to the apartment.

Uneasy, Swan turned off the teleholo. Somehow Gibbs seemed a little too chipper. As he left the teleholo booth, he looked around at the pristine, clean spaceport. When he had left Earth, the port had been grungy and dirty. People packed the place from wall to wall. As a cop in Southern Arizona, he had been all too aware that many of those people had made their homes in the spaceport. In Doomsday's aftermath, Swan had been prepared to encounter an Earth worse off than the one he had left behind. Instead, he found a clean and pleasant homeworld. It gave him the creeps.

Leaving the spaceport, Swan hailed a hovercab and gave the driver directions to Gibbs' apartment. On the journey, he studied the city he had grown up in. The route they traversed proved as clean and pristine as the spaceport had been. However, he used his cybernetic eye to take snapshots up side streets and back alleys. Most were as dirty as he remembered, though in one he noticed a work crew scrubbing a building's brickwork. Ahead of the cab, Swan noticed a smoke plume. As they passed, he took a snapshot with his eye. As his brain processed the image, his stomach almost emptied onto the cab's floor.

Bodies were stacked up like cordwood, in the middle of a dirty street. Police officers gathered around the bodies with flame-throwers, igniting the pyre. The cab's movement had blurred the image, but he thought he could make out his former boss, Sheriff Wilmot, among the assembled officers. Swan closed his eyes, trying to shut out the image. After a moment, he remembered the command to wipe the image from his eye.

The hover cab settled to the ground in front of Timothy Gibbs' apartment building. Swan entered a credit code and stepped out. He noticed several walls had been scrubbed clean, but others still showed graffiti and gang tags. Once cleaned up, the apartment complex would be a wonderful place to live, but gangs had been active in the recent past. That made little sense to Swan, who remembered Timothy Gibbs as a brilliant computer tech in the making – someone who should be able to afford a higher-class apartment. However, competition for even the best jobs was fierce and even the best and the brightest were lucky to be employed at all on an all-too-crowded Earth.

Swan found Gibbs' apartment and rang the buzzer. He blinked in surprise when Gibbs opened the door without using the video interface to check his identity.

"Come in," said Gibbs.

Swan entered the apartment. Like the city itself, it looked as though the apartment was being rennovated. Clean dishes sat stacked on a chipped but scrubbed linoleum counter. Gibbs led Swan to a torn and tattered couch that reeked of disinfectant.

"Can I get you some coffee?" asked Gibbs.

Swan nodded. "I've been worried ever since our teleholo call was cut off the other day."

Gibbs poured the coffee and nodded. "I know. That was a rough day and the next day was even worse." He stepped back toward the couch and handed Swan the cup. "Things have moved fast since then, though."

"Things?" Swan's brow furrowed.

"It's hard to explain." Gibbs dropped into a chair opposite his friend. "After college I couldn't find a single job in computers. I'm sure my poor people-skills never helped. Still, I was good with computers. I found a job maintaining starliner interfaces. After a time, the starliner company folded, as did three others I worked for. Since then, I've been fixing teleholos for a small shop down the street."

Swan shook his head. "That's a waste of resources, my friend. You should have been working on the most cutting-edge technology." He pointed to his cybernetic eye.

Gibbs nodded. "I am now. After all this time, I found someone who appreciates my talent and it's paradise."

"Who?" Swan leaned forward and placed his coffee cup on the table.

"The Cluster. They want me to build a legacy." Gibbs sat back in the chair, heaved a deep sigh and closed his eyes. "Sorry to leave you, my friend, but it's time to get back to work. Make yourself at home. I'll be back before long." A moment later, Gibbs' features went slack.

Swan jumped off the couch and checked Gibbs' pulse. Relieved to find it, he examined his friend with his cybernetic eye. He was alive and healthy. Everything seemed to indicate he had just fallen asleep – everything except his brainwave patterns. Swan had experience studying brainwave patterns during interrogations. However, he had never seen any so active as those in this apparently sleeping man.

The *Nicholas Sanson* jumped into Earth's solar system near Mars. Laura eased the ship around the red planet and then steered it into a gentle, arcing course toward the Earth itself. Now that they had entered the solar system, Natalie could pick up transmissions from Earth.

Ellis sat on the edge of his seat. "Has the Cluster seen us enter the solar system?"

"If they've noticed us, they're not saying or doing anything about it," said Natalie.

"Do you want me to perform a pre-orbital scan?" Laura looked over her shoulder at Ellis. "It could alert the Clusters to our presence."

Ellis nodded. "I suspect they know we're here already and they either want us to come to Earth or they don't care."

Laura nodded and began the scan. Natalie chewed on her nails as she monitored news reports on her brain implant. Yermakov wiped more sweat from his brow then stood and walked over to Natalie's station. "How does it sound?" he asked.

Natalie turned and seemed to look through Yermakov. "It sounds normal … and frightening."

"Sir," interjected Laura. "I'm detecting three Clusters in orbit around the Earth."

"There're at least four Clusters." Yermakov looked at Ellis. "We don't know how many in all. But at least one of them isn't here."

Ellis digested the information. Kirsten emerged from her office, looking a little pale – suffering the after effects of the jump to the solar system. The captain stood and flashed a brave smile at her, then turned his attention back to Natalie. "Can you find a news broadcast?"

Natalie nodded and the holographic view changed to a newscaster sitting behind a desk somewhere on Earth. The newscaster reported that the number of "Doomsday Dead" was leveling off. Several graphs popped onto the display and orbited the newscaster's head.

"Natalie, please pause the broadcast," said Kirsten. The newscaster stopped speaking and the graphs remained still. Without Natalie's intervention, the graphs would have vanished after a brief appearance on the screen. Kirsten walked up and examined the information. Her hand flew to her mouth. "Over sixty percent of the Earth's population is dead," she gasped.

A palpable silence fell over the command deck.

Ellis broke the silence. "But the Cluster doesn't want humans dead." He stepped forward and examined the charts himself, then signaled for Natalie to resume playback.

The newscaster went on to discuss the president's recent successes. Jenna Walker had found housing for all the people of the Earth. She had announced new approaches to medical care, education and farming along with new fuel sources. The president and a supportive senate anticipated an immediate reduction in taxes.

Fire and Manuel entered the command deck as Smart and Ellis walked around the newscaster's image. Kirsten read a report about how Southern California and Arizona's air quality had improved. "This is bizarre." Her eyebrows knitted. "It's like the Earth has been hit with an epidemic of depression."

Fire walked up and stood next to Laura's console. "This report sounds like Earth is becoming a nice place to live, though." She put her hands on her hips.

Kirsten motioned for Fire to look at the same statistics she examined. Fire whistled as she looked at the astonishing death rate.

"We already know the Cluster can tap into emotions," said Ellis. "They seem to be tapping into some dark ones."

Manuel shrugged. "But the Cluster didn't need to go to so much trouble. Why make people kill themselves when it has so much firepower at its disposal? It could just decimate the planet's surface if it wanted to."

Fire's brow furrowed. "If the Cluster's looking for symbionts, what havoc would so much destruction wreak on the survivors?"

Ellis grunted. "But according to the newscast. Depression didn't hit everyone. It sounds like the politicians have broken through layers of dogma." He shook his head. "Taxes haven't been reduced in over five centuries."

"From the Cluster's perspective, can all humans be successful symbionts? What would the Cluster do with those who wouldn't submit?" Fire frowned. "Sending dark emotions to the unsuitable would be trial by fire. The most unsuitable, would destroy themselves. The ones not able to be symbionts, but still survivors, might be scared enough to look for guidance to make things better for the 'true believers.'"

They listened to more of the report. The newscaster reported that gang violence had ceased in metropolitan areas around the globe. If not for the death statistics sitting in front of him, Ellis would be tempted to believe the Cluster's appearance had benefited humanity. He placed a cigar in his mouth, but did not light it.

"Entering orbit in ten minutes," reported Laura. "The Clusters still haven't responded to our presence."

Ellis removed the cigar. "Proceed with orbital entry. The Cluster doesn't seem to be shooting at anyone. I don't think we have anything to fear at the moment."

Manuel licked his lips. "Okay, we're at Earth. Now what do we do?"

"Our mission is reconnaissance," said Yermakov. "We have these newscasts recorded. Can't we just take this information back to Alpha Coma?"

Mark shook his head. "I'm afraid not. All we have is

circumstantial evidence that the Cluster is behind the deaths."

"Pretty good circumstantial evidence, if you ask me." Yermakov's words had a sharp edge.

Fire shook her head at the first mate. "We know the Cluster can manipulate emotions and it's here. That's opportunity. However, we don't have a motive. As far as we know, the Cluster wants to form a symbiosis with humanity."

"We need to go to the planet." Ellis returned to the command chair. "We need to find out what's happening, first hand."

"Where do we go?" asked Manuel.

Kirsten inclined her head. "We don't want to attract attention. We're a mapping ship home from a voyage. The first thing I'd do is check in."

The captain nodded. "Mr. Yermakov, would you please prepare the launch for a flight to TransGalactic Headquarters in Japan." He placed the unlit cigar back in his shirt pocket.

Yermakov looked glum. "Aye, sir."

In the Columbia District, Surgeon General Eva Cooper strolled across the White House lawn. She needed some fresh air after reading reports of people being found around the world in a comatose state. The people were among the best and brightest minds. They weren't dead like the Doomsday Dead, just absent from their bodies, somehow. Above the force field surrounding the compound, sat the bluest sky Cooper had ever seen. The president had taken credit for the improvement in air quality. The surgeon general snorted. While she knew the president's initiatives would improve air pollution, she also realized the improvements that had already occurred resulted from fewer people on the planet, not any policy change.

Eva Cooper gasped when she looked up to see Jenna Walker approaching her. The president smiled and waved. She wore a light, summer dress that revealed tantalizing hints of skin around the upper breasts and thighs, which caused an embarrassing heat to rise in the doctor. Blushing, Cooper waved back.

The president came alongside Eva and linked arms with

her. "I love walking out here," said the president. "Planetary Security doesn't feel the need to watch me like a hawk when I'm under the force field." The two strolled over the grass, arm-in-arm in ardent silence.

Eva wanted to lean her head against Jenna's shoulder and allow herself to be carried away in the moment. Fear kept her facing straight ahead. Part of her feared the president's power. What's more, Jenna had communicated with the Cluster, but something more discomfited Eva. She feared falling in love with Jenna Walker.

Jenna stopped beside a flowerbed, knelt down and smelled a red rose. "I've missed you, Eva," she said in hushed tones.

"I've missed you, too." Eva said the words, but doubted her feelings. "I've been worried about you." The second sentence held more certainty and conviction.

"Why?" asked Jenna – a smile like sunshine lit up her face. "I've never felt better in my life." Jenna's smile faded as she looked into Eva's downcast features. "I'm sorry I haven't been around more. After our morning together – after Arlington – I've wanted to get back together, to talk, and maybe explore our feelings more."

"Jenna," – the president's smile brightened again when Eva used her first name – "my feelings are confused; but more about you and the Cluster than you and me."

"I see." Jenna looked from Eva to the rose. "Dick tells me the Cluster hasn't spoken to you."

Eva nodded, not certain whether Jenna saw or not. "What does it mean? What is the Cluster?"

Jenna walked along the path a little further, then paused, but did not turn to face Eva. "The Cluster is, maybe, the most ancient form of life there is. She's older than the Titans and she's beautiful. From her perspective, Earth's problems look like child's play to solve."

"How does she talk to you, Jenna?" Eva took a few cautious steps toward the president.

"I'm not sure. It's like she talks to the very essence of my being; my emotional core, as it were." Jenna's voice held a dream-like quality. She knelt beside another rose bush. "I remember words, but I don't know if she actually spoke."

"The dead, Jenna," whispered Eva. "What about the Doomsday Dead? You said the Cluster was responsible in your speech the other day, but then you absolved it." Eva's voice developed a razor edge. "How can you absolve the Cluster for killing over half the planet's people?"

Jenna stood, her back tense. "To grow the most beautiful garden, you have to cull the weeds. The Earth became overridden with weeds."

"If I can't speak to the Cluster, does that make me one of the weeds?" asked Eva, horrified.

Jenna turned slowly, her head inclined. She reached out and wiped a tear from Eva's cheek. "No, you're a beautiful flower."

Eva looked into Jenna's eyes and wanted to fall into them. She wanted Jenna to hold her and … the thought hung for several moments, pregnant and unspoken. "I'm the beautiful flower and you're the gardener," she burst out at last, then spun on her heel and ran as fast as she could back to the White House. She could hear Jenna calling her name.

Eva didn't stop running until she reached her office. She threw open the door, slammed it behind her and locked it. Throwing herself into her chair she put her face in her hands and cried for several minutes – irrational, blind fear and betrayal overrode every other emotion. She wanted to believe Jenna – wanted to believe the Cluster had come to Earth for good. But, human lives compared to weeds? She could never believe the president would view herself as some kind of master gardener over all the planet's lives.

Several beeps sounded, pulling Eva from her reverie. She wiped her eyes, reached for a tissue, and blew her nose. Activating the teleholo, Eva read an alert saying the TransGalactic Mapping Vessel *Nicholas Sanson* had just entered Earth's orbit. Her computer had been scanning for it. The ship that had first encountered the Cluster had come home.

Eva looked up the location of TransGalactic's headquarters. She chartered a transport for Japan. Arrangements made, the surgeon general stood, straightened her coat, and left the White House Complex, determined to get some answers.

The launch from the *Nicholas Sanson* carried John Mark Ellis, Kirsten Smart, Suki Ellis and Manuel Raton to Japan. Ellis called for permission to land at Tokyo Spaceport – mentioning their business with TransGalactic Corporation. "You're cleared for Shikoku," came the voice from city control.

"No way!" exclaimed Kirsten. "I've never been cleared directly for Shikoku. It's always too crowded."

"If we're cleared, let's go for it. I don't wanna walk too far," grumbled Raton.

Ellis nodded and acknowledged city control saying they were rerouting to the Shikoku spaceport. As they came down, automated controls directed the launch, keeping it clear of traffic. Even so, the launch kept on a straight path. It didn't dodge or swerve as Ellis expected when coming down into a congested city.

Kirsten seemed to understand Ellis's concern. "What's happened to all the traffic?"

Fire and Manuel looked at each other, then looked out the windows. "Looks like a lot of hover cars to me." Manuel's gaze flitted between several sets of hovers.

"You're from a rural planet," said Ellis. "This might be heavy traffic for a place like Tejo City back on Sufiro – but it's nothing for Japan."

The launch settled onto the landing platform. Ellis, Kirsten, Fire, and Manuel stepped out and were surprised to find a cab waiting at the spaceport, which could take them to TransGalactic. As they skimmed over the city's streets, they noticed few pedestrians.

The cab driver attempted to make conversation. "It's a great day, isn't it?"

"It is a nice day," said Fire. "But, we've been off planet and just learned about all the people committing suicide."

"Yeah," said the cabbie. "They're just a bunch of losers. I think the planet's better off without 'em."

Ellis looked to the others, not believing the cab driver's response. He was grateful when the cab sat down in front of the TransGalactic building.

They left the cab and entered a cavernous foyer. Their footsteps echoed as they approached an unoccupied reception desk. "This place gives me the creeps," said Fire. "Too quiet."

"It shouldn't be so quiet," affirmed Kirsten as she led the way back to an elevator tube. They rode in silence to the building's top floor. Ellis remembered visiting the building with Clyde McClintlock and G'Liat. They'd come to meet the company's Senior Mathematician – a formidable woman named Kumiko Meiji.

Kirsten led the party into Meiji's office. Waist-high pedestals littered the large room. Over each pedestal floated stars and grid lines. The holographic projections were the aids every human-built star vessel in the galaxy used to navigate. Near the room's center, a well-dressed woman sat in a lotus position on the floor. Her eyes stared forward in wonder. "Ms. Meiji," exclaimed Ellis.

"Kumiko," called Kirsten. She knelt down on the floor and checked her friend's pulse.

"What's going on?" asked Manuel. "Is she in some kind of trance?"

The four jumped when an office door opened. A woman with a beak-like nose and wide, curious eyes entered. Stepping past the four, the woman knelt down next to Kumiko Meiji and looked at her eyes and then listened to her breathing. The woman shook her head and stood up, studying the four. "Are you from the *Sanson?*" she asked.

Brow knitted, Ellis nodded and offered his hand. "Yes, ma'am. I'm Captain John Mark Ellis."

The woman breathed a relieved sigh. "I'm Dr. Eva Cooper." The woman accepted Ellis's hand. "I hoped I'd find you here."

Kirsten's eyes widened in disbelief. "The surgeon general?"

"The same." She flashed a pleasant smile.

"What's wrong with her?" Manuel indicated Ms. Meiji.

"I don't know." Cooper shook her head. "Thousands of people around the world have ended up just like her. It started after the Doomsday Deaths, but there are a lot fewer people like this, so they weren't noticed at first. They don't seem in any danger, but they're not responding. It's like their minds are elsewhere."

"What's going on?" asked Fire, hands on her hips. "People are dying. People are comatose. For the most part, people don't seem to care."

"I hoped you would have some answers," said Cooper.

Mark folded his arms. "I think it's time to sit down and compare notes."

"Not here." Again, Cooper shook her head. "The president and her staff can trace my travel. We need to find someplace private."

Kirsten narrowed her gaze and looked from Cooper to Ellis.

"We'll go to Nantucket," announced the captain. "My home is there. If we go in the launch, it'll throw them off if they come looking."

"Lead the way." Cooper indicated the door. Ellis nodded, looking forward to going home.

Chapter Eight

MASTER AND COMMANDER

"I've never experienced anything like Doomsday," explained Dr. Cooper once the *Nicholas Sanson's* launch lifted from the Shikoku Spaceport in Japan. "It just seems as though everyone I knew had grown hopeless – had no more reason to live."

"What about you?" asked Fire, who sat next to the surgeon general. "How did you feel?"

"Helpless." Cooper shrugged. "Most people in the president's cabinet have known one another for years. Like most surgeons general over the last few centuries, I'm not an insider. Even so, I've been working with Dick Richards, President Walker and their aides for the last two years. There have been tough times and crises but President Walker's spirit always amazed me. Richards' outward calm impressed me." She took a deep breath. "However, on Doomsday, both Richards and Walker just seemed sad. So did almost everyone else on the cabinet."

Kirsten Smart, sitting next to Captain Ellis at the front of the craft, turned in her seat and faced Dr. Cooper. "I take it you weren't sad … at least not in the same way."

Cooper's brow furrowed. "Now that you mention it, no. Sure, I was sad because my friends and colleagues were downcast, but I wouldn't call it full-blown depression."

"So," said Raton from the back of the launch. "What made you different?"

"I wish I knew," said Cooper. "As far as I know, I'm the only person in the president's inner circle who hasn't spoken to the Cluster."

John Mark Ellis looked over his shoulder. "People have been speaking to the Cluster?" He remembered his own experiences. First, at the planet Sufiro right after the war between New Granada and Tejo, he'd been convinced the Cluster had attempted to communicate with him. Since then, he'd talked to the Cluster twice. The first time had happened while he commanded the Destroyer *Barbara Firebrandt* and he'd tried to rescue the freighter *Martha's Vineyard*. The second time was while the *Sanson* had been in the Clusters' home system.

"I can't quite explain it," said Cooper. "They say they've spoken to the Cluster, but I've heard and seen nothing except for those people who drop into a kind of absent state, like your friend Ms. Meiji back in Japan."

Ellis nodded and looked forward. "The Cluster seems able to tap into people's emotions. The one time I 'spoke' to the Cluster, I passed out on my own ship's command deck."

Kirsten looked out the window. The launch had entered near-Earth orbit and now dropped around the planet toward North America. "It sounds like the Cluster can talk to anyone at any time." She faced Mark, eyes rounded with concern. "What's to prevent the Cluster from contacting you right now?"

Ellis chewed his lower lip. "Nothing, I suppose," he answered at last.

Kirsten nodded and faced forward. She touched several buttons, activating the launch's backup controls. "I doubt I'm any more immune to the Cluster than you are, but the Cluster does seem to have taken special notice of you. I figure we'd better be ready, just in case."

"Good thinking," called Manuel.

Fire looked at Cooper. "So, what happened after Doomsday? Everyone seems to be in denial about the event."

"That's true," said Cooper. "The president has been frightening since then. She talks about it as though it were the best thing that ever happened to the planet. She called the people who died the 'weeds' and she referred to herself as a 'gardener' tending those of us who were left."

"I suspect the Cluster is the real gardener," mused Ellis. He checked the controls and pushed the launch's joystick forward. "Slowing for final descent."

"Shall I call for clearance at Boston?" asked Kirsten.

"Might as well try for Nantucket itself." The captain shrugged. "Given our experience at Japan."

Kirsten nodded and made the call. Flight control cleared the launch to land at the tiny Nantucket spaceport. Ellis guided the launch downward, through a cloudbank. Nantucket Island appeared below them. Even from their height, the captain could discern familiar sites: the old mill alone on a hillside, the Unitarian Church's rounded steeple towering above Nantucket village's other buildings, the green rolling terrain that covered the island like a carpet. He took a deep breath and reached out, taking Kirsten's hand. He was home at last.

"I'm glad to be here," said Kirsten. "I just wish the circumstances were better.

Ellis nodded, then guided the shuttle toward a small spaceport frequented by cargo shuttles and private spacecraft belonging to the wealthy. He landed, they undid their harnesses, then left the craft. Manuel frowned as he emerged from the launch. "Back in the land of fog and rain," he grumbled.

Fire took his hand and squeezed it as she gave him a reassuring smile. "We'll get back to Sufiro before long, I promise."

Ellis shot a glance back at his mother, then turned forward. "Let's see if we can find a ride at the terminal." He led the way toward a squat, gray-shingled structure, which looked far too quaint to be a spaceport terminal. As they walked across the desolate spaceport, Ellis noticed a silver egg-shaped craft – a Rd'dyggian star vessel. His brow furrowed, but he continued toward the terminal. He opened a white, wooden door and stepped inside.

"John Mark Ellis!" exclaimed the short, wiry man with white hair who stood behind the counter as the group entered. "Why you're a sight for sore eyes." Then he examined the entire group and his eyes fell on Fire. "And Dr. Ellis, too. We've missed you here on the island."

Ellis reached out and shook the man's hand. "I can't tell you how much I've missed the island, Charlie." The captain turned and introduced the group to Charlie Rogers, who'd run the Nantucket spaceport for as long as he remembered. "Charlie, is there anyway we can get a ride into the village? We're in kind of a hurry."

"No problem," said Charlie. "I can take you into town my-self."

"Don't you need to be here when other ships arrive?" asked Kirsten, aghast.

"No need to worry about that, young lady. No one else has landed in the last two days. Even if traffic picks up for some reason, I'll only be gone a few minutes." Charlie stepped from behind the counter and led the way through the glass doors to a hover car parked in the lot outside. The small group clambered in and Charlie closed the doors. He started the car and left the parking lot.

"Are there some Rd'dyggians on the island?" asked Ellis as Charlie thumbed the network receiver, trying to find music.

"Ayup. I'm sure you'll find out about him soon enough." Charlie's brow crinkled as the speakers remained silent.

"Him?" asked Ellis. "You mean there's just one?"

"Ayup." Charlie shook his head and gave up finding any music.

The hover car wound its way through Nantucket's narrow streets. Kirsten gazed in wide-eyed wonder at the ancient buildings, covered in gray shingles as they had been since the 17th century. Many streets were plascrete, but they crossed a street paved with worn cobblestones. At last, Charlie set the hover car down in front of a gray house with white shutters, which looked much like its neighbors. A whitewashed widow's walk topped the house. Centuries before, women used the platforms to look out at the sea and wait for their sailor husbands to return. Fire looked up at it and frowned. Ellis noticed and remembered she had been up there the night his father, Jerome Ellis, had died.

"Thanks much, Charlie," said Ellis as one after the other, the group extracted themselves from the hover car.

"You're welcome," said the spaceport attendant. "Let me know if you need anything." He closed the doors, lifted the hover car and disappeared down the street.

Ellis led the way up the path to the front door. He reached out to take the knob when the door opened from within. He looked up and found himself face-to-chest with an eight-foot tall Rd'dyggian warrior. "I knew you would return," said G'Liat.

"What are you doing here?" asked Kirsten, hands on her hips.

Ellis pushed past the warrior who more than filled the doorway. "I thought you were on your way back to Rd'dyggia."

Manuel tilted his head to the side. "I presume you know this man."

"Damn right I know him," spat Kirsten. "He killed Clyde McClintlock in cold blood."

"Is that a reason to despise him, or to go up and shake his hand?" Manuel's mustache twitched as his mouth threatened to break into a grin.

Both Kirsten and Fire shot Manuel a withering look. He put his hands in his pockets and looked down at the ground. G'Liat, stooped over because the ceilings were a foot shorter than his eight-foot stature, turned and followed Ellis. The captain faced an antique chronometer, turned it and wound it, then reset his wrist chronometer to match. "Why are you here?" asked Ellis, looking up.

"I'm here to study the Cluster," said G'Liat in a practiced terro-generic accent with no trace of the natural Rd'dyggian singsong.

"That tells us why you're on *Earth*," interjected Kirsten who had followed the warrior inside. She dropped herself onto the couch. "You haven't told us why you're in this house."

"I knew you would return here." G'Liat's glistening black eyes never left the captain. "I've been on Earth for several days now. There are reports of people all over the planet who have fallen under the Cluster's influence. I even suspect the Gaean Alliance's president is under its influence."

"What do you know about the president?" Cooper pushed a few blond strands behind her shoulder.

"All I know is what I see on the news, Dr. Cooper," G'Liat turned away from Ellis and moved toward the staircase. Even hunched-over the massive warrior displayed a frightening grace. "I have noted rather odd announcements from the president under the circumstances. I've also noted reports saying the surgeon general of the Gaean Alliance has gone missing."

"You still haven't answered Kirsten's question." Fire stepped between G'Liat and Cooper, meeting the warrior's fierce, glass-like gaze with her own deep brown eyes. "Why have you invaded my home?"

"Your son shares a certain … rapport with the Cluster. He is also able to control his contacts with the Cluster well. I hope to find answers to the Cluster's motives," explained G'Liat.

Cooper shrugged. "I have to admit, that's why I'm here. I want to know what's going on as well."

"The difference, Dr. Cooper, is that your motive is to help humans." Kirsten turned and narrowed her gaze, as though evaluating the warrior. "I'm not quite sure what his motive is, but it's not to help humans."

G'Liat turned on his heel, causing Kirsten to gasp despite her forced calm. "You are correct. I am not here to serve humans. I am here to serve Rd'dyggians. However, if humans are destroyed, what's to stop the Cluster from moving on to my planet. I have no interest in seeing humans destroyed."

Fire gritted her teeth and took a step toward the warrior. "I accept your motives, but you still don't have the right to sleep under our roof."

"I have not been sleeping here," said G'Liat. "I have been sleeping on my chartered ship. Perhaps you saw it at the spaceport?"

"All right." Ellis put his hands up. "I'm tired of the games. What were you doing here when we arrived?"

"Monitoring." G'Liat stepped past Ellis toward the stairs and gestured for him to follow. "You may find this interesting. Perhaps even concerning."

Ellis followed G'Liat up the stairs. Fire and Dr. Cooper trailed behind. G'Liat opened the door to the guest bedroom. "Coffin," said Ellis and Fire together. Samuel Coffin lay on the bed. Several days' stubble grew on his chin. His wispy, silver hair, though tousled was not matted. He'd not been tossing and turning in the bed.

Cooper stepped past the others and checked the old man's pulse and put her ear to his chest. "He's like the others," she announced.

"Just like Ms. Meiji," breathed Ellis.

"His mind is not here," said G'Liat. The Rd'dyggian warrior pointed to a table where a device made from a lustrous, translucent substance like mother-of-pearl lay. Ellis recognized it as a Rd'dyggian brain interface unit. G'Liat could use the device to see other beings' thoughts.

The captain ground his teeth, at once incensed that the device was used on his friend without consent, but also confused by the warrior's exact meaning. "What do you mean his mind is not here?"

"His brain lives, but there is no activity," explained G'Liat.

Cooper shook her head. "That's not consistent with the other cases I've studied. Brain wave activity doesn't discontinue while a person is in the Cluster trance."

G'Liat inclined his head in a studied imitation of human behavior. "Yes, but I imagine the president and her cabinet speak to Clusters orbiting the Earth. Two Clusters were gone when I arrived. One has returned."

"And you didn't examine Ms. Meiji's brainwaves," Ellis observed.

Cooper chewed her lower lip and nodded agreement.

Fire stepped to the bed and sat on it, next to Coffin. She picked up his hand and patted it, an instinct to comfort, even though his brain appeared to be elsewhere. "What you are suggesting is almost inconceivable. The mind can't be transplanted. Not even Rd'dyggians can do brain transplants."

G'Liat's purple mustache wriggled in undisguised annoyance. "But, Rd'dyggians have succeeded in mapping brain waves, put them in memory cells, and let them control a computer independent of any other outward input." He turned and looked at Ellis. "The Cluster is much more ancient than the Rd'dyggians. I'm certain its abilities outstrip ours."

Ellis sighed. "I hate to admit it, but you might be able to help us."

"John Mark," gasped Fire.

Ellis waved his mother's interruption aside. "But, I think it's time you return to your ship." He took a step forward and lowered his voice. "I warn you, though. Please do not return to this house without an invitation from me."

"Now that you are home, I have no need." The warrior turned on his heel and left the room.

Once G'Liat had left, the atmosphere in the Ellis home

relaxed and people began sorting out rooms and luggage. Fire and Manuel took the master bedroom, though Ellis found himself stifling some consternation that Manuel would be sleeping in his father's bed. Manuel excused himself to do some shopping for dinner. While he was gone, Kirsten reminded Ellis that Manuel had been sleeping in that bed already. By the time Manuel returned with the groceries, Ellis had resigned himself to the situation.

Meanwhile, Ellis and Kirsten decided to sleep in his old room. The double bed he'd grown up with proved just big enough for the two of them. They left Coffin "sleeping" in the guest bedroom, figuring it was the best place for him. Dr. Cooper contented herself with sleeping on the couch in the living room.

While Manuel and Fire busied themselves preparing dinner for the full house, Ellis contacted Yermakov aboard the *Sanson* to let him know where they were and what they had seen. "Skipper, I don't want to stay here any longer than I have to," said the first mate. "I think you've found out enough for a good report."

Ellis nodded. "The problem is, I still don't know how or why the Cluster killed off over sixty percent of the planet's population. I also don't know what's happening with the people who are in a trance-like state. All I have are guesses."

Yermakov rubbed his eyes. "I just don't want to become a victim in order to find out, sir."

The formal "sir" startled the captain. He looked at Yermakov again and noticed the worry lines around his first officer's mouth. "We won't be much longer, I promise."

"Thank you, sir," said Yermakov. "*Sanson* signing out."

Glum, Ellis deactivated the teleholo, but his spirits lifted with the smells coming from the kitchen. Manuel had whipped up some seafood enchiladas and a simple jicama salad and served it with a Chilean white wine. Fire lifted the glass and took an appreciative sip. "I spent my first years on Earth in Chile." She looked at Manuel. "Maybe if the Cluster ever leaves, we should visit."

Ellis rolled his eyes. Kirsten put her hand on his forearm and looked at Manuel. "I didn't know you were such a good cook."

Manuel's eyes glistened with moisture. "My mother and father taught me." His parents had been killed on Sufiro. "The chilies here aren't very good, but the seafood, I have to admit, is excellent."

Everyone fell upon their food with delight. Out of the corner of his eye, Ellis saw Cooper take a pill with some wine. He wasn't certain, but he thought the pill might be the emotion-stabilizing drug, Proxom.

Once they finished the meal, Cooper and Kirsten picked up the plates and stacked them in the cleansing unit. Ellis stretched and yawned. "I think the wine's making me sleepy," he said.

Fire looked at her wrist chrono. "It's been a long day. We should turn in soon."

Kirsten tapped Ellis on the shoulder and the two went upstairs, arm-in-arm. They looked in on Coffin, and then went to their own bed. Once under the covers, Ellis took Kirsten in his arms. She trembled. "What's wrong?" he asked.

"I'm scared," she whispered. "Things are just wrong. I'm afraid if we stay too long we'll get caught up in it."

Ellis nodded. "I know, but, I feel like we need to learn a little more before we can suggest a plan of action to the senator."

Kirsten took a deep breath and released it. "I agree. It doesn't scare me any less."

Ellis kissed Kirsten and then turned out the light. He rolled over and fell asleep with her snuggled up against his back.

During the night, Ellis rolled and found his face pressed into canvas. Blinking, he sat up, then rolled out of a hammock and into another body, then down onto a ship's wooden deck. Grunting, he rubbed his back and sat up as a sailor cursed at him, then rolled over and went back to sleep. Ellis looked around in the semi-darkness until his eyes adjusted. Dark as the space was, wan light seeped through from above, as though it were day outside. He sat in an old wooden ship's hold, filled wall-to-wall with snoring people in hammocks. Brow creased, he eased himself to his feet and made his way along the wall, stumbling once or twice as the ship rolled until he noticed a ladder leading to the deck above.

Ascending the ladder, Mark Ellis found himself on a whale

bark's main deck. He looked up at a sky bright with stars, and then stepped over to the rail and looked at the black, light-warping maw the ship orbited. "My God," he whispered.

"Young Ellis?" came a raspy voice from the ship's stern.

Ellis looked around and up to the command deck. There in a black coat and white trousers, looking younger than he remembered, was Samuel Coffin. "So, this is where you've gotten to, old friend." Ellis moved to the ladder leading up to the command deck.

Coffin's eyes twinkled. "I should have known you'd show up here eventually."

"Where are we?" asked Ellis as he joined Coffin on the command deck. "I presume that's a black hole, but it's the biggest I've ever seen." He waved his hand around at the sky. "The density of stars is incredible. Are we…"

"We're at the center of the galaxy," affirmed Coffin.

Ellis stepped to the starboard rail. Matter swirled around the great black spheroid – material in an accretion disk drifted into the black hole's event horizon. "Are we really here or is this an illusion?"

"Old Folger and I think this is somehow real. Also, Kumiko Meiji." He indicated the ship around them and the flapping canvas above. "All of this must be an illusion for our benefit, but somehow we are aboard a ship that's, in fact, at the galaxy's center."

Ellis looked at Coffin aghast. "Did you say Kumiko Meiji?"

"Ahh," said Coffin. "I didn't think you'd remember her. She visited Nantucket while you were still quite young."

"She's my boss at TransGalactic," explained Ellis. "Presuming it's the same Kumiko Meiji." He tried to shove his hands in his pockets and discovered he wore a pressure suit – strangely comforting in such surroundings. "So, why are we at the galactic core?"

"Because I ordered us here." Coffin joined Ellis at the rail. "It's quite a sight, but I think we should move on tomorrow. I think we've taken all the measurements we can get." He paused and looked around. "Besides, this seems to be a rather popular destination."

"What do you mean?"

"Another ship arrived two days ago," explained Coffin. "We think it was a different Cluster, projecting a different illusion. It resembled a rocket ship, not a sea vessel. Our midshipman said more computer types crewed that ship than this one."

"I presume researchers and teachers comprise this crew."

Coffin nodded. Ellis took a deep breath and looked around. He noticed a young woman at the ship's wheel and a man in the bow. In a crow's nest atop the main mast, a man kept lookout, as though for distant whales. Then Ellis noticed a series of little flags along one line. "Who are you signaling?" he asked.

Coffin shrugged. "I may be this ship's captain, but I don't know all of her secrets yet. The flags just seem to change from time to time without my command."

Ellis frowned as wind blew past the ship and rustled his hair. As the wind shifted, contentment rolled over him. A few moments later, the breeze shifted again and something like ire washed over him.

"The illusion is frighteningly realistic," said Coffin. "Right down to the wind."

"Right down to the wind," echoed Ellis, his brows knitted. He looked up and noticed the signal flags had changed. "This Cluster is signaling another one." He looked into Coffin's eyes. "When the other ship was here, what did they do?"

"I'm not sure," said Coffin. "They moved from star to star. My best guess is that they were conducting a survey of some sort," said Coffin.

Ellis looked around at the many stars and shivered. Then he turned with the wind and tried to see where it blew. Just to the port of stern, he thought one star didn't look quite right. "Do you have a telescope?"

"Of course." Coffin retrieved a spyglass from his belt and handed it to Ellis, who opened it and looked at the bothersome star. Somehow, it was not a star, but a divot in space. It reminded him of the nodal points ships used to jump from star to star; the paths that ships like the *Nicholas Sanson* mapped.

He collapsed the little telescope and gave a confident nod. "We're communicating with someone else. EQ communications use the same nodal points that starships use to jump from system to system." He pointed to the place he'd examined with the telescope. "There's a jump point right over there."

Coffin's shaggy brow furrowed. "Who are we communicating with?"

"I don't know," said Ellis, "but I want to find out." His eyes fell on the whaleboat secured to the bark's stern. "May I borrow a boat?"

"We're not using them out here." Coffin chuckled, but his shaggy eyebrows came together and he frowned. "But, how can you make an interstellar jump in a whaleboat?"

"How can we be orbiting the black hole at the galaxy's center in a whale bark?" Ellis met Coffin's gaze. "There must be some open channel between us here at the galactic core and the Clusters orbiting Earth. Otherwise, I could not have arrived here. Last I knew I was on Earth. You've been out here a few days. Somehow, my mind moved from Earth to here. I can sense it on the wind."

Coffin nodded. "You may have the boat, but be careful, my friend."

"Trust me, I will."

Kirsten awoke as early morning sunlight streamed in through the bedroom's windows. She flashed a mischievous grin and snuggled up to Mark's back. His breathing was shallow as though he were awake, or near the surface, but he didn't respond to her at all. "Come on, sleepyhead, up and at 'em." She rolled him onto his back.

His open eyes stared unblinking at the ceiling and she gasped as she reminded herself that he still breathed. She checked his pulse and confirmed its steady rhythm. With a worried frown, she climbed out from under the covers, found a terrycloth bathrobe, and went across the hall. She knocked on Fire and Manuel's door.

Wearing only boxer shorts, a bleary-eyed Manuel Raton opened the door and blinked a few times. "What is it?"

"It's Mark," gasped Kirsten. "I think he's gone ... he's gone wherever it is people are going ... where Mr. Coffin and Ms. Meiji went."

Fire stepped up behind Manuel. Kirsten's eyes went wide when she realized Fire wore nothing at all. Ignoring her reaction, Fire stepped past Manuel and Kirsten and entered Mark's room. She checked her son's pulse and breathing, then reached over and closed his eyes.

Kirsten watched from the doorway, holding her robe closed. "What do we do?" she asked.

Looking up, Fire sighed. "First thing is get Dr. Cooper up here and have her give him a more proper examination – make sure he's in the same state as Coffin. From there we have two choices. We can wait until he and Coffin return or we can bring G'Liat here and see if he can tell us anything with his machine." Noticing Kirsten's pointed gaze, Fire looked down at herself and shrugged. "Sorry," she mumbled as she returned to her own room and half closed the door behind her. On the other side, a drawer slid open.

"I don't want to involve G'Liat," protested Kirsten to the closed door. "He's a murderer – he doesn't even see humans as ... well ... humans. It's more like we're animals in his eyes."

Manuel, now wearing jeans, emerged from the bedroom, pulled a T-shirt on and shrugged. "I've been a cop a long time; humans can be animals. I think we need to use whatever resources we have at hand, no matter how distasteful."

Fire appeared at the door, buttoning a pair of pants. "I'm afraid you may be right. Thing is, one of my dad's best friends was a Rd'dyggian pirate. Arepno could be a little odd, but he was a good soul."

"That's the problem," protested Kirsten. "I don't think this G'Liat is a good soul at all."

Fire grabbed a tank top from the bed and nodded. "I appreciate your concern. Mark is my son after all and I don't trust this G'Liat either." She pulled on the top. "Let's get Dr. Cooper up here, then we can discuss this more after breakfast. Agreed?"

"Agreed," said Kirsten. "While you're getting the doctor, I'll get dressed."

Once Kirsten had dressed, Cooper came upstairs and examined Mark. As expected, she reported he'd entered the same state as Coffin. Meanwhile, Manuel went downstairs to start breakfast. When the women smelled the rancid, sulfuric smell of burning eggs, they ran downstairs to find Manuel slumped over the kitchen table. Kirsten turned off the fire and dumped the eggs in the sink while Cooper checked Manuel.

"Is he…?" asked Fire, with a worried frown.

"Alive, and in the same state as Ellis and Coffin as best as I can tell," said Cooper.

Fire looked at Kirsten, who nodded. "I hate to say it, but I think it's time we got G'Liat," she said.

John Mark Ellis rowed away from the *Pequod* in the whaleboat. He felt the oars push against water, though he couldn't see any. Coffin had given him provisions: food, blankets, and a first aid kit. He didn't know how useful those things would be. As the divot in space grew closer, a current-like force grabbed the boat. It didn't take long for him to reach the node. Looking back, the *Pequod* was lost among the stars. He had no sense of scale, but his instincts told him he approached the speed of light.

As he entered the nodal point, he expected he would experience something like a starship jumping from point to point in the galaxy. Instead, Ellis found himself in a deep indigo void. As his eyes adjusted, he noticed currents moving through the void, resembling a jetstream through clouds. Pinpricks of light shone through, twisted into corkscrews. He soon realized the view echoed aspects of his experiment wearing a virtual reality helmet during mapping jumps on the *Sanson*. Of course, there would be a different color palette. The helmet assigned colors based on a programmer's discression. He didn't know if he viewed a simulation from a different source or "reality." As he pondered this, the rowboat pitched forward and Ellis's stomach lurched. He followed a bend, then flipped sideways.

A moment later, he stood on solid ground facing a door.

The boat and the provisions had vanished, though his clothes hadn't changed. Ellis opened the door and stepped into an electronics lab.

A drafting table stood against one wall, while the room's lone occupant sat hunched over a workbench, a test probe in one hand. Ellis approached the man. His shoes creaked and the man looked up. "Ah," he said. "You must be new here."

"Well…" Ellis ran his hand through his hair. "I just got here, if that's what you mean. But, I'm not sure where this is."

The man smiled. "My friend, you've just found paradise." He put down the test probe and shook Ellis's hand. "My name is Timothy Gibbs and for the first time in my life, I'm getting to build the computer I've always dreamed of."

Ellis's eyebrows came together. "Who are you building the computer for?"

"For the Cluster, of course," he said. "It's their legacy."

"Tell me more," said Ellis.

Gibbs looked at his wrist chrono. "Let me show you around and I'll explain as I go." He moved toward a door at the room's far side. "I'm afraid I don't have much time. I managed to leave a friend back at the apartment. I'm sure he's worried. He just arrived from Sufiro when I had to leave for work."

"You have a friend from Sufiro?" asked Ellis. "I know some Sufirans. What's your friend's name?"

"Ed Swan," said the man.

Ellis's jaw dropped for a moment before he regained his composure. "Yes, show me around. Let me know when it's time for you to go. I have a message for your friend."

G'Liat stood over John Mark Ellis, his hands balancing the Rd'dyggian brain scan device on the captain's head. The device was designed for Rd'dyggians, whose brains were in their chest cavity. After a few moments, G'Liat looked up. "That's odd," he said with a look of near-human puzzlement on his face. "Ellis was gone, just like Samuel Coffin."

"Was?" asked Kirsten.

"I'm now registering brain activity again," said the eight-foot tall warrior. "He's much nearer again, like most humans. It's as though his brain pattern had been sent to a distant point, but now it's come back to a Cluster close to the Earth."

"How can that be?" asked Fire.

"I don't have enough data yet," said the warrior. "However,

I've never seen anything like this in any of the people I've examined."

"Perhaps you should examine Manuel," suggested Fire.

"Perhaps," agreed the warrior, retrieving the brain scanner.

"Examine Manuel for what?" Raton leaned against the bedroom door, stroking his mustache. He stepped over to the window and pushed it open, breathed in the damp, salt air and grinned. "Man, it's a beautiful day." He turned and looked from Kirsten to Fire. "Did someone get those eggs I left on the stove before they burned?"

Chapter Nine

BEYOND SYMBIOSIS

va Cooper and Fire Ellis watched Manuel Raton as he ate his oatmeal and toast with a peaceful, contented look on his face. Fire led Eva aside. "I grew up with Manuel on Sufiro. I know his moods. I've seen him raging mad at injustice, worried about friends in trouble, satisfied after solving a dispute, and even joyous when things went his way. I've never seen him so serene."

"You know," said Manuel from the table, "the Cluster has made things so peaceful here on Earth, I wonder what it could do for other worlds, like Alpha Coma or Sufiro."

"I don't know if I want to find out." Kirsten wrinkled her nose. "I don't care how nice the Earth seems. I care about the sixty percent of Earth's population who died."

Fire sat down at her breakfast plate and pointed a spoon at Manuel. "How do you know what the Earth was like before? You didn't even grow up here."

"But I spent time here before the Cluster, with you." Manuel leaned forward. "My father and mother told me how they lived on the streets of El Paso and Juarez, not even able to afford a place to live. That's all been fixed."

"In the most draconian of ways," said Kirsten. She threw her napkin on the table and picked up her dirty dishes.

G'Liat reclined on the couch and studied the interchange. He made a show of examining his fingers for a moment, then looked up again. "So, what was it like to communicate with the Cluster?"

Manuel's mouth worked, but he couldn't quite get the words out. "It's hard to describe," he stammered at last. "It was like being gathered into my mother's arms and told everything's all right." His content smile dissolved into a deep frown as he remembered his own mother, murdered on Sufiro. He turned away from the warrior's gaze.

Eva looked from Manuel to G'Liat and back again. "You're in law enforcement, Mr. Raton. How can you condone what the Cluster has done?"

Manuel's brow wrinkled as though he contemplated a difficult problem. "I don't..." he began, but stopped. "I don't know how to explain," he resumed after a moment. "I almost wish the Cluster had come sooner, not later. I wonder if my mom and dad would still be alive."

"Who knows? If the Cluster had come sooner, perhaps your parents would still be dead and Sam Stone of Tejo would still be alive," said G'Liat from the couch.

Eva's brow furrowed and she looked at Kirsten.

"I refer to the man who ordered the execution of Manuel's mother and father," explained G'Liat.

Manuel glared at the warrior. "How do you know Sam Stone?"

G'Liat held his arms out to the side. "I know many things."

Fire gritted her teeth at the Rd'dyggian's reply. The tele-holo signal sounded. Fire continued to stare at G'Liat as she stood, then broke her gaze when she went to the other room and answered the call. A moment later, she returned. "Kirsten, it's a call for you. It's Simon aboard the *Sanson*."

Kirsten nodded and followed Fire back to the teleholo. After completing her errand, Fire returned and sat down.

Eva took a last bite of her oatmeal and washed it down with some coffee, then sat back and eyed G'Liat with a sly grin. "You're testing, aren't you? You're trying to find out if there's a way to break the brainwashing the Cluster has done."

Before G'Liat could answer, Kirsten appeared at the door. "Simon's just told me that several people aboard the *Sanson* have just ... zoned out, like Manuel and Mark. Even our pilot, Laura Peters seems to have been in contact with the Cluster."

"And Suki Firebrandt Ellis ... or so it would seem." G'Liat stood up from the couch. Hunched over, he approached her. Her eyes were open and staring, but she didn't blink when he waved his orange six-fingered hand in front of them.

Eva stood and moved to Fire. Kneeling beside her, she took

her pulse and checked her breathing. She looked up at Manuel whose smile had returned. "She's with the Cluster now," he said. "There's no need to worry."

Kirsten leaned against the great stone fireplace and sighed. Eva stood and joined Kirsten. She looked up at a beautiful seascape on the wall. After a moment, her eyes fell down to a rack of pipes. She picked one up and considered the great wars medical science had waged against smoking and obesity. Looking back at Manuel, she began to think she might be seeing an addict.

"G'Liat," said Eva, "what would happen if we took Mark and Fire back aboard the *Sanson* and got them out of the Cluster's range?"

For a moment, G'Liat's mustache wriggled, then he shook his head in a human-like gesture. "That strikes me as a bad idea." The warrior picked up Fire's dishes and took them to the cleansing unit. "We don't know what, in fact, has happened to their brain patterns. What would happen if the time came for them to return to their own minds and the body was not here to receive it?"

"You think it could kill them?" Eva returned the pipe to the rack.

"I don't have enough data for a solid hypothesis," said G'Liat. "However, I can think of one possibility."

"So, are we trapped here until everyone is back in their own body?" asked Kirsten as she moved from the fireplace to the couch.

"If you do not wish to desert your friends," affirmed G'Liat. As Kirsten opened her mouth to protest, G'Liat raised his hand. "Knowledge is power in this case. The more you know, the better your ability to save your friends from the Cluster. The longer you wait, the more you will know."

Eva looked at Manuel. "I don't like it. I'm afraid we may all succumb to the Cluster … or worse."

G'Liat finished clearing the table. "That's the chance you must be prepared to take."

❁

In Southern Arizona, Edmund Swan paced back and forth in Timothy Gibbs' apartment, trying to decide what to do. He'd spent two nights while his friend sat motionless in an armchair. Several times, Swan thought about calling the police or an ambulance – some kind of emergency help. Every time he considered it though, he remembered the police officers burning bodies in the street. He didn't know whom he could trust and began to think it had been rash to come to Earth so unprepared.

Tim Gibbs' eyes fluttered open. "Good, you're still here," he said. "I've just met a friend of yours named Mark Ellis."

Swan's jaw dropped. "You *met* Mark Ellis. Where?"

"At work." Gibbs spoke the words as though he'd been outside the apartment and not sitting in his armchair for the better part of two days. Gibbs stood and went to the bathroom. When he returned, he ordered roast beef, mashed potatoes, vegetables and bread from the food preparation unit.

Swan joined his friend at the kitchen table. "So, where do you work?"

Gibbs' brow creased and he looked at his plate. "I'm not sure ... I think it's an orbital complex. Your friend, Ellis, seemed most interested." He took another mouthful of food and washed it down with some water. "Oh, I almost forgot, Ellis had a message for you. He said his mother, Manuel Raton, and some others were on Nantucket Island. He knew you'd want to talk to them."

Swan smiled. "You bet I do. May I use your teleholo?"

Laura Peters stepped onto the *Nicholas Sanson's* command deck. She moved to the pilot's station and commanded it to bring up her standard display, which looked identical to a pilot's console on a Gaean Navy vessel.

Natalie Papadraxis at the communication's console eyed her with concern and Simon Yermakov stood up from the command chair and stepped to her side. "How do you feel?" he asked.

Heat rose to Laura's cheeks and she looked down at the console, checking ship's status to avoid meeting either Simon's or Natalie's eyes. "Embarrassed mostly," she muttered. "I should have been able to fight the Cluster – keep it out of my mind and keep working."

Natalie put her hand on Laura's shoulder. "There's no reason to be embarrassed, Laura. I've felt the Cluster's power. There isn't anything you could have done."

"Isn't there?" Laura shot back. She looked up at Natalie, her jaw clenched. "Why me? Why did the Cluster single me out?"

Simon tugged on his trouser legs and squatted down next to Laura's chair. "That's an excellent question." He looked down at the deck and then up again. "I'm sorry, but I have to ask – what was it like?"

Laura took a deep breath as she considered her answer. "It was comforting … the most comfortable place I've ever been. I forgot about the ship, forgot about my duty. It seemed like I needed to relax and clear my mind before taking on a bigger task, something more important but…"

"But, there's nothing more important to you than your duty to the ship and crew," Natalie spoke in calm, reassuring tones.

Laura nodded and sniffed.

Simon stood. "Don't be too hard on yourself. We'll leave just as soon as we can." He stepped around the pilot's console and into the main holographic tank. The projection showed the Earth and the position of all orbiting ships and satellites along with three Clusters. One Cluster increased speed and moved away from the Earth. He continued to watch it for a few minutes, his brow furrowed.

"Display crew roster here." Simon stabbed his finger at a point in the air. A list of names appeared where he had indicated. "Remove all personnel off-ship," he commanded. Mark, Suki Ellis, Raton and Smart's names vanished. "Highlight all personnel in medical during the last day who were treated for Cluster-induced trauma." Several names were highlighted, including Laura's and Chief Engineer Mahuk's. Simon paced a little ways off and turned to look at the Cluster leaving Earth. Laura followed his gaze and noticed the Cluster accelerated.

"Show me the departing Cluster's destination," ordered

Simon. He pointed at the Cluster he meant. A yellow line shot out from the Cluster. "Show any jump points on that course projection." A red, blinking dot appeared in the Cluster's path.

Laura, intrigued by Simon's actions in the holo tank, stepped forward and joined him. "Where's that one going?"

"Show jump point destination." Simon pointed to the co-ordinates above the blinking jump point.

Laura's eyes widened. "That's the center of the galaxy," she said. "What do you suppose it wants there?"

He shook his head while Laura examined the list floating in the tank. She looked over to Natalie. "Are you still taking Proxom?"

Natalie looked up from her console and smiled. "I hate to say it, but yes. I know there's a risk it'll interfere with my implant, but it keeps me from having nightmares about the Cluster."

Laura looked at Simon. "Sir, I don't want to ask this … but you take Proxom, don't you?"

Simon sniffed and looked away for a moment, watching as the Cluster reached the jump point and vanished. He looked back to Laura and nodded without speaking. Laura returned her attention to the list. "Computer, highlight all crewmembers currently with Proxom prescriptions."

"Classified information," protested the computer.

"Override." Simon's order held a rare, authoritative tone. "This is a matter of ship's security. First officer's authority."

Ten crewmembers' names, including Simon and Natalie's were highlighted in green.

"No one taking Proxom has been affected by the Cluster," said Laura.

Simon shook his head. "That's not enough to go on. It's only ten crewmembers."

"But," protested Laura. "Proxom is an emotion stabilizer. Wouldn't it make sense that people on Proxom might have some immunity to the Cluster?"

Simon nodded. "A good hypothesis." He left the holo tank. "Thing is, I think we need more data to be sure." Just then, he stumbled. Turning on his heel, he looked back at Laura. "Did you feel that?"

She took a step. The deck didn't feel level. "I think so, but

I'm not quite sure."

"Check it," he ordered and continued to the command chair.

Laura sat down at her station and poured over data from the sensors. As a mapping vessel, the *Nicholas Sanson* had equipment tuned to the galaxy's gravitational currents. The ship felt its way from jump point to jump point, mapping the course as it went. Unlike most space vessels, the *Sanson* rocked and swayed as competing gravitational forces from different bodies in the galaxy tugged at it.

Laura gasped at the data appearing on her display. "Sir, there was a density wave spike just moments ago."

The ship listed over at a slight tilt. Most people who stood on *Sanson's* deck would probably not have noticed it, but Simon and Laura looked at each other. Again, Laura checked her sensors. "We're detecting a major gravitational shift, sir."

"Point of origin?" asked Simon.

She looked up. "It's from the galactic center, sir."

Samuel Coffin stood at the *Pequod's* aft rail looking at the point of light where John Mark Ellis had rowed the whaleboat a few hours earlier. He hoped he would see his friend row back and let them know what he'd found. He feared that Ellis had in fact disappeared forever.

Kumiko Meiji joined Coffin at the aft railing and followed his gaze. "Still no sign of Ellis?" she asked.

Coffin shook his head. Just then, something silver flashed near the point of light. He watched it for several minutes. Soon, he realized another ship had appeared – the same silver spaceship he had seen before. It moved around the black hole and stopped. A blue beam shot out from the ship's bow and struck a distant star.

Meiji gasped when the star started to move. "That's impossible."

Coffin nodded without saying a word. He looked around and motioned to Elisha Folger. "Mr. Folger. I think it's time to go."

"All hands!" called Folger, but his voice cracked. He moved forward two steps and called again. "All hands, prepare to make sail!"

The midshipman Coffin had seen when he'd appeared aboard the *Pequod* scurried up the ladder to the aft deck. "Sir," he called. "We have new orders from the admiralty." The boy handed a paper to Coffin.

Coffin took the paper and read the orders. "We can't do this," he said as he handed the note to Meiji.

"We couldn't move stars around even if we wanted to," she said when she finished reading. "And I don't see any reason why we'd want to."

The midshipman shook his head. "I'm afraid it's out of your hands now."

He pointed forward and a yellow beam shot from the *Pequod's* bow toward a distant star.

John Mark Ellis sat in Timothy Gibbs' drafting room staring at a set of plans. Gibbs had explained how he had designed a storage device, which could hold almost limitless data. The device required a supermassive black hole – one just a little larger than the black hole at the galaxy's center. Directing Quinnium particles through the black hole at precise frequencies could allow the data to be accessed.

As Ellis examined the plans, he realized the supermassive black hole would also collimate vast amounts of energy, creating a radio-frequency jet. If enough stars were pulverized, it would create a gas halo around the black hole, changing the frequency of the radio energy projected from the galactic core to something quite different from radio jets in other galaxies. With care, the halo's density could be varied and the signal could be made to pulse at a modulated frequency.

Ellis rubbed his chin. "A beacon," he said aloud, even though he was alone. The Cluster has been using humans to help design and build a memory core at the center of the galaxy and the core included a beacon to alert others to its presence.

The captain sat back and took a deep breath. He knew

what the Cluster wanted to build, but he didn't know why and a chill crept up his spine as he considered the "others" the Cluster might want to contact. Did the Cluster know another species? If so, how powerful might they be?

He looked around at the room he occupied. There were state-of-the-art computer terminals and teleholo units. Drafting and test equipment littered the tables. Looking up, tasteful art adorned the walls. He couldn't help thinking that much as he liked Van Gogh's "Starry Night" he would much prefer a sea-scape. As he watched, the painting morphed into a seascape like one that hung in his own house above the fireplace.

Ellis looked down at his body and realized he had not eaten or relieved himself in several hours. What's more, the realization did not inspire any urges within him. As he looked down, he wished he wore something more comfortable. As he watched, the pressure suit morphed into a white shirt and blue trousers. He smiled to himself, not so much because he wore more comfortable clothes, but because these two experiments demonstrated something he had suspected since arriving aboard the *Pequod* – he was not someplace in body, but someplace in mind.

When searching for the Cluster, G'Liat had encouraged Ellis to practice interacting with and manipulating his dreams. Now Ellis understood how that could be a useful skill. Then he shuddered, as he considered whether G'Liat could have understood this aspect of the Cluster from the beginning. He couldn't worry about that now.

Somehow, the Cluster had copied his brain patterns and moved them to a place where he could think and act. It was as though a file had been copied from one computer – his brain – to another computer. He guessed the other computer must be a Cluster.

Ellis looked back at the drafting table. If the Cluster could copy his memory, life, and experiences – everything that was him – to some new location, the Cluster might be looking for a place to copy all its experiences. Such a place would have to be a vast storage cell.

He patted his shirt pocket and found a cigar, just as he thought he might. He put it in his mouth and lit it. "If someone doesn't like the smell," he grumbled, "they can wish it away."

Looking at the teleholos on the table, he had a thought. Sitting down at one, he entered the code for his home on Earth. He caught his breath when his mother did in fact answer. "Mom. It's John Mark. Can you hear me?"

"I can hear and see you." She flashed a grin. "Where are you, Mark?"

"I'm not sure," he admitted. "I think I may be 'aboard' a Cluster ship, but I'm not positive. How's everyone at the house?"

"I'm not sure, either," she said. "I've been taken someplace else, as well." Her brow creased. "It's a comfortable place. It reminds me of dad's homestead on Sufiro. The Cluster has been talking – at least I think it's talking." She shook her head. "I feel like the Cluster has nothing but good intentions for humanity."

Ellis shook his head. "Mom, the Cluster is building something big at the galaxy's center – a giant memory core. The problem is, I don't know why, yet."

Suki Ellis gasped. "I think it's time to go. I need to leave."

"Tell the others," called Ellis. "If you see them, tell them about the memory core."

Fire's face disappeared from the teleholo. Mark pounded his fist on the table and rolled the cigar to the other side of his mouth as he contemplated the situation. He drew on the cigar then exhaled, realizing he had to get back to the *Pequod*. There, perhaps he and Coffin could compare notes and develop a strategy.

He stood and went back to the door through which he'd entered the lab. As he expected – or rather, as he willed – the *Pequod's* whaleboat bobbed in the water alongside a pier. A light shone in the distance – similar to the one he'd entered when he'd left the *Pequod*. The captain untied the rope from the pier and climbed in the boat.

Suki Firebrandt Ellis blinked several times as the kitchen on Nantucket materialized around her. She tensed when G'Liat's massive head appeared. "Welcome back," said the Rd'dyggian warrior. He looked at her for a moment before he returned to the couch.

She blinked several times, then looked around the room. Kirsten sat with her at the table and Dr. Cooper sat in the easy chair next to the fireplace. "Where's Manuel?"

"He went to answer a teleholo call," answered Kirsten.

A moment later, Manuel appeared at the hallway door. "We just got a call from Edmund Swan. He's in Southern Arizona and he received a message from Mark."

"So did I," piped in Fire.

G'Liat swung around and looked at her. "You communicated with Ellis? While your mind was with the Cluster?"

She shrugged. "I guess so."

"Edmund's holding on the other end. He wants to know if there's something we can do to help each other," interjected Manuel.

Fire stood, put her hands on Manuel's shoulders, and looked into his deep brown eyes. "How do you feel?"

"Just fine," he said, the vacant smile creeping onto his features. Then, he shook it off. "I guess I'm actually a little confused. A part of me says not to worry about the Cluster – or the death it's caused. That same voice keeps saying this is all for good."

Fire nodded. "Yes. I keep having the same feeling, but who's good? Ours or the Cluster's?"

"Ours," Manuel blurted out, then stopped and chewed on his lower lip. He looked into Fire's eyes. "I don't know. I want to say ours. I feel I ought to say ours … but I don't know."

The teleholo chimed again.

Manuel looked over his shoulder. "Edmund's waiting."

Fire shook her head. "That's not the reminder signal. A second call is coming in." She stepped past Manuel into the hall and went to the room where the teleholo was. Manuel followed Fire. "Hi Edmund," she said. "We have a second call coming in. Let me add them into the call." She pushed a button. Edmund Swan sat in a small apartment. Projected next to it was the *Nicholas Sanson's* command deck.

Simon Yermakov stood next to the pilot's console with his hands behind his back. "This is Simon, is Ms. Smart available? We have something to report."

Fire looked up at Manuel who looked as though he wanted

to protest, but left to retrieve Kirsten. "She'll be right here." She turned her attention to Edmund Swan. "Ed, Manuel tells me you received a message from Mark…"

Swan nodded. He looked to his right. He would see the split screen on the teleholo he used and seemed uncomfortable about speaking in front of an unknown person.

"Sorry," apologized Fire. "Simon Yermakov is first officer of Mark's ship, the *Sanson*." She couldn't help but notice as a pained expression crossed Simon's features. She looked at Simon. "Edmund Swan is Manuel's deputy from Sufiro."

"Pleased to meet you," said Edmund.

Simon nodded in response.

Edmund looked back toward Fire. "Mark did get in touch with me through a friend." He adjusted the holographic pickup on his end and expanded the view. A man sat in a chair, eyes closed. "His name is Timothy Gibbs and I think he's building something for the Cluster."

Just then, Kirsten entered the room with the teleholo and put her hands on the back of Fire's chair. She nodded at Simon.

"John Mark thinks the Cluster is building a memory core at the galaxy's center," said Fire.

"Using the black hole," affirmed Edmund. "Timothy had a theory such a device could be built. He recently joked about wanting to build it, but the problem was getting someone to give him a black hole."

"If someone's manipulating stars near the center of the galaxy, that would explain the readings we're getting," piped in Simon. He looked up at Kirsten. "We've been detecting large scale gravity waves for the last twenty minutes or so."

Fire looked up at Kirsten, eyebrows lifted in an unspoken question. Kirsten put her hands behind her back. "We're so far from the galactic center, it's a little like sensing a Southeast Asian tsunami in California. The gravity shifts are so slight, we won't feel them here on the Earth, but the *Sanson* is designed to detect shifts in the galaxy's overall gravitational field."

Fire frowned. "That doesn't sound at all good."

Kirsten's brow furrowed. "It depends, if they move just a few stars, the main thing it'll do is wreak havoc with jump points around the galaxy – a pain, but something mapping vessels like the *Sanson* are equipped to handle."

"What if they move more than a few stars?" asked Fire.

"I don't know," admitted Kirsten.

Edmund Swan rubbed his chin and looked from Simon to Kirsten and Fire. "Why does the Cluster want a giant memory core anyway?"

Kirsten lifted her chin. "I suspect the person who knows is sitting there right next to you."

Swan looked back at Timothy Gibbs and nodded. "I think you may be right, but he's not exactly communicative right now."

"I think I know someone who can help," said Kirsten, her jaw set.

Fire stood and put her hand on Kirsten's shoulder. "You don't mean G'Liat?"

Kirsten nodded. "If Gibbs' mind is stored in an orbiting Cluster, then there's a chance he can put us in touch with him. Otherwise, if Gibbs comes back, G'Liat can still help us get to the bottom of this – help us learn how many stars the Cluster is going to move and why they're doing it."

"Manuel and I will go with him," said Fire. "We know Edmund and can help out."

Kirsten shook her head. "No, I need to go with him. He'll need someone who can help interpret whatever we learn from Gibbs."

"G'Liat seems quite capable…" began Fire.

"G'Liat knows many things, but he isn't a trained physicist." She looked to Swan. "We need to know how to find you."

"I'll send the address," said Swan.

Fire tried to find the right words to say. "I know you don't like G'Liat…"

"We've worked together before; we can work together now. It's all right." The corporate officer straightened and looked back at Simon. "Did you have anything else to report?"

Simon sniffed and rubbed his nose on his flannel shirtsleeve. "Nothing definitive, but we suspect Proxom may interfere with the Cluster's symbiosis with human minds."

"That makes sense." Kirsten looked down at Fire. "It sounds like something Simon should investigate further with Dr. Cooper."

Fire nodded then looked up at Simon. "I'll have Dr. Eva Cooper give you a call so you can compare notes."

"The surgeon general?" asked Simon, wide-eyed. "Sounds like you have quite a party at that house."

Kirsten reached across to the teleholo control pad and retrieved a data disk with the coordinates to Timothy Gibbs' apartment in Southern Arizona. She looked up at Swan. "I suspect we'll see you in a couple of hours."

"Looking forward to it." He switched off his call.

Kirsten smiled at Simon. "I'll check in once we get to Arizona."

"Take care, Kirsten." Simon turned and nodded to Natalie who terminated the call.

Kirsten and Fire stepped from the teleholo room and walked down the hall. Fire looked at the photos lining the wall. They contained men and women who resembled her son and her late husband. Some wore military uniforms. Others wore casual, civilian clothes. Almost all the photos had been taken aboard ships. One photo in particular caught and held Fire's attention. It showed her father-in-law standing with Samuel Coffin. Behind them was a sperm whale's ridged back.

At the door to the living room, Kirsten looked back to see what kept Fire. "What's that?" she asked.

Fire grinned. "We're trying to figure out what motivates a creature that's all intelligence but has a limited capacity to affect the world around it." She pointed to the whale in the picture. "I think I know someone who can help us."

Chapter Ten

LEGACY

Manuel Raton sat on a deck chair on a small boat as it careened out into the open ocean. He reached into his pocket, retrieved a handkerchief, and blew his nose. The moist air combined with the Proxom Eva Cooper had given him made his nose run. The ocean swells tossed the boat from side to side and Manuel worried he would lose his lunch. The Proxom might be keeping the Cluster out of his head, but between his stomach and his nose, he had little room for other thoughts.

Before he and Fire had left Nantucket, Eva Cooper had spoken to Simon Yermakov aboard the *Sanson* and compared observations. She agreed that Proxom might suppress the Cluster's ability to reach into people's brains. She had enough of the drug on hand to ration out three days' doses to the people in the house before they left on their respective errands. G'Liat didn't take the drug, protesting that Proxom was poisonous to Rd'dyggians.

Manuel's stomach and nose calmed for a moment and he looked up. Fire stood at the boat's wheel. She wore a simple formfitting black shirt and pants. Her hair blew backwards in the wind. He wished he could appreciate the sight more. She might be a woman in her late forties, but he still found her gorgeous. He thought if Fire stopped the boat, perhaps he would feel better and they could go below decks – the bed down there looked quite inviting. As Fire set her jaw and scanned the horizon, he realized such recreation would be out of the question. They had an objective. They sought an old family friend: a sperm whale named Richard.

Richard had told Mark Ellis about G'Liat and thought the warrior might help him understand the Cluster. Now, Fire hoped the whale might provide some insight into the Cluster itself. Manuel had a sudden thought. Standing, he accompanied Fire at the wheel. "How do we know the Cluster isn't affecting the whales the same way as humans?"

Fire looked at him and sighed. "We don't," she admitted. "However, the Clusters don't seem to have had any effect on G'Liat while we've been here. I suspect the Cluster is only targeting humans. Anyone else is off their radar."

Manuel frowned. "I hope you're right." He looked down at the boat's radar and tracking equipment beside the wheel. "Speaking of radar, how are we supposed to find this Richard, anyway?"

Fire shrugged. "Like all sperm whales, he follows a migratory pattern. Mark kept records." She reached down and activated the holographic display. "We're heading for the approximate area where he should be."

Manuel studied the display for a moment. "That's about one hundred square miles of ocean! How do we find him in all that?"

Fire smiled and shook her head. "Typical man … can't be bothered to ask directions." When Manuel lifted an eyebrow, Fire laughed outright. "There's bound to be other sperm whales in the area. If we don't find Richard first, we ask them."

The boat hit another swell and Manuel released a loud belch. "I'd better sit back down."

"I was thinking about making some lunch," said Fire. "Care for any?"

At the question, Manuel's stomach lurched and he ran for the boat's rail.

Edmund Swan found himself once again alone with a silent, motionless Timothy Gibbs. He stepped over to the kitchen, ordered some coffee and contemplated a walk, but decided against it when he remembered the smoldering bodies piled up in back alleys. Taking the coffee, he moved to an armchair opposite his friend and sat down. He hoped the Rd'dyggian named G'Liat and the woman named Kirsten Smart would arrive soon.

Just as he lifted the coffee cup to his lips, the door chime sounded. Startled, he sloshed some coffee onto his shirt and swore while looking at his wrist chrono. It seemed inconceivable that G'Liat and Smart could have arrived already.

He stood, went to the door, and opened it. Instead of a Rd'dyggian warrior and a stout woman, Swan faced a tall, thin man with a haunted expression and salt-and-pepper hair. The deputy sheriff swallowed hard when he realized the man pointed a hepler-225 right at his stomach.

Swan held his hands out at his side. He examined the man with his cybernetic eye and noted his elevated pulse and respiration. "Who are you?"

The man looked around Swan at Gibbs' seated form, then back at Swan. "We intercepted your teleholo call to Nantucket. We think you can help us."

"Who exactly are you?" Swan's eyes narrowed.

The man licked his lips and looked hard at Swan as though trying to decide how far to trust him. After a moment, he lowered the hepler pistol a little. "My name's Jerry Lawrence. I'm with the resistance."

"Against the Cluster?"

Lawrence shook his head. "We shouldn't talk here. We have reason to think they know what we're saying." He cast a meaningful look at Gibbs.

Swan set the coffee cup on a shelf next to the door and looked at his wrist chrono again. "I've got friends coming."

"I know," said Lawrence as he turned and started down the hall.

Swan stood frozen on the spot for a moment, then pursed his lips and followed Jerry Lawrence.

Kirsten and G'Liat flew to Southern Arizona aboard the chartered Rd'dyggian spacecraft. Like G'Liat, the Rd'dyggian pilot called Rizonex seemed unaffected by the Cluster. Kirsten wondered whether that meant Rd'dyggians were immune to the Cluster's influence or whether the Cluster wasn't targeting them.

The Rd'dyggian craft made the journey from Nantucket to Southern Arizona in less than an hour. Despite the craft's speed and its sparse accommodations, the journey proved smooth and comfortable.

They landed at the Southern Arizona spaceport and took a cab to Timothy Gibbs' apartment complex. Kirsten had never been to Arizona before, but noted the quiet streets and the striking, blue sky. She suspected Arizona had been much more like the rest of the planet before the Cluster's arrival. As she stepped from the cab, she felt as though she had entered a blast furnace. Looking back, she noticed that G'Liat also seemed uncomfortable. "This heat seems to bother you almost as much as me," she said, trying to make conversation.

G'Liat typed a credit code on the cabby's keypad then turned to face Kirsten. "The heat here is bad, but it bothers me less than the low humidity."

Kirsten looked at him. His orange skin had grown dry and flaky. She nodded, then entered the apartment building followed by G'Liat. The ceilings in the modern apartment complex were higher than in Ellis's ancient house, so the warrior could walk upright. They found Gibbs' apartment and rang the chime. They waited for an answer, but none came. Kirsten pushed the door chime again, then folded her arms and began tapping her foot. "Do you suppose he stepped out?" asked Kirsten.

"It seems doubtful." G'Liat reached into a compartment within the case he carried and retrieved a small device. Setting it against the keypad, he thumbed a control stud and waited a moment before looking at the readout. Though awkward given the Rd'dyggian's large fingers, he keyed a sequence into the lock and the door opened.

Kirsten took a step forward, but the Rd'dyggian held out his arm and entered the apartment first. Kirsten followed close on the warrior's heels and looked around. Seeing the man sitting stock still in the armchair, Kirsten pointed. "Do you suppose that's Timothy Gibbs?"

G'Liat nodded. "Presuming we're in the correct apartment."

"I checked the number," said Kirsten. "It's got to be the right place."

Once G'Liat examined the room, he approached a shelving unit next to the door. He picked up the coffee cup and held it to his nose. The purple mustache-like feelers entered the liquid and then shot back. "The coffee's still hot," explained the warrior, returning the cup to the shelf. "Swan has not been gone long."

Kirsten shifted from one foot to the other as she looked around. "Well, I hope he gets back soon."

G'Liat carried his traveling case to the kitchen table, set it down, and opened it, revealing the brain scan device within.

"Don't you think we should wait for Swan?" she asked.

"We don't know where Swan has gone, or how long he'll be." Seeing Kirsten's disapproval, G'Liat inclined his head. "Still, it will take time to prepare the device. We should be ready."

Kirsten dropped into the armchair across from Gibbs and frowned as she stared at the man's blank features. "Okay, go ahead and prepare the device, but you'll hold off using it until I give the word."

"I respectfully remind you that I am no longer a member of your crew." The warrior folded his arms.

"So noted," said Kirsten. "Neither are you a citizen of this planet. I want to find out what happened to Swan and talk to him before we start poking around in this man's brain."

"As you wish." The warrior turned back toward the kitchen table. "However, the danger builds every second we delay."

"I know," said Kirsten. "I know."

As before, John Mark Ellis rowed toward the portal. Once he arrived, he again entered the strange void space with streaming lights like a rushing current. He concentrated on the illusory boat. He didn't want to contemplate what would happen to him if the small craft vanished. Perhaps he could continue without it, but he didn't want to test that. When he emerged, he once again found himself near the black hole at the galaxy's center. He looked around, attempting to get his bearings. His brow creased as he observed a silver craft, which looked almost alien to him until he realized that it was a primitive Earth rocket. He smiled when he realized that the ship resembled something he'd seen in a science fiction vid from the mid-twentieth century.

However, as he watched, the smile fell away. A yellow energy beam emerged from the ship's bow and shot toward a distant star. At first, he didn't understand the beam's function, but then, little by little, the star moved.

Ellis turned and faced the *Pequod*. As with the silver ship, the whaling ship projected a yellow beam toward a star. Looking closer, the captain thought he noticed activity on the whale ship's deck, like a scuffle or fight. He grabbed both oars and began to row with all his strength.

The captain soon realized he no longer made headway toward the *Pequod*. Instead, he moved away from the whaling ship and back toward the node. "No!" he shouted, trying to impose his will on the events he witnessed. He tried rowing again. Despite his best efforts, he shot into the light that took him back to the lab – back to the Cluster orbiting the Earth.

Unseen by Ellis, a small probe orbited a star not far from where he rowed with all his might. The probe also couldn't see Ellis, but for different reasons. Ellis couldn't see the probe because he concentrated on rowing. The probe did not see him, since he was, in fact, nothing but an electromagnetic energy stream existing outside the realm of visible light.

What the probe did see were two silver clusters of spheres – one nearby and another rather distant. Each cluster projected a yellow energy beam toward a star, which then began to ease through space. The probe relayed the images it recorded back to Saturn's largest moon, Titan. On Titan, a large teddy bear-like creature watched the probe's telemetry on a holographic display with rapt interest. She had a silver-gray pelt and was her people's matron and the galaxy's leader.

She knew that by moving stars around in the galactic core, the Cluster would wreak havoc on the galaxy's gravitational tides and cause significant damage.

Her people had been the Cluster's slaves for over a

million millenia, though. As a result, she knew two things. The Cluster – or the Intelligence, as her people knew it – loved its appendages. The Cluster would do everything in its power to keep humans and their home solar system safe. By extension, she believed her own world would also be safe.

Teklar also knew that if she warned the galaxy's populace, the Cluster might seek either vengeance upon her people, destroying them; or even worse, the Cluster might enslave them again. Therefore, Teklar watched the display and did nothing else.

Jerry Lawrence led Edmund Swan to a building a block away from Tim Gibbs' apartment complex. Inside, they climbed a flight of stairs and walked down a dark hallway. Swan adjusted his cybernetic eye to let in more light. As he did, he noticed the graffiti in this building had not been scrubbed clean and the wood had a musty smell.

At last, they stopped at a door and Lawrence keyed a sequence into the computer touchpad.

Stepping inside, Swan counted four women and five men huddled around a teleholo watching the news. One woman turned off the teleholo and stood. The others all turned careworn expressions toward the deputy sheriff. "You must be Edmund Swan," said the woman.

Swan gave a curt nod.

"We're the Southern Arizona faction of the resistance against the Cluster." The woman glanced from side to side, as though she feared Swan would laugh at her.

Swan looked around at the people gathered. "There's only ten of you…"

"I know." Lawrence shrugged. "There are cells in other cities…"

"But, I'm afraid our numbers are shrinking as the Cluster contacts more people." The woman stepped forward and offered Swan her hand. "My name's Maria Gonzalez." She then introduced the others in the room. "I believe you already know Jerry."

Jerry flashed a half-hearted smile, thumbed the safety on his gun, and tucked it in his waistband.

"What do you want with me?" asked Swan.

"You're the same Edmund Swan from Sufiro who organized the New Granadan resistance against Tejo, are you not?" asked Gonzalez.

Swan nodded. "I am. What does that have to do…"

Gonzalez put her hand on Swan's elbow and led him to a chair. "We're civilians, Mr. Swan. Jerry Lawrence used to repair teleholos. Carlos there –" she pointed to a man with scraggly black hair "– used to be a plumber. I was a local elementary school principal. No one here is what you would call military material, but we've seen what the Cluster is doing and we don't like it. We want to stop it." She sat down, put her hands on her knees and looked into Swan's eyes.

"What about the police?" Swan feared he already knew the answer.

"Those who survive," said the man called Carlos, "are all controlled by the Cluster."

"We need someone like you," pleaded Jerry, "who has military experience as well as experience with the Cluster to help organize us."

Swan snorted. "Including people in other cities, how many of you are there in all?"

"About a hundred and fifty so far." Gonzalez sounded as though she appologized for the small number.

"But there are only four Clusters," Lawrence chimed in.

"Do you have any armaments?" asked Swan. "Any ships?"

Lawrence retrieved the gun from his waistband. "Just a few hand heplers."

Swan closed his eyes. A moment later, he opened them and looked at each face in the room. They were horrified at losing loved ones and friends. They didn't understand how their world had changed so much in just a few days. They feared the Cluster would absorb them and they'd die in the process. "I'll be honest – I don't see what chance we have, but I'll help if I can."

Hope glimmered in several people's eyes. "That's all we ask," said Maria Gonzalez, her own eyes bright with moisture.

"I need to get back to Tim Gibbs' apartment," explained Swan. "I was supposed to meet someone. They might be able to help me get word out – help us find a ship, maybe some more armaments."

Maria Gonzalez nodded. "Good," she said. "Go meet your friends then come back tomorrow and let us know what you learn."

Gonzalez and Swan stood and shook hands. The deputy sheriff tried to find more words, but he dropped his gaze to the dirty floor and returned to Timothy Gibbs' apartment.

Manuel Raton looked over the boat's rail. As the day wore on, he grew more accustomed to the boat's rocking and swaying. He'd spent most of his life living in inland towns or cities, well away from oceans. As a young adult, he'd traveled between the continents of New Granada and Tejo on a large ocean-going vessel on the planet Sufiro. He remembered that voyage as a happy time. On the voyage, he'd attempted to bond with another young man, Sam Stone. Manuel's frown deepened as he recalled the greed that overtook the self-absorbed young man and how that greed had compelled Stone to kill Manuel's parents.

The boat slowed and he looked toward the bow. Fire pulled back the throttle. "Is everything all right?" Manuel frowned.

"Yeah. We're approaching the area where Richard should be." Fire activated the boat's autopilot and stepped back toward the aft rail. "Deep thoughts?"

Manuel shook his head. "Just thinking about the last time I was out this far at sea."

"You look like you're feeling better," she said.

He nodded and patted his stomach. "Still a little queasy, but I'm doing a lot better than a couple of hours ago, that's for sure."

"Glad to hear it." She took him in her arms and he leaned his head against her shoulder.

They stood that way for a moment. "Are you ever sorry we got back together?" asked Manuel.

Fire shook her head. "Not at all." She stood back, looked into Manuel's eyes, and smiled. "I do miss Jerome Ellis, but you and I have been friends since we were both children. There are few people I trust as much as you."

"I've just been afraid…" Manuel's voice hitched.

"That I'm in some kind of rebound … going with you just because I feel I need someone in my life." Fire shook her head and chuckled. "I'm surprised at you. I'd think you of all people would know me better than that."

Manuel smiled, took her in his arms, and kissed her. When he released her, he noticed something in the distance, over her shoulder – almost like a shimmering crystal.

"What's the matter?" she asked.

He pointed. "Is that a whale spout?"

She turned and narrowed her gaze. "I think it might be." The two stepped back toward the wheel. Fire steered the boat toward the spout. She pointed to a metal cabinet beside the wheel. "There are translators in the bottom drawer."

Manuel knelt down and retrieved the translator units. He handed one to Fire then put the other on his head and adjusted the microphone. As they approached, Manuel realized there were several whales ahead. Even though his stomach gave a slight lurch, he moved toward the boat's bow to get a closer look.

He didn't know much about whales, but there had been many pictures in the Ellis house. Almost all of them showed creatures with massive square heads and tiny, almost underdeveloped, lower jaws filled with sharp teeth. These whales were different. Their heads were rounder in front and more wrinkled on the top. Their jaws dominated their faces and when one opened its mouth, it had no teeth. Instead, its mouth had something that resembled white hair.

Fire activated the boat's hover controls and lifted it out of the water, so the engine's noise wouldn't disturb the whales. He looked back, his brow creased. Fire stepped forward and put her arm around Manuel's shoulder.

"Those whales don't look like the pictures at the Ellis home," complained Manuel.

"That's because they're humpback whales," said Fire. They

watched as one whale rolled onto its side, revealing a long, paddle-like flipper. "They're a different species than Richard."

"Can they help us find him?" asked Manuel.

"I doubt it," said Fire. "Humpbacks don't care for humans. It's best if we keep our distance."

"Why don't they like humans?"

"Because humans almost hunted them to extinction." Fire looked up toward the sky. "We didn't stop until the late twenty-first century. That's when Myra Lee first recognized that the whales and the Titans spoke to one another."

Manuel sighed, feeling a momentary pang of regret at being born a human. Too many people, like his friend Sam Stone, had proven to be monsters. He looked back to the whales. "Can we at least listen to them, hear what they're saying?"

"We can try," said Fire. "Remember, humpback whales speak in song. They don't talk to each other quite the same way we do."

Manuel put his hand to his ear and listened to the receiver. The whales discussed the land-apes who plied the water on floating islands. Fire pointed to some smaller whales in the distance. "I think they're talking about us," she said.

"How ironic," sang one whale, "that the land-apes are at the mercy of creatures such as us; creatures who do not build tools; creatures who but swim the depths of space."

"They know about the Cluster?" Manuel whispered to Fire.

"Whales know about a great many things." Then Fire shushed him, tuned her translator, and then nodded. Tapping Manuel on the shoulder, she pointed to the setting and indicated that he should also adjust his translator.

When he did, he heard a different song. "For us, the art is the song, the composition, the memory of what was and the dreams of what will be. For the land-apes, the art is the death, plunder of the world and taking more than they give back."

"How are the land-apes different from the spermaceti?" came an eerie refrain. Fire inclined her head as she listened and tapped a button on her translator.

"For the spermaceti, the art is the hunt, the chase, the challenge. They hunt and are hunted. They exist in balance with the world."

Fire turned off her translator and stepped back toward the boat's wheel, then put the unit next to the computer. Manuel stepped up next to her and watched as she started a program. A moment later, coordinates appeared above the holographic dais.

"What's that?" asked Manuel.

"That's where we'll find sperm whales," said Fire. "You see, part of what makes humpbacks hard to understand is that their songs are multi-layered and contain more information than just the words. When they mentioned the sperm whales, they also happened to tell us where we could find them."

"And Mark's friend, Richard?"

Fire shook her head. "No, but if we find a sperm whale pod, they'll be a lot more willing to talk to us and help."

Manuel pursed his lips while looking out at the humpback whale pod. "I'm surprised any whale would help humans after what we've done to them."

Fire nodded. Then, with the boat still in hover mode, she turned away from the humpbacks and drifted a distance away before dropping back into the water so they could continue their quest.

When Edmund Swan returned to Timothy Gibbs' apartment, he found an eight-foot tall Rd'dyggian warrior in a black turtleneck shirt glaring at a stout woman wearing a TransGalactic blazer and blue slacks, her hands on her hips.

Swan cleared his throat and the two looked up at him. The woman's surprise at his entrance seemed genuine. Though the Rd'dyggian also looked surprised, Swan couldn't help but feel the surprise was just an affectation.

The woman stepped forward, her hand extended. "You must be Edmund Swan. Good to meet you at last. I'm Kirsten Smart." As the deputy sheriff took her hand, Smart looked into his mismatched eyes and her breath hitched. She inclined her head toward Gibbs. "How's he been doing?"

Swan released Smart's hand. "Who can tell? He's been like that almost all the time I've been here."

"But he does have periods of consciousness?" asked Smart.

"Every ten hours or so he wakes for an hour then goes back under." Swan looked down at his wrist chrono. "He's due to wake any minute."

Swan looked up at the Rd'dyggian warrior and pursed his lips. All the Rd'dyggians Swan knew liked to wear loose-fitting garments and made large, loping movements. This one stepped up to Swan with almost delicate precision and introduced himself. Seeing the open case on Gibbs' kitchen table, Swan stepped past G'Liat and examined the device within using his cybernetic eye. "I've heard about these brain scan devices," he said. "I don't know how I feel about them."

"As a law enforcement official," said G'Liat, "I would think you would find such a device useful for interrogation."

Swan gritted his teeth. "Devices like that violate too many basic rights." He shook his head. "Using one would require a grave emergency."

"That's just what we were discussing when you walked in," said Smart. "G'Liat wants to use the device on your friend now, but I was trying to persuade him to wait until your return."

In a heartbeat, the warrior slipped between the deputy sheriff and Smart. Swan took a step back. "What I want to know is where you had gone. Why weren't you here?"

Smart shot the warrior an angry look and Swan opened his mouth to answer, but a shuffling from Gibbs' armchair interrupted everyone. The computer technician blinked in surprise at the new people in his apartment. He flashed a self-conscious smile and waved as he rushed to the bathroom and closed the door behind him. Once finished, he emerged and went to the kitchen.

"Tim," said Swan, "I'd like you to meet two friends of mine: Kirsten Smart and G'Liat."

Gibbs punched his order into the food preparation unit then turned on Swan. "Edmund, I don't mind you being here, but please ask before you invite other people into my home."

Swan started to speak but Smart held up her hand. "We won't stay long," she said. "We've heard a little about the project you're working on."

"We're curious," interjected G'Liat. "We'd like to know more."

Gibbs brightened for a moment, then his eyes narrowed as he evaluated G'Liat. "Rd'dyggians are warriors and pragmatic to the extreme. Why would you be interested in an advanced computer project?"

Smart's jaw dropped. Even though she didn't have much love for G'Liat, such a racist statement from the engineer shocked her. G'Liat cleared the distance from the table to Gibbs in a single step and looked down into the engineer's face.

"I will remind you, Mr. Gibbs that Rd'dyggians were in space while your kind were still killing each other with animal bones." His icy tone sent chills down Swan's spine.

Swan took two steps forward and put a hand on G'Liat's chest. "Tim's been working long shifts." He tried to conjure the right words to pacify a dangerous situation. He examined the Rd'dyggian warrior with his cybernetic eye, but found the readings hard to interpret. He faced his friend. Perspiration dotted Gibbs' upper lip.

Gibbs looked down at the floor. "I'm sorry. I didn't mean to offend." A moment later, a chime sounded, indicating his dinner was finished. Jumping to his feet, he upset the chair. Hands shaking, he removed the meal from the unit and carried it around the eight-foot tall warrior to the table. With a certain grace, G'Liat righted Gibbs' chair and held it for him.

Smart looked up at G'Liat with a frown, and then joined Gibbs at the table. "I'm afraid we've gotten off on the wrong foot." When Gibbs looked up, she smiled. "I'm a cartographer for TransGalactic."

Gibbs chuckled, shook his head and then he took a bite of food. "You'll have your work cut out for you," he said.

"My ship has sensed gravitational shifts from the center of the galaxy. From what Edmund tells me, this might be related to what you're doing."

Gibbs nodded. "The Cluster is an ancient lifeform with knowledge spanning eons. They want a place to deposit that knowledge, so others can benefit." He stood from the table and stepped over to his teleholo. He brought up a schematic that showed the black hole at the galaxy's center, with intense energy plumes shooting out into intergalactic space. A gas cloud veiled the dense mass. "We're building a relativistic quantum computer."

Smart and G'Liat both approached the teleholo and examined the image displayed as Gibbs returned to the table and continued eating. "So," said G'Liat, "why does the Cluster need a relativistic quantum computer? It seems they can store and analyze the information they've gathered."

"They're dying," Gibbs responded. "There used to be more of them than there are now. They want to make sure the information they've gathered is preserved. They've had symbiotic relationships with other lifeforms – sensual creatures who interact with the world around them. They want to experience what it is to be a creature with appendages first hand. They're lonely and they see this as a way they can experience true camaraderie with others."

Smart chewed her lower lip for a moment before looking up at Gibbs. "Do you mind if I use your teleholo to call my ship?"

"Be my guest," said Gibbs.

As Smart called the *Sanson*, Swan sat down with Gibbs at the table. "So that's what this is all about? The Cluster wants new experiences and they want to save their knowledge for posterity?" When Gibbs nodded, Swan looked up at G'Liat. "That doesn't seem so bad, does it?"

"It all depends," said the warrior as he stepped toward the table. "Who gets to access the data?"

"Anyone," said Gibbs. "The design includes a beacon with coded instructions on how to retrieve the information and how to add one's consciousness to the database."

Swan noticed that Smart was deep in conversation with the *Sanson's* first officer. He stood up from the table and joined her as the first officer whistled. He knelt beside a woman typing on a console. A holographic simulation of the black hole appeared. After a moment, bright light flared and Swan had to look away until the light dissipated.

"Are these masses correct?" asked the man on the ship, wide-eyed.

Smart looked up. "Mr. Gibbs, are the masses you used for

your simulation the same ones you're using in the memory core?"

Gibbs nodded and wiped his mouth on a napkin.

"What's the matter?" asked Swan.

The doll-like figure stood up on the little dais. "Bringing that much mass together would trigger a shock wave throughout the galaxy," he explained. "It would strip the atmospheres from a million stars. Long before that happens the tachyon burst from this event would devastate life as we know it. Zahir, Rd'dyggia, Titan, Earth … and all their colonies…" Simon looked down at his feet then back up. "Kirsten, if they complete this project, life as we know it is over."

Smart, Swan, and G'Liat all looked at Gibbs.

Gibbs looked from one face to the other. "The Cluster says they'll protect us here on Earth. They can control the tachyon burst so we'll be safe in this solar system."

"That still leaves everyone else," said Smart. "Humans on Alpha Coma and the other colonies, not to mention all the people in the galaxy." She avoided looking at G'Liat.

G'Liat made a low, menacing growl while Swan dropped into a chair and put his face in his hands. He thought about his friends on the planet Sufiro. Smart thanked the ship's first mate and then terminated the connection. Without another word, she left the apartment, needing to get some fresh air.

John Mark Ellis awoke in his room on Nantucket and found himself looking into Eva Cooper's blue eyes. She gasped, then brushed blond hair behind her back. He blinked a few times and she helped him sit up, then handed him a pill and a glass of water. Without thinking about it, Ellis took the pill and gulped the water.

"Thanks." Ellis handed the glass back to Cooper. "May I have more?"

"Certainly." Cooper stepped across the hall to the bathroom where she refilled the glass. "You must be dehydrated after two days asleep."

Ellis swallowed the second glass of water and then nodded.

With that, he leapt up and stepped across to the bathroom. After he finished, he looked up and down the hall as he padded back to the bedroom. "Where are the others?"

Cooper filled Ellis in on the last two days' events while he rifled through the closet looking for some clothes. "I'm glad mom went out to talk to Richard. I think if anyone can help, he can. The Cluster's building something at the galaxy's center and I don't like what I saw at all." He looked out the door then at Cooper. "How's Coffin?"

"He's been doing quite well for someone who's been asleep for so long. I've been giving him some sucrose solution to keep him from dehydrating. I was just about to check on him when I noticed you waking up." She looked at his pajama bottoms and blushed. "I'll go check on him and let you get dressed," she said.

As Ellis pulled on his pants, he tried to remember what he'd seen just before he awoke. The image of the scuffle on the *Pequod's* deck came to his mind. He threw on socks and shoes, then stepped across the hall.

Cooper looked up from Coffin and swallowed hard. "His life signs have dropped. I don't know why – maybe he's been too long without food and water, maybe it's something else."

"I need to get back," said Ellis. "If I can get back to the Cluster, I think I can save him."

"Oh no." Cooper stood up. "I don't think that's going to be possible for at least 24 hours." She pulled out a chair and indicated that Ellis sit down. As he did, she explained what they had learned about Proxom inhibiting the Cluster.

"So that pill you gave me?" asked Ellis.

"Was Proxom," she said.

Ellis took a deep breath, rubbed the sleep from his eyes, and then tried to think. "Something major's happening." Ellis looked to his friend, lying on the bed. "He's going to need help."

"Where are we going to get that help?" asked Cooper.

"Let's get Kirsten, G'Liat, and Swan back here," he said. "Then I think we need to have a talk with the people who should be helping us."

"Who's that?"

"The people who used to be subject to the Cluster," said Ellis. "The Titans."

Part III: Battle for the New Earth

"And there appeared a great wonder in heaven; a woman clothed with the sun, and the moon under her feet and upon her head, a crown of twelve stars: And she being with child cried, travailing in birth, and pained to be delivered. And there appeared another wonder in heaven; and behold a great red dragon, having seven heads and ten horns, and seven crowns upon his heads. And his tail drew the third part of the stars of heaven, and did cast them to the earth: and the dragon stood before the woman which was ready to be delivered, for to devour her child as soon as it was born."

Revelation 12: 1-4

Chapter Eleven

PASSION

Fire yanked down on the throttle and spun the wheel to avoid hitting the dark gray form, which had leapt from the water in the boat's path. Manuel fell out of the deck chair and rolled into the boat's rail. "What the hell?" he cursed as he pushed himself to his knees and rubbed his neck.

Fire activated the antigraviton generators so the boat hovered over the water, then turned on her translator as the whale turned toward them. It spoke in staccato clicks. "The cycle continues."

Fire summoned the solemnity the proper response required. "The cycle continues." She studied the whale and smiled as she recognized Richard. Manuel struggled to his feet and joined Fire at the rail.

"Suki Firebrandt Ellis," said the whale.

Manuel inclined his head and listened to the static-like vocalizations for a moment before turning on his own translator box in time to hear the whale say, "It is good to see you again."

"I presume you're Richard," ventured Manuel.

"The name suits me. It approximates what my kind call me and I like how it's similar to the name of a famous whale from human fiction." The whale swam close to the boat and turned so one eye looked up at Fire and Manuel. "I do not know you, land ape."

Manuel looked at Fire and shrugged.

"He is called Manuel Raton," said Fire. "He is a friend of … my calf … John Mark Ellis."

The whale lifted its tail from the water and slapped it down on the surface. "How is John Mark Ellis? Is he well?"

Fire shook her head. "I wish I could tell you for sure." She looked down at the deck and tried to find the right words. "He lives, but last we saw him, his mind had left his body. We

143

believe a thing called the Cluster stole it."

"Ah." Richard swam a short distance away from the boat. "John Mark spoke to me of the Cluster when he last visited. It is a thing in space that understands the hunt and the death. I told John Mark he should seek out the philosopher called G'Liat."

"He did," said Fire. "G'Liat helped John Mark find the Cluster; helped him follow it to its home, a cluster of ancient stars. There, John Mark communicated with it. Now his body is back on Earth. G'Liat is here as well."

The whale swam a little further away and said, "Whales care not for matters of space."

"You can't just ignore the Cluster," called Manuel. "It's over our heads, orbiting the Earth."

Richard made a long, gentle arc and circled back to the boat. "I do not ignore the Cluster. Suki Firebrandt Ellis just told me the Cluster has stolen John Mark Ellis's mind. That matters to me, but I am powerless – just as I had been when a giant squid carried my calf down to the depths – just as I'd been when my mate came to the end of her time. I am not a tool builder."

"Neither is the Cluster," interjected Fire. "What we need is understanding."

"What would a tool-builder offer you?" asked Manuel.

Richard exhaled and a waterspout washed over the deck, drenching both Fire and Manuel. "John Mark Ellis and his father offered me friendship. Beyond that, I do not know what a tool builder could offer me. I have no need for tools, no desire to build."

Fire's eyes narrowed. "Why not?"

"What have tools given you?" Richard swam away a short distance, circled around and came back. Fire sensed the whale grew restless.

"Tools give us the means to support ourselves." Manuel rubbed his hands through his hair. "They give us the means to feed ourselves."

"My teeth and jaw do the same for me," observed Richard.

"Tools have allowed us to travel far, to explore," suggested Fire. "Without tools, we couldn't have built this boat to be out here with you."

"True," said Richard. "But why must you be out here? What drove land apes to leave their migratory paths?"

Manuel narrowed his gaze. "Curiosity. The desire to learn and pass knowledge from one generation to another."

Richard slipped below the water and came up on the other side of the boat. Fire stepped over to the opposite rail. Manuel joined her. "What you describe is like the humpback whale songs," said Richard after a brief silence.

"Except it's different." Fire's brow furrowed as she considered how best to explain. "The humpbacks make a living record of their travels. With pencil and paper, we can write down our thoughts. With books and computers, we can store our thoughts for generations to come. I can read my grandmothers' and great grandmothers' exact thoughts if I choose to do so."

Richard exhaled again and slipped under the water, saying, "the cycle resumes."

"Is that it?" Manuel began to shiver.

Fire shrugged, then went to the cabinet and retrieved two towels and wrapped one around his shoulders.

"Humpbacks have a living memory." Manuel gripped the towel and looked up at the sky. Above, wispy cirrus clouds thickened into overcast. "Living memories are passed down through oral tradition. They change with time. Some things are forgotten. Other things are added. What if the Cluster's memory is like the whales'?"

"How could that be?" asked Fire. "From what G'Liat and John Mark have said, it seems like the Cluster is little more than a giant computer itself."

"But it's also alive." Manuel tugged on his mustache and glanced over at the boat's control panel. "People remove data from computers and write new data in its place."

A voice issued from the translator units, startling Fire and Manuel. "The cycle continues." Returning to the starboard rail, they faced Richard again. "You said that G'Liat is here on Earth?"

Fire and Manuel looked at each other, then back at the whale. "Yes," said Fire.

"I must speak with him. You have posed several interesting ideas, but they are difficult to understand. Whales understand not the ways of land apes nor understand the ways of space. Perhaps G'Liat can help me understand. Then, perhaps I can help more. I am concerned for John Mark Ellis. I will help if I can." Before Fire or Manuel could respond, the whale said, "the cycle resumes," and slipped back under the water.

"I think we've been dismissed." Fire shrugged, then stepped back to the wheel and turned the boat around, back toward Nantucket Island.

Kirsten was surprised that G'Liat had not killed Gibbs. She tried to imagine how many would die if the Cluster succeeded. If she'd had a gun, she would have been tempted to pull the trigger and kill Gibbs herself. However, G'Liat explained how Gibbs would be more useful alive than dead. Kirsten didn't quite know how to interpret his explanation, but agreed with Swan's assessment that they might be able to persuade Gibbs to help them from the inside. Even so, Kirsten had no desire to remain with Gibbs any longer. "I don't know about you two," she said once Gibbs had fallen back into a trance, "but, I want to get back to Nantucket."

Swan chewed his lower lip for a moment, then looked up at Kirsten. "I want to go with you, but there's something I need to do here." G'Liat looked up with keen interest and Swan fell silent and turned away from the warrior's gaze.

"Let's take a walk," suggested Kirsten.

Though he showed no outward emotion, G'Liat continued to watch as Kirsten and Swan left the apartment.

As they walked down the hall and rode in the elevator, Swan told Kirsten about the resistance.

"It sounds like a lost cause," said Kirsten as they stepped from the building into the Arizona sun's glare.

Swan swallowed hard. "Probably," he admitted. He took a few steps down the street and looked around at the structures, then up to the sky. "I never thought I'd see blue sky in Arizona." He held out his arms. "Out beyond the city there's desert – a little, anyway – and maybe Saguaro cactus can grow and Palo Verde trees can provide a little shade again. Maybe the scent of mesquite will perfume the air after a monsoon rain."

"It's a beautiful thought." Kirsten flashed a slight smile.

Swan dropped his arms to his sides. "I can't change what the Cluster has done, but Earth belongs to humans – not just the ones who live here, but those humans on the colonies as well – not just to mindless zombies like Tim Gibbs, but to those who will appreciate the sights and smells." He looked down to the ground then back up to Kirsten. "You're doing your part to stop the Cluster. I have to do my part. My part is helping the resistance here in Arizona." He stepped forward and took her hands. "The problem is, I can't do it alone. I need Manuel or Mark – if he's awake again – to get a message to Ellison Firebrandt on Sufiro." Swan reached into his shirt pocket, took out a piece of paper and a pen, and wrote a note, then handed it to Kirsten.

"I'll do my best." Kirsten folded the paper and put it in her pocket. She turned back toward the apartment complex, but Swan had not joined her. "Aren't you coming?" she asked.

He shook his head. "Lock up when you leave. I just want to take a walk."

Kirsten smiled despite the lump in her throat, then nodded and went back into the building. She and G'Liat traveled back to the island aboard the ship the Rd'dyggian warrior had chartered. During the short journey, Kirsten stared at the pilot, Rizonex. She wondered how much he knew and whether his opinions about the Cluster differed from G'Liat's. Rizonex's hands rested on the console along with G'Liat's. Through the computer, the two Rd'dyggians could share their thoughts without vocalizing. It seemed possible the pilot knew everything G'Liat did.

Landing at the island's spaceport, old Charlie Rogers once again greeted them in cheerful tones, which sent a shiver down Kirsten's spine. He drove the two back to the Ellis house. G'Liat went to the door while Kirsten tried to pay. "No need for John Mark's friends to pay me. It's my pleasure to have some company," said Charlie.

Kirsten joined G'Liat at the door, unlocked it, and entered. She smiled when she noticed John Mark having lunch with Dr. Cooper. She crossed the room and put her arms around him from behind. "I'm glad to see you back," she whispered in his ear. She then frowned as she noticed his dour expression.

Mark reached up and patted Kirsten's hand. "It's good to see you," he croaked. "It's just that Coffin's in trouble. I think he's dying."

Dr. Cooper looked down at her plate. "And I'm afraid I didn't help any." She looked back up at Kirsten. "I gave Mark Proxom as we discussed."

G'Liat entered and pushed the door closed. Mark Ellis nodded at the tall warrior. "I'm glad to see you back. The Cluster's building something big at the galaxy's center and we need all the help we can get."

"We know." G'Liat explained what they'd learned from Timothy Gibbs and Kirsten reported what they'd learned from the *Sanson*.

"Didn't Edmund Swan come back with you?" asked Mark, once they finished their narrative.

Kirsten cast a meaningful glance at G'Liat then looked back at Mark. "He decided he needed to stay behind."

"I suspect he's been asked to join a resistance movement," said the warrior. "A futile gesture, though. To defeat the Cluster we must pool our resources."

Mark looked at Kirsten. With a nod, she acknowledged G'Liat's assessment.

Mark and Kirsten sat down on the couch, next to each other. The captain took out a cigar, but after a sharp look both from Kirsten and Eva, he didn't light it. Instead, he just held it in his teeth as they discussed what they had learned. "What I don't understand," said Mark around the cigar, "was what happened to me. It seemed like I had gone to some strange dream world."

"I suspect you had." Stooped over, G'Liat moved around the coffee table and sat in the remaining chair. "Somehow the Cluster seems able to copy your memories, your thoughts, everything that makes you an individual and place that essence into themselves."

"I gather I spoke to Gibbs aboard a Cluster in Earth's orbit." Mark removed the cigar from his mouth. "However, there's another Cluster – maybe two, now – at the center of the galaxy."

G'Liat considered that. "The Clusters must have some way

to communicate with each other. It's probably an EQ channel like we use for starship communication."

Mark's brow creased. "So, you think my 'spirit' found a way to ride from one Cluster to another? That's what I suspected."

"Indeed, what you describe is like a data packet transferred from one computer to another," affirmed G'Liat. If the giant warrior could have shrugged, Kirsten suspected he would have.

Mark stood and stepped over to the fireplace. Despite Kirsten and Dr. Cooper's silent objections, he lit the cigar. Kirsten sighed and looked around the room until her gaze settled on the stairs. "So, what do we do about Coffin?" she asked. "If he's in trouble, then Ms. Meiji at Mao must also be in trouble, as are others. Their minds may be alive in the Cluster but what happens if their bodies die here on Earth?"

"We need to do something." G'Liat stood. "If the Cluster is copying humans' personalities and memory matrices, it's possible the data still exists in the brains of those humans here on Earth. Could injecting those humans with Proxom cause them to revive?"

Eva gasped. "What would that do? Would there be two copies of each person – one in the person's body and one in the Cluster's memory?"

"Possibly," said G'Liat. "It would explain certain … observations. A person who is under an orbiting Cluster's influence is having data transferred back and forth – a copy is being made as they work. Those on the more distant Clusters are too far away for such instantaneous transfer." He started to move toward the door.

"Where are you going?" asked Kirsten.

"Back to the ship." He opened the door. "It has been a long and tiring day and I wish to consult the shipboard computer, to see if I can learn more about Proxom's properties and refresh my memory on brain transfer experiments." The warrior left, closing the door behind him.

Mark exhaled smoke with a sigh. "He is right. We need to know more, before we proceed, but I think we have a source for more information."

Kirsten understood at once. "The Titans. We could be there tomorrow on the *Sanson*. Edmund Swan also wants us to get a message to your grandfather. From Titan, we could jump to another star system, send the message, and be back within the hour. What are we waiting for?"

"I want to go back to the Cluster." Mark stepped toward the kitchen table. "I want to see if there's anything I can do to help Coffin and the others from within. I think I can move from one Cluster to the others better than most. I might be able to do something to help."

Kirsten smiled. "I understand. We can send Simon to Titan."

Mark tossed his cigar into the fireplace. "Let's wait for mom and Manuel to get back and see what they've learned from Richard. She might want to go to Titan as well." The captain stroked his mustache. During his mother's last foray to Titan, she'd managed to break into the Titans' computer system to discover their connection to the Cluster in the first place. "In the meantime, I think I could use some fresh air." He looked to Kirsten. "Care to go for a walk?"

"I'd love to," she said.

After Mark and Kirsten left on their walk, Eva Cooper found herself alone. She went upstairs to check on Coffin. Finding his condition unchanged, she realized she could use some fresh air as well. She went out the front door and walked to the white picket fence surrounding the Ellis family house. She looked both directions and decided to turn right – back toward the spaceport.

As she walked, Eva drank in the landscape. Her ancestors had been American and she found the sense of history – the Americana – around her both comforting and somehow discomfiting. She paused at a Revolutionary War memorial and took in the names of those from Nantucket who had died to end the British Crown's oppression. As she moved on, she considered how few they had been compared to the number who had died in a single night due to the Cluster's emotional onslaught.

Half a mile from Ellis's house, the buildings began to thin out and Eva strolled up a slight grassy incline. She continued walking until she came to a large windmill in the middle of a field. A plaque on the building identified it as the "Old Mill" and went on to describe how a millstone inside once ground wheat into flour. She looked up at the windmill's blade and the gray sky beyond and thought about President Walker and crops that needed tending. Walking around the Old Mill, she found a door and tried to open it. The door proved to be locked and she couldn't see the millstone within. Even so, she considered that even the best crops get ground into powder.

Looking at her wrist chrono, Eva realized she should get back to the house to see if anyone had returned. On her way back, she passed a small observatory. Across from it sat an extensive graveyard. Cooper pursed her lips as she looked out across the sea of tombstones and realized that most of the island's residents were, in fact, dead. Her eyes caught several dates: 1682, 1723, 1955, 2230. How much human experience had been buried in this one graveyard? How much would be lost forever if the Cluster succeeded in its mission?

With a sigh, Eva continued on her way. She arrived at the house just as the sun reached the horizon. Mark and Kirsten had returned from their walk. Fire and Manuel had also returned from their excursion.

As Eva sat down, Manuel turned to Kirsten. "What I still haven't figured out is if Swan's here on Earth, who the hell is minding the store back on Sufiro?"

"Who knows?" said Kirsten. "Swan didn't tell me and I didn't think to ask."

Manuel rolled his eyes. "I doubt he bothered to leave anyone in charge. We'll be lucky if we have a planet to go home to, even if we *do* beat the Cluster." He dropped onto the couch and Fire sat down next to him.

They began to discuss plans. They agreed that Fire and Manuel should go to Titan while Mark would stay on Earth and see if he could get back to the Cluster once the Proxom wore off.

"The problem is," said Mark, "they booted me out. They may not let me back."

"But, you do have to try." His mother leaned forward. "Besides, Richard wants to talk to you and G'Liat. Even if you don't make it back to the Cluster, you can do more good there. You and Richard understand each other."

"Who knows what thoughts G'Liat might try to put in your friend's mind," said Kirsten. Eva couldn't tell whether she was joking or serious. Before she could decide, Kirsten stood up. "I almost forgot." She reached into her shirt pocket, took out a scrap of paper, and handed it to Manuel. "Edmund asked me to have you deliver this message to Ellison Firebrandt."

Manuel unfolded the paper, read it and laughed. He handed it to Fire who read it, then punched Manuel's shoulder. "You know Edmund's serious, don't you?" asked Fire with an expression that seemed at once bemused and worried.

"Yeah, but wouldn't it be better if I went to Arizona to help him? Doesn't he trust old Manuel?"

"I wouldn't," said Fire and Kirsten choked back a laugh. "Thing is, it sounds like Edmund needs dad to send a spaceship for his plan to succeed."

"Why go to Ellison? Sure he has contacts, but the only ship he has is the *Legacy* and it's been grounded for almost fifty years." Manuel turned serious as Fire's bemusement vanished, leaving a worried frown behind. "Wouldn't it be better if we just went to Alpha Coma and found someone to send reinforcements?"

Fire folded the note and put it in her pocket. "You know my father – he'll find a way to get Swan the help he needs. There's always Arepno." Her voice grew distant. After a moment, she looked at Kirsten and smiled. "I'll make sure dad gets the message."

Mark activated the teleholo in the living room and contacted the *Sanson*. He filled his first mate in on the plans. The first mate seemed relieved to be able to put some distance between himself and Earth. A moment later, he issued orders. "Set course for Titan, Ms. Peters. We'll leave as soon as Ms. Ellis and Mr. Raton are aboard."

"Aye, aye, sir," responded a woman Eva didn't know. She presumed that must be Ms. Peters.

After a brief discussion with the first mate, Mark turned off the teleholo and turned to his mother. "Just go to the space port and signal *Sanson* from the launch. Simon will bring you aboard via remote control."

Mark hugged his mother and shook Manuel's hand. Eva considered those people buried in Nantucket's vast graveyard. How many of them had spoken their last good-byes in a moment like this?

That night, the house seemed strangely quiet as Mark, Kirsten, and Eva ate dinner. Throughout the meal, Kirsten caught Eva stealing glances at her and Mark and she wondered what the doctor thought. Eva's brow was knitted and her eyes were moist, as though she were sad. She poked at her food and when not stealing glances at Mark and Kirsten, she gazed off into the distance.

Mark, on the other hand, seemed ravenous. It made sense – he hadn't eaten for over a day. The captain didn't seem to notice Eva much at all, or Kirsten for that matter, as he wolfed down his food. When Kirsten had walked with Mark earlier in the day, he had been preoccupied, thinking about how to return to the Cluster. As she ate dinner, Kirsten found herself glad that Eva had given him a dose of Proxom and she would have the captain to herself for at least one quiet night before everyone went their separate ways again.

"President Walker said the Cluster had spoken to her emotional core." Kirsten jumped when Eva spoke. "Captain, what was it like for you to be with the Cluster so long?"

Mark wiped his lips on his napkin and thought. "Seductive," he said at last. Earlier in the day, Mark had described what it had been like to wake up aboard the *Pequod*, in orbit around the black hole at the galactic core. "The Cluster fed me an extraordinarily real vision. It would have been easy to stay there."

"Were you in control?" asked Eva. "Or, was the Cluster?"

Mark frowned and seemed to consider the question. "I could move around within the reality I perceived. I could manipulate that reality to some degree…" He shook his head. "The problem is, I enjoyed being in that reality so much, I didn't push the boundaries as much as I could have."

"It was … seductive," echoed Eva. She sighed. "Jenna Walker is being seduced and so are most of the people on this planet. Those who are alive, that is."

Kirsten thought she detected a deeper hurt than simple concern for the Earth's Commander-in-Chief. A knot formed in Kirsten's gut as she realized how close she had come to losing Mark. She put an arm around his shoulder and squeezed, then looked into his eyes. They seemed to stare through her for a few seconds before they refocused on her. After a moment he smiled at her. She withdrew her arm, finished dinner, and then cleared her plate and glass from the table.

Mark stood and retrieved a third helping while Eva finished her first and Kirsten stepped over to the couch and turned on the teleholo. It almost surprised her to see a favorite comedy show rather than another newscast. The show gave Kirsten a fleeting sense of normalcy before goose bumps stood up on her arms and she had to change channels.

"It must have been something to grow up on this island," said Eva.

"It was," said Mark as he finished his dinner and cleared his own place at the table. "I suppose it's a little like growing up at the center of the universe."

Kirsten turned and shot him a glance.

"Those of us who grew up here – had families on Nantucket for generations – are islanders. Everyone else is an off-islander." He smirked.

"Does that include the Cluster?" asked Eva.

"Yeah." Mark put his plate in the cleaner. "I suppose the Cluster would be the ultimate off-islander."

"How does the galaxy's real center compare to Nantucket?" asked Kirsten.

Mark settled down on the couch next to her. "Not as many summertime tourists," he said. "But, the swimming is nowhere near as good."

Kirsten found a movie about the first humans to travel to Saturn. The ship they'd used had been a heliogyro – a type of solar sail that resembled a pinwheel. Kirsten shook her head, thinking the ship on the teleholo wasn't much different than the wooden sailing vessel Mark had described being aboard at the galactic core.

As she watched the movie, Kirsten's eyes began to drift shut. She made an exaggerated yawn and stood. "I think it's time for bed." She stood and held her hand out to Mark. Caught by a dramatic moment in the movie, Mark almost begged off until he met Kirsten's gaze. He flashed a guilty smile and took her hand. She turned off the teleholo, then turned to Eva. "Good night."

"Good night," called Eva, who seemed lost in her own thoughts.

Up in the bedroom, Kirsten closed the door as Mark sat on the bed and pulled off his boots. She unbuttoned her blouse and then hung it over the room's chair. He reached up and took her hand and she sat on the bed next to him. They kissed and his cool hands roved her back as she unbuttoned his shirt. She explored the hairs on his chest, then moved over his nipples and, at last, pushed the shirt the rest of the way off his arms.

A moment later, Ellis stood and closed the shutters on the windows. As he did, Kirsten removed her slacks. He smiled as he turned. She reached up and unbuckled his trousers, then lowered them to the floor next to hers. She smiled, noticing his arousal. He sat next to her and massaged her breast. Her breath caught as her nipple hardened under his thumb's gentle caress.

They changed positions and she stroked his penis for a moment, satisfied to hear a deep guttural sound in his throat. She guided him to her vagina and she sighed as he filled her. He began a slow, rhythmic thrusting. This time when she gazed into his eyes, she had his full attention. "I'm glad Nantucket's the center of your universe," she said. "I'm glad you came home."

Ellis shook his head. "Nantucket's not the center of the universe. You are."

She allowed herself to believe him and met his thrusts with her own.

Chapter Twelve

RESURRECTION

A loud beeping sound caused Manuel Raton to sit bolt up-right in bed in a cold sweat. Strong but slender hands caressed the hairs on his chest and eased him back down onto the bed. "What the hell time is it?"

"I set the alarm for 10 a.m. ship's time," mumbled Fire as one hand drifted to Manuel's belly. Her hand continued downward while she nuzzled his neck.

"Why's it still dark outside?" Manuel looked toward the window and blinked in confusion.

Getting the reaction she sought, Fire rolled atop Manuel and took him within her. "That's because we're aboard the *Sanson*, you idiot."

He met her thrusts.

"Of course, it's about four in the morning Nantucket time," she added.

"We should have gotten to bed sooner." He reached up and twirled her long, silver-streaked black hair with one finger. His hand moved down, to cup her full breast and she sighed in response.

"We got to bed in plenty of time," Fire breathed. "What we should have done is gotten to sleep sooner. We should be at Titan within the hour." She leaned forward and kissed him, delighting in the way his bushy mustache tickled her lip. With that, the two stopped talking and escaped into the moment.

A short time later, with the sheets curled around their feet and Fire pressed against Manuel's side, he asked, "So, any idea what we'll say to the Titans? Are we just going to barge in there and ask why they haven't sent in the cavalry?"

"More or less," she laughed, "but I thought I might try a little more tact. We'll need to go through channels. Natalie

Papadraxis is supposed to have called ahead and scheduled a meeting with Valentin Lifshitz, the human ambassador to Titan." She kissed Manuel on the nose, then clambered out of bed and walked over to the shower unit. She turned it on, and stepped in.

Manuel yawned and stretched, then stood and laid out his clothes.

"Aren't you going to join me?" asked Fire.

"I thought you'd never ask." Manuel grinned and joined her in the shower.

As she soaped his back, Manuel considered the Titans. Aside from the Cluster, they were the most ancient race in the galaxy. At one time, the Cluster had subjugated them the same way the Cluster subjugated humans now. They provided creativity and a means to accomplish tasks – giving the Cluster a purpose. "What if the Titans don't know how to defeat the Cluster?" asked Manuel. He turned and she soaped his chest.

"They were subject to the Cluster for millennia. They must have some idea about how to defeat them." Fire's brow knitted.

Manuel took the soap and began lathering Fire's back. "Yeah, but in the end, they ran from the Cluster, they didn't defeat them. Maybe they're still just as helpless."

Fire sighed. "Still, they managed to escape." She turned and smiled as Manuel took extra time soaping up her breasts. "In the end, we're in the same position. We don't need to defeat the Cluster. We just need to stop them."

Manuel stepped under the running water and rinsed off, then stepped aside to allow Fire to have the water. "Yeah, but the Titans lived in fear for millennia after the Cluster had subjugated them – fear that the Cluster would find them again. Don't we want to put an end to the Cluster once and for all?"

Fire didn't answer. Instead, she turned off the water, left the shower stall, and found a towel. She tossed another towel to Manuel, then dressed in silence. They found their way to the ship's mess hall where the pilot, Laura Peters, waited for them. "Mr. Yermakov wanted me to tell you we've been granted permission to enter orbit around Titan. I'll pilot the launch down to the surface."

"Thanks," said Fire as a cook handed her a plate with a

green chile quiche and some hash browns.

"So, when are we scheduled to meet with Ambassador Lip-shit?" Manuel cast a sidelong glance at the quiche, but after his first bite, he continued eating with enthusiasm, then gulped down his first cup of coffee.

"Lifshitz," corrected Fire.

Laura frowned in disapproval. "All she received was an automated message telling us which landing bay to use." She stood to retrieve her own coffee and refilled Manuel's cup. "I'm guessing the ambassador will meet us, or send word where to meet him."

"Doesn't that seem a little odd?" Manuel asked the question around a mouthful of quiche.

Fire inclined her head. "Why? I'm sure the ambassador and admiralty are busy with this crisis. In a way, we're lucky to get a meeting at all."

Manuel looked thoughtful as he drank his second cup of coffee. "You know," he said, "maybe you should take the message from Swan to your father to the command deck – just in case we run into problems or there's a delay."

Fire took the note Kirsten had given her from her pocket and looked at it. "Maybe you're right." She looked up at Laura. "Do you think Simon would send this message if we ran into an emergency?"

Laura held out her hand, took the paper, and read the message. "I don't see why not." She stood and stepped over to the intercom. "Natalie, where are you?"

"In my quarters," she said. "I'm getting ready to go up to the command deck."

"Can you swing by the mess hall on the way?"

"Sure." A few moments later, Natalie appeared in the mess hall's doorway. Laura handed her the note.

"If anything happens to us, you must jump out of the solar system and send that message," said Laura.

Natalie's smile evaporated. "What do you think is going to happen?"

"I don't think anything is going to happen," reassured Fire. "But, a good friend trusted me to do this. I don't want to let him down."

Natalie's smile reappeared. "Okay." She turned on her heel – her full, flower-print dress swishing around her ankles – and left for the command deck.

"Do you think she'll get the job done?" asked Fire once she knew Natalie was out of earshot.

"She's a good kid," said Laura. "If it's important, it'll get done." The three finished breakfast in silence, then Laura led the group to the launch bay. After Natalie gave her clearance to depart, she charted a course for the human pressure dome.

Though she had seen it before, Fire gasped when the launch left the hold and Saturn's golden spectacle appeared before them – the planet's icy rings glimmered in the sun's rays. Below the launch were Titan's red-orange clouds. From time to time, a faint light glimmered off another star vessel's black Erdonium hull. She had often wondered how the galaxy's capital could have remained hidden to humans for so long. However, she noticed that even undisguised spaceships proved almost invisible. Hiding from primitive human cameras might not have been a significant challenge for the Titans after all.

As they dropped toward the cloudtops, Fire noticed much less traffic than normal traveling between the surface and orbit – much like Earth. Soon, the Titan capital city came into view: A vast array of silvery, translucent domes, similar to the Cluster's silver spheres filled a valley surrounded by rugged peaks. A liquid methane river wound its way from the mountains down toward the domes.

The launch descended toward a dome. A hatch in the top irised open and the launch settled onto a platform, which descended into the dome. An automated message announced that the launch had been secured. Fire, Manuel, and Laura undid their seat restraints and stepped out. As with the spaceports on Earth, this one seemed too quiet. No crews appeared to service the launch and neither the ambassador nor his staff could be seen.

A shiver crept up Fire's spine as she led the way from the landing bay into the main pressure dome. They looked around at the buildings under the domed ceiling. The human pressure dome on Titan served as an administrative complex and people usually bustled around from building to building on errands from the consulate to the admiralty. The dome was silent except for a few imported birds singing in the trees. Their cries echoed in the vast space.

"I don't like this." Manuel's hand went to his hepler pistol. Fire put her hand on his arm. "Let's see if we can find out what's going on." She pointed to a tall structure. "I believe that's the consulate over there." As they began walking, other footsteps thudded on a nearby pathway.

Three people approached from a large, squat structure reminiscent of the Pentagon on Earth. A gray-haired woman with piercing blue eyes led the group. She wore a Gaean Navy uniform with two golden epaulets on her shoulders, which made her look imposing. The two people behind her also wore Gaean uniforms. The woman stepped up to Fire, who extended her hand. The woman made no attempt to return the handshake. "My name is Marlou Strauss," the woman introduced herself. "Sorry I couldn't meet your vessel when it arrived."

"John Mark's told me about you." Fire flashed a wry grin. "I'm Dr. Suki Ellis and we hoped to meet with the ambassador."

"I'm afraid that won't be possible," said Strauss. Behind her, the Gaean officers drew their sidearms. "You will come with me."

Manuel made a noise a little like a growl. "Here we go again," he muttered.

Twilight illuminated the sky outside his bedroom window as Mark Ellis awoke, but the sun had not yet risen over the horizon. Sitting up in bed, he looked over at Kirsten, lying on her side, snoring softly. He crept out of bed, slipped on his trousers, shirt, and shoes and stepped from the room. He needed some time to clear his head and think. The Proxom would wear off in a few hours, but when it did, he didn't know how he would return to the Cluster. Mark peeked into Coffin's room. The old man looked so frail and still, that he feared his friend had died. Setting his jaw, Ellis vowed to discover what was happening to his friend.

He continued down the stairs. Eva Cooper lay on the

couch, the blanket off her bare shoulder. He stepped past her, then out the front door. He walked through the front gate and turned toward town, passing several gray-shingled houses, most quite similar to one another, yet each one with its differences. Even though it was early morning, the island should not have been so quiet. Weeds had taken over several flowerbeds. Many houses had shingles that had weathered to the point they needed replacing, yet no one worked on repairs.

The captain turned down the cobbled main street and walked past history. Houses once owned by ship captains gave way to shops run for tourists. He glanced in one shop's window, where a lightship basket hung, covered in cobwebs. Behind it stood a wooden ship's wheel with a thick coating of dust. The sign in the shop's window said "open." Ellis tried the door and found it unlocked. He plucked the lightship basket he'd seen through the window from its hook. It was a replica of the baskets certain ships once used to guide other ships into Nantucket Harbor at night. Mark blew the cobwebs from the basket then called out: "Hello!"

Not hearing an answer, he hung the basket back on the hook and left the shop, goosebumps forming on his arm. He turned off Main Street and strolled through back roads toward Brant Point, a small sandbar that jutted out into the ocean. A squat lighthouse occupied the sandbar. With no one around, the captain removed his shoes, then stripped off his trousers and shirt. He hung them over a railing at the lighthouse's door. He stepped into the waves rolling onto the beach and sighed as he squished wet sand between his toes. Though the icy water sent chills along his arms, he continued on and waded out to where he could swim. He swam several yards out and then turned back.

A willowy blond woman stood on the beach. Though he was Suki Ellis's son, Ellis found it difficult to leave the water while the woman watched.

"You'll catch your death out there," called the woman.

Hearing her voice, Ellis realized Eva Cooper stood on the beach. "What are you doing out here?" he called back.

"I heard you leave, so I followed you." She inclined her head and grinned. "You really shouldn't stay out in that cold water, you'll get hypothermia." When Ellis still hesitated, she said, "I'm a doctor. It's not like there's anything I haven't seen."

Blushing, Ellis clambered onto the beach. Realizing he hadn't brought a towel, he shook the water off as best as he could and, shivering, pulled clothes onto his body. The cloth clung to his wet skin. Cooper handed him her sweater and he pulled it on.

"What can I do for you, Doctor?" asked Ellis with chattering teeth.

She sighed. "I don't think I can wait any longer. I need to put Samuel Coffin on life support, but I need some basic equipment." The two began walking back toward Main Street. "The problem is, I don't know where to get it."

"Would a hospital have what you need?" he asked.

The doctor nodded.

"Let's get some breakfast, then I'll take you to the hospital. Between you being the surgeon general and me and Coffin being old-time Nantucketers, I'm sure we can beg or borrow the equipment you need."

As they turned onto Main Street, Cooper peered into the shop Ellis had entered earlier. "Presuming there's anyone left at the hospital."

Mark shivered and he wasn't certain whether swimming in the cold water had chilled him or if her words rang all too true. They walked in silence back to Ellis's house.

As Mark opened the door, he smelled coffee, onions, and peppers and grinned. His smile fell away when he saw G'Liat standing at the counter. The large knife he wielded looked petite in the warrior's huge six-fingered hand. The knife flashed several times – almost faster than Mark's eyes could follow and an onion lay in pieces on the cutting board.

Kirsten sat at the table and held out her hands. "He just invited himself in," she said. "I didn't know what else to do."

Mark stepped over to the table, took Kirsten's hand, and gave it a gentle squeeze. "It's okay."

The warrior reached over, turned out a perfect omelet onto a plate and handed it to Kirsten. "Ms. Smart has just told me about the conversation your mother had with the whale you call Richard." The warrior cracked three eggs into a bowl and began whipping them with a whisk. "I came over to check on you and Coffin. Hearing this news, I believe you should eat breakfast and we should leave as soon as possible."

Mark held up his hands. "Wait just a minute. Dr. Cooper's just told me she needs to get life support equipment to keep Coffin alive. I need to take her to the hospital to get the equipment. He's one of my oldest and dearest friends. I can't just let him die."

G'Liat added ham, onions, and bell peppers to the just-cooked eggs in the pan and folded the omelet. "Ms. Smart can look up directions to the hospital on her handcomp. I believe it is imperative that we go see Richard as soon as possible." He slid the omelet out onto a plate and handed it to Mark.

Mark looked at Kirsten, who poked at her own omelet. "I hate to admit it, but I think he's right. I can help Eva get the life support equipment together." She took a deep breath and then blew it out. "Mark, the whole planet's at stake. If Richard can help, you and G'Liat need to talk to him. Your mother just confirmed things we suspected, she didn't find any actual answers."

"What happens if the Proxom wears off? I want to get back to the Cluster, but I want to be here when I try." He tasted the omelet and nodded grudging admiration at the Rd'dyggian warrior who had started a third.

Eva poured herself a cup of coffee and sat down at the table. "You've got several hours before the Proxom wears off," she said. "I don't think you'll have a chance before then."

G'Liat finished cooking the third omelet, gave it to Eva, then sat down and stared at Mark. "We can go talk to Richard and be back in just a few hours."

Mark didn't answer. Instead, he continued to work through breakfast, and then he looked into Kirsten's eyes. She flashed an encouraging smile, then reached out and squeezed his hand.

Mark sipped his coffee. "Then I suppose I should get some dry clothes on and we should get going."

"Do I want to know why you and Eva sneaked out of the house this morning? Or, why you came back sopping wet?" asked Kirsten.

"Probably not." Mark leaned over and planted a kiss on

her cheek. He stood, handed Eva her sweater and made for the stairs.

Arepno sat in guest quarters in the Rd'dyggian dome on Titan and sorted through data he had collected. When he and Swan had first arrived in the Gaean system, ship activity had appeared normal. He'd seen a ship jump into the system and another jump out. After depositing Swan on Earth, he returned to Titan to check in with Rd'dyggian central command. As he prepared to leave orbit, the Titans denied his ship departure clearance.

As a Rd'dyggian, Arepno always questioned orders, but he doubted a direct query would provide the answers he sought. He requested quarters in the Rd'dyggian dome and began reviewing the data he'd collected. While on Titan, he searched the database and discovered that the "doomsday phenomenon" struck the human dome on Titan as well as Earth. If anything, it was worse for the humans on Titan. Over eighty percent of them had died. Of those who survived, some ninety percent were reported to be in a comatose state.

The numbers didn't surprise Arepno. As with the Rd'dyggian dome, diplomatic and military personnel staffed the human dome on Titan. Those were specialized jobs requiring intelligent people. The Cluster would have little need for some of those jobs. For others, it could have great need. Arepno also noted that the Titans had gone to considerable effort to suppress all information from the human dome.

After a day on the moon, his first officer reported a steady increase in the number of ships in orbit. Arepno checked the computer records and learned that only Titan ships had ever been granted permission to leave orbit and depart the solar system. The Cluster itself never appeared to interfere with any ships trying to leave but the Titans never granted departure clearance.

Growing more curious about the human dome's status, Arepno requested permission to visit. An automated message from the human dome refused the warrior's request. He then decided to take matters in his own hands.

Arepno went down to the Rd'dyggian dome's ground level and checked out a space suit and a land rover. He drove out across Titan's frigid, reddish surface. He pulled up a holographic map. Even with the map's help, he had to count how many silver domes he passed to avoid getting lost. At last, he reached the human dome. He drove to the airlock and, as he expected, he was again denied admission. Using an emergency override code he'd found on the Titan central computer, he opened the outer door. He stepped in and closed the door behind him. Again, it did not surprise him when no air filled the chamber and the inner door failed to open.

He tapped an intercom button and pushed his faceplate to the microphone so his voice could be picked up. "This is Captain Arepno of Rd'dyggia. I was outside the dome on a routine survey when my onboard computer malfunctioned. There may have been micrometeorite damage. This is an emergency request for atmosphere so I may check my suit for damage."

The automated systems could not refuse that specific request. Soon atmosphere poured into the airlock. Arepno removed his helmet and breathed in the stale air. Then, he retrieved a small box from a pocket on his space suit. Opening it up, he held it to his mouth and exhaled. Tiny dust grains flew into the air – each one containing a micro-miniature camera and transmitter. He replaced the box, then replaced his helmet and faced the intercom. "Suit checks out, please evacuate chamber and open the outer airlock door."

The precious atmosphere was drawn back in through the vents, along with the miniature cameras and audio sensors. They would be pulled through the recycling system, then pumped throughout the dome.

The airlock's outer door opened and Arepno returned to his land rover and went back to his quarters in the Rd'dyggian dome.

Since returning to his quarters, he monitored the data coming back from the human dome using a headset separate from the Titan network. He took care not to monitor the probes too often. He assumed the Titans spied on him in the same way he spied on the humans. Though he would have liked to unleash his cameras in the Titans' city, he didn't dare for fear they would be detected right away.

For the most part, little in the human dome interested Arepno. The common areas between buildings were often deserted. Once in a while, some lost-looking soul would leave a government building and go to a familiar restaurant, only to find it closed, then either proceed to their housing unit or return to the office building they'd emerged from.

One of Arepno's cameras did find its way into the ambassador's office. He lay on the floor, eyes staring at the ceiling. Arepno could not tell whether the ambassador was alive or dead. However, he guessed Lifshitz still lived and the Cluster had absorbed his mind – as it had done with many of Earth's politicians.

Arepno turned his attention to reports of ships arriving at Titan. If he had been a human, he would have smiled. Instead, his purple mustache-like growth wiggled a little. John Mark Ellis's ship, the *Nicholas Sanson* had appeared in orbit. He activated cameras on his ship and watched the *Sanson's* launch as it descended and then entered the main human dome.

He then put on his headset and searched for signs of the craft's occupants. After a brief search, he located them on a camera hovering near an outer area's ceiling. The microphone hovered too far away for him to hear what the people said, but zooming in, he could see Ellison Firebrandt's daughter, Manuel Raton, and a third human. He presumed her to be the launch's pilot. Another group of humans left the Navy headquarters. Arepno thought the human admiral, Marlou Strauss, led the second group. He couldn't be certain, though, since humans could be so similar to one another. Strauss and her party drew weapons and led Suki, Manuel and the other woman away.

Arepno removed the headset and considered what he should do. Ellison Firebrandt had saved the warrior and his crew's lives. The warrior turned and sent a scrambled signal to his ship to be relayed to the *Nicholas Sanson*. He then stood and waved his hand over a storage locker. The force field in the top dissipated and Arepno began pulling out the tools he would need for the operation's next phase.

Aboard the *Nicholas Sanson*, Simon Yermakov paced back and forth. He would have been relieved to be away from Earth and the Clusters, except that the Clusters' activities at the galaxy's center made him uneasy. The Clusters needed to be stopped. He just never imagined himself so necessary to the process of stopping them. He dropped into the command seat and looked at the chrono display. He had yet to receive word from Laura, Fire or Manuel. That fact alone didn't bother him. For all he knew, it could take them a day or two before they learned something from the Titans. Still, he had expected Laura to check in soon after the shuttle had landed.

Natalie inclined her head to the side, as though she listened to a signal. After a moment, she turned toward Simon. "I'm receiving the strangest signal." Natalie's brow furrowed. "I wonder if the Proxom is interfering with my communications implant after all."

Simon stood. "Can you put it on the intercom?"

She reached down and pushed a button on the holographic console. A series of chirps, whistles, long plaintive notes and growls issued from the speakers.

Simon approached the communication's console. "If I didn't know better, it sounds like a sea creature from Earth, like a whale or a dolphin."

Natalie's eyes went wide and looked up at Simon. "No, that's not from Earth at all. I just realized – it's Rd'dyggian."

"Why aren't we getting a translation?" Simon knelt down next to Natalie's console.

She touched several buttons and checked several displays. In the holographic tank at the front of the command deck, numerous yellow dots appeared, marking the positions of orbiting ships. She pointed to a blinking red dot. "That Rd'dyggian ship seems to be sending this. It's on a tight-beam frequency with an embedded decryption algorithm." When Simon shook his head, she explained: "They're sending a coded signal right at us. When our computers intercepted the signal, an embedded program installed itself in our computer and began decoding the signal."

"Why is it in Rd'dyggian?" asked Simon standing and moving toward the holographic tank. "Why didn't they just send the message in terro-generic?"

Natalie shrugged. "It's possible it's meant for another Rd'dyggian ship and we just happened to be in the way."

Simon entered the holographic display. "I don't see any other ships beyond us on that line of sight. Can you translate the signal?"

"Sure." Natalie turned to her console with a vacant smile while Simon continued to walk around in the holographic tank, trying to see whom else the Rd'dyggians might be attempting to communicate with.

A moment later, a singsong voice issued from the speaker. "This is Captain Arepno calling the TransGalactic Mapping Vessel *Nicholas Sanson*. This is an emergency. A human admiral has abducted Dr. Suki Ellis, Manuel Raton, and a woman from your crew. I will attempt a rescue. You should leave orbit right away. Jump away from this solar system. Do not request permission. Rendezvous at Alpha Coma."

Simon licked his lips. "What the hell does that mean? They were abducted? By a human admiral?"

Natalie looked down at her hands. After a moment, she looked up at Simon. "I think Laura suspected something like this might happen." She reached into the little satchel she had on her belt and took out the slip of paper Laura Peters had given her. "Laura said we should send this message to Sufiro if anything happened to the landing party."

"Laura said?" asked Simon, throwing his hands up. "Just who commands this vessel anyway?" He took the note from Natalie and stalked toward the command chair. After taking a deep breath, Simon relaxed and read the note. As he did, his eyes grew wide and his shoulders slumped as though the weight of the crisis had just descended full force upon him.

"Do you know who this is for?"

"It's for Ellison Firebrandt, the pirate who founded Sufiro," said Natalie.

Simon nodded. "It's a call for help from the resistance on Earth." He stepped forward and handed the note back to Natalie, then returned to the command chair. He sat there for several minutes looking down at the controls. He knew Kirsten Smart had not wanted him to command the *Sanson* because he had not been decisive enough. Now, he was faced with the worst possible decision. If he left, he'd be abandoning Suki Ellis and Manuel Raton, along with a member of his crew. However, if what the Rd'dyggian had reported were true, they would be rescued. He wasn't sure he could trust this Captain Arepno, but the Rd'dyggian had gone to great lengths to get the message to the *Sanson*. He could return to Earth and ask Ellis and Kirsten what to do, but that would mean Kirsten had been right about him and he couldn't make decisions on his own. What's more, Simon believed he *should* go to Alpha Coma and report what they had learned.

He brought up a chart and ran a few quick calculations. The jump points were already changing due to the Cluster's interference at the galaxy's center. Even so, it would be easy enough to jump out of the solar system, deliver the message to Ellison Firebrandt, then continue on to Alpha Coma. If the Rd'dyggian was right, he'd have his missing crewmember back. If the Rd'dyggian had lied, he could return with help.

Standing up, Simon tucked his flannel shirt into his trousers, then stepped forward to the Pilot's console. "Natalie, inform the crew we're leaving orbit. Do not, I repeat, do not request permission to leave orbit from Titan Central Command."

Natalie smiled at Simon and then started her task. In the meantime, Simon brought up his own version of the pilot's console and began searching for jump points. The one for Alpha Coma was more distant than he liked, but he charted a course for it while noting other, nearby jump points.

"All decks report ready to depart orbit," said Natalie.

Simon cast a self-conscious glance back at the command seat, hoping there would be someone – Ellis, Ms. Smart, anyone – to give the order. He swallowed hard, then pushed a lever forward and fired aft thrusters. In the holographic tank, a blinking red dot representing *Sanson's* position appeared and it began moving toward the jump point for Alpha Coma.

"The Titans have just ordered us to stand down." All dreaminess had vanished from Natalie's voice. "They say they have armed missiles and will destroy us if we do not resume orbit."

"Tell 'em to go to hell," said Simon, through gritted teeth.

"Do I have to?" asked Natalie, eyes wide. "I don't think they'll like that much at all."

Simon's laugh bordered on hysterical. "Don't tell them anything, then." He reached over to his own intercom. "Engineering, this is Yermakov on the command deck, I need all the power you can give me."

"What's going on up there?" asked Chief Engineer Mahuk. "Are we running away from Titan?"

"We are." Simon knew Ellis would say something like "cut the chatter, Mister." Instead, he decided to give the third in command more details. "We need to get to Alpha Coma and get help. Things are going wrong way too fast."

Mahuk must have heard the quavering in Simon's voice. "Steady on, Simon," he said, exuding calm. "You're the first officer and I'm right behind you, my friend. I'll give you everything I've got." Mahuk's words strengthened the first officer's resolve.

"Oh no," breathed Natalie. Simon turned to see Natalie staring at the holographic tank, wide-eyed. "They've launched the missiles. They'll overtake us before we get to the jump point for Alpha Coma."

Simon looked up at the display. Two new points closed on them. He scanned the display for new jump points. Seeing one nearby, he altered course. The missiles turned in a leisurely arc and followed them.

"Simon, that jump point will take us out to the rim…"

"Strap in, Natalie," he said. "Call an emergency jump warning." He activated the intercom again. "Mahuk, get ready to jump on my mark." Natalie announced the emergency jump warning behind him. Simon looked into the holographic tank. The two missiles continued to close on them. A green light started blinking on his console. "Mahuk," he cried. "Jump!"

Roberts hovered back and forth outside the old teleholo booth within the grounded privateer vessel, *Legacy*. Ellison Firebrandt, his hair loose about his shoulders, stepped from the booth and nodded to his old friend. "The *Nicholas Sanson* just relayed a message from Edmund Swan. He needs our help on Earth."

Roberts sighed and looked up and down the corridor. "Is there no one else who can help?"

Firebrandt's gaze narrowed. He lifted his finger and opened his mouth.

Roberts held up a hand to stave off a lecture. "I'm not trying to run from a fight, old friend. But this is an ancient ship. We only have a skeleton crew available and – like it or not – we're two old men who haven't seen action in nearly fifty years."

"You're right on all counts." Firebrandt retrieved a rubber band from his trousers' pocket and tied his hair back. "The *Sanson* is going to make for Alpha Coma. I hope they can find help there as well, but with the Cluster moving stars in the center of the galaxy, the jump points are changing faster than they can be charted. It might take them a while to make it to Alpha Coma and then back to Earth once they do. Mark, Edmund, and Fire need our help, now." He reached down and grasped his friend's shoulder. "Call in the crew. Have them assemble on the command deck."

Roberts floated into the teleholo booth to carry out the captain's orders while Firebrandt went to his cabin. Since Edmund Swan left Sufiro, Roberts and Firebrandt had gathered a crew of fifteen. Some were old, trusted friends, but all had experience either with freighters converted from aged privateers like the *Legacy* or with systems aboard the antique vessel. Over the past days, Firebrandt and Roberts had forgone the harvest and worked with the fifteen crewmembers, getting them ready in case someone needed their help.

Within an hour of receiving the call from the *Sanson*, Roberts had gathered the crew on the *Legacy's* command deck. The deck had been restored to its one-time glory. The metal surfaces shone under the lights. The wooden handrails that lined the deck had been polished. One gunner's rig had been modified so Roberts could operate it from his hover chair. Ellison Firebrandt himself wore the uniform-like outfit he favored for special occasions. It was a black jacket over a white turtleneck shirt with black trousers. A blood-red stripe ran down each leg.

"By now, I'm sure you've guessed that we've received an emergency call from Earth." Firebrandt paced back and forth at the front of the command deck and looked into each crew-member's eyes. "This is much sooner than I hoped, but, given the Cluster's power, it's perhaps not sooner than we feared." He paused and flashed a reassuring smile at Anne McClintlock. "I don't know how much we can do, but we have a ship with new weapons, a good engine, and loaded with fuel. The first officer of the mapping vessel *Sanson* tells me the Cluster is tak-ing actions that could destroy Sufiro, Alpha Coma, and every other human colony. It's essential we do everything we can to help. The man coordinating this operation is Edmund Swan – a man I trust implicitly, and I'm sure many of you do, too." Firebrandt looked at Juan Raton – Manuel's brother who had fought alongside Swan in the war against the Tejans.

"Now, this class of vessel," continued Firebrandt, stepping over to the rail and patting the wall, "was never designed to land or take off from a planet. However, those of you famil-iar with EQ engines," and he cast a meaningful glance at the mechanics he'd hired, Mary Seaton and Junior Kimura, "know they work using controlled Quinnium bursts. A gravitational jump point is one way to control the burst and send a ship in a particular direction. However, this ship is equipped with a special generator, which can direct a burst and jump a short distance without being at a jump point. We can use that ability to jump from the surface to orbit."

Junior Kimura held up his hand. "Won't that do consider-able damage to the land around the ship?"

Roberts hovered forward, next to Firebrandt. "It'll do less damage than a rocket would. I suspect it'll destroy the house around us, but not much more. We've cleared several acres around the house just to be safe, but I expect we'll still be able to harvest our crops when we return."

"Presuming the frost doesn't get it first," said Firebrandt with a wry grin. "Any other questions?" He looked around at the nervous, but determined faces. His chest puffed out. It had been a long time since Firebrandt had spoken to a crew who would follow him anywhere. "Let's get to work."

"All hands, to your stations," barked Roberts.

With less than military precision, the *Legacy's* new crew shuffled off to their stations. Juan Raton, Anne McClintlock, and Mary Seaton remained on the battle deck. Anne took the central network station at the deck's starboard side while Juan took station at the starboard gunner's rig. Mary sat down at the engine control terminal on the deck's port side while Firebrandt stood at the ship's wheel console at the deck's center.

"You may bring the engines on line, when ready," said Firebrandt. "Mr. Roberts, please close all airlocks and make us ready for spaceflight."

Seaton activated several controls, then asked for a report from Junior. Several red lights flickered on at the engine console. Roberts moved next to Anne McClintlock at the central network station. Together they brought other ship's systems on line, including life support, the new graviton generators, and navigational systems. As ordered, Roberts closed all the airlocks, sealing the ship off from the rest of the homestead. Firebrandt retrieved a pipe from his pocket, packed and lit it, then checked systems on the wheel console. By then, the red lights on the engine console had turned green.

Firebrandt started typing on the wheel console. Equations appeared in the holographic tank.

As he worked, Seaton announced, "Engines on line, sir. Junior's checking system integrity, but he believes we'll be ready to jump in about fifteen minutes."

"Excellent," said Firebrandt, his teeth clenched around the pipe stem. "Roberts, I just calculated a jump from the planet's surface to a position outside Sufiro's gravitational well. Will you please check my calculations and make sure I'm not going to send us into the sun?"

McClintlock looked at Firebrandt with wide eyes and Roberts laughed. He brought up Firebrandt's jump algorithm and checked it over. After a moment, he nodded, impressed. "For an old space dog who hasn't done this in fifty years, you did pretty damn good." The first mate drifted over to the captain. "Once we get to orbit, we'll need to analyze hull integrity and perform a full systems' check."

"I know," said Firebrandt. "Are the launches ready to go in case this doesn't work?"

"They are," said Roberts. "We'd be able to get everyone back to the planet as long as the ship doesn't explode on jump."

Firebrandt nodded and took a few puffs of his pipe. He looked down at the crystalline computer network below his feet, blinking as it sent information from one system to another. Roberts followed his gaze and remembered their former crew. He wondered about the man called Computer who had interfaced with the ship's network so well. He wondered if Nicole Lowry still commanded an Alpha Coma Navy ship. Last he knew, Kheir el-Din had retired to a distant colony world and enjoyed spending time with his grandchildren.

Firebrandt allowed his pipe to burn out.

"Junior says we're ready to go," reported Mary.

"Sound the jump warning." The captain placed his pipe in his pocket and grabbed the handles on each side of the wheel console. Roberts hovered back to the computer terminal. He lowered the hover chair to the deck. Magnetic clamps grabbed onto the grating. Next to him, Anne McClintlock had trouble with her restraints. Roberts reached over and helped her.

The captain scanned the deck, then swallowed hard. "Broadcast a countdown from ten throughout the ship." His hand hovered over the button that would activate the intraship jump engine he'd acquired many years ago.

Roberts often wondered why no one had come looking for it. He shook his head to clear his thoughts, then touched a control on the hover chair. "10... 9... 8..." he began.

Sweat beaded on Firebrandt's forehead.

"7... 6... 5..."

Juan Raton grasped the handles on either side of the gunner's rig.

"4... 3... 2..."

A light flickered red on Mary Seaton's engine console. She tapped it and it flickered back to green.

"1," said Roberts.

Firebrandt pressed the jump button. Reality collapsed.

Jumping into the fourth dimension played havoc with anybody's senses. Human beings are creatures of three dimensions and when they're transported into the dimension that runs parallel to time, the brain gets confused. To Roberts, it seemed as though the floor dropped out from beneath his chair, despite the firm clamps. All light vanished and he swore he could hear the smell of burning electronics.

As the jump ended, Juan Raton held the handles on either side of the gunner's rig and screamed. He opened his eyes and took a few deep breaths. "Sorry," he said.

Firebrandt had collapsed to his knees. Roberts unclamped his hover chair and sped to the captain's side. The captain waved him off. "I'm all right." He turned toward Anne. "Turn on the viewer, let's see where we are."

The holographic viewer sprang to life. Shimmering blue-green, Sufiro hung in the tank like a great globe with shimmering stars in the background. Juan Raton gasped and a tear ran down Ellison Firebrandt's cheek.

"We made it," said Roberts.

"We're adrift and tumbling," reported Anne, "but we're outside Sufiro's gravitational well and all life support systems seem to be functioning." She reached over and typed in a command Roberts had taught her. "Thrusters fired. We've stabilized our position," she reported.

"Junior says we've burned out a few engine relays," said Mary, "but we have spares and we should be ready to jump again within the hour."

Ellison Firebrandt looked around the battle deck and smiled. "Well done, everyone." He looked at Roberts who hovered beside Juan. "Inspect the hull then report to me in my cabin," he said to Roberts.

Before leaving the deck, Roberts drifted forward and gazed at Sufiro. He remembered Suki Mori, who had loved him as well as the captain. Her ashes had been scattered on the planet below. "I'll be back, I promise." He then turned and joined Juan to inspect the ship.

Chapter Thirteen

FUGITIVES

Within the *Sanson's* holographic tank, Simon Yermakov appeared to stand between the Perseus and Orion arms of the Milky Way Galaxy. Wavy blue lines indicated previously charted jump paths from one star system to another. Wavy green lines indicated how those paths would have changed assuming certain gravitational shifts at the center of the galaxy.

Chief Engineer Mahuk strode onto the command deck and shook his head, bewildered. "What is all that?"

Simon stepped through a stellated galactic arm to stand next to the hologram. He pointed to a yellow sphere in the Orion arm that represented the Sun. "That's where we jumped from." Then he pointed to a red sphere in the outer most part of the Perseus arm. "This is where we are now." He pointed to the end of a blue streamer a few inches to the left. "This is where we should have come out of jump according to the charts."

Mahuk joined Simon in the tank. A green streamer came close to connecting the yellow and red spheres. "This must approximate the path we followed," guessed Mahuk.

Simon smiled. "It's close. I used our mapping programs to model the way the jump points are moving due to the Cluster's interference at the galaxy's center."

Mahuk narrowed his gaze. "Can we use this to get back to Earth?"

Simon left the holographic tank, leaned on the pilot's console, and looked down, not meeting the engineer's eyes. "The Cluster hasn't stopped adding stars to the black hole at the center of the galaxy. The jump points will keep changing until they stop or someone stops them. This projection is good for an

176

hour or two at most." He looked up at the chief engineer. "How are the engines doing?"

Mahuk held out his hands. "The engines still lack the fine tuning for a mapping jump, but we can do a coarse jump again when you give the word."

"Good." Simon nodded. "We need to jump soon, or else we'll be stranded here – out on the rim." He stepped back toward the holographic display. "However, I don't think we should return to Earth."

"If not Earth, then where?" asked Mahuk.

"We need to get back to Alpha Coma and let them know what we've learned so far." Simon pointed to the chart. With another jump, I might be able to refine this model. I might be able to predict what's happening to the jump points – at least well enough they can get a few ships to Earth."

"Do you think that will do any good?" Mahuk's brow furrowed. "No one has ever been able to attack a Cluster ship and survive."

Simon puffed out his cheeks. "It's not our job to ask that question. Our job's just to get the information back to Herbert Firebrandt on Alpha Coma."

Mahuk stepped forward and patted Simon's shoulder. "You're beginning to sound a lot like Captain Ellis." Simon's throat tightened and his knees weakened, as though he'd suffered a physical blow. The chief engineer chuckled. "Simon, that's meant as a compliment. Keep this up and you'll end up commanding the ship."

The tightness in Simon's throat became tension in his neck muscles. "Somehow, I don't think Ellis is going anywhere."

"Maybe not." Mahuk shrugged. "Still there are many ships in TransGalactic's fleet. You're working on a promotion, my friend." With a cheerful smile, Mahuk took a few steps away then turned around. "I'll prepare the engines for jump. You get things ready up here and give the word." With that, he stepped into the elevator.

Simon activated the intercom. "Natalie, break's over, I need you back on the command deck." He returned to the holographic tank and pointed to a green ribbon near their current position. The ribbon terminated near Alpha Coma Berenices. "Computer," he called. "Store this course in the navigational system." He went to the pilot's console and charted a course to the new jump point for Alpha Coma.

As Simon pushed at the holographic lever that applied forward thrust, Natalie entered the command deck and took her seat at the communications station. "Natalie," he said, "activate sensors. We'll need to feel around for the jump point's exact position. They're moving around a bit."

She nodded and did as Simon asked. A three-dimensional display appeared over her console, showing the ship along with gravitational density measurements. She touched her forehead. "Simon, two Titan ships have just jumped into the area. They're ordering us to return with them to Titan."

Without thinking about it, Simon increased the thrust to full and chewed on his lower lip. "Why are they trying to stop us?" asked Simon aloud. "You'd think they'd want to see the Cluster stopped, too."

"They're scared," said Natalie.

Simon looked around at her.

"They're afraid we won't be able to stop the Cluster and things will get a lot worse." She pointed to her forehead. "I've been listening to the Titan frequencies. There's been chatter." She looked at another screen. "The Titans are pursuing us."

Simon turned back to his own console. "We're approaching the jump point. Give me some direction." He backed off the forward thrust.

"Gravitational density increasing about twenty degrees to port."

Simon typed a command into his console and a steering column appeared. As he turned the ship, Natalie reported again. "Gravitation density now increasing fifteen degrees below us." He pushed the column forward, dropping the ship's nose. "I guess they've closed to firing range," said Natalie.

"Why's that?" asked Simon.

"They've just launched two missiles."

"Keep your eyes on the gravitational density and warn the crew that jump is imminent. I want everyone strapped in and ready to go."

"Two degrees back to starboard." Natalie sounded the first jump warning. As Simon turned the ship, her indicator blinked green. "I think we're right on top of it." She looked over at her other display. "The missiles are closing pretty fast."

Simon shut down the forward thrust. "We're getting out of here." He pushed the intercom button. "Mahuk! Jump now!"

Used to the long, protracted mapping jumps, Simon gasped when the displays already showed a completed jump. He gaped at the display for a moment, then looked back at Natalie. "Did the missiles interfere with jump?"

"No." Natalie changed the holographic display to show a real-time view. They faced Alpha Coma. "We arrived right on target." She pushed a button and several red dots appeared around the planet.

"What are those?" asked Simon.

"Military vessels." Natalie shuddered "I count thirty-two of them." She turned and looked at Simon. "I hope they don't start shooting missiles at us."

"As long as they're not Titan ships, I think we'll be okay." He tried to sound reassuring, but feared his voice shuddered. "Call Herbert Firebrandt and let him know we're back. I want to talk to him."

Roberts let himself into Ellison Firebrandt's cabin. He looked around and smiled. The room was paneled in wood except for three lighted alcoves covered over with stained glass. A brass lantern swayed back and forth on a chain. He pondered for a moment how long it had been since he'd seen the lantern swinging, instead of standing still. Firebrandt reclined in a large, overstuffed chair, snoring.

The first officer nudged his hover chair closer to the captain and his smile melted into a worried frown. He thought about his arthritis and looked at Firebrandt's white hair. With a look back at the door, he considered the inexperienced crew and hoped their adventure wasn't the folly of two old men bored with farming. He reached out and touched Firebrandt's forearm.

The captain startled awake and sat up. "What time is it?" He rubbed his eyes.

"Ship's hull integrity is good, sir." Roberts avoided the captain's question. "Junior Kimura says the EQ engines are ready for jump."

Firebrandt looked at Roberts as though seeing him for the first time. His gaze drifted around the cabin and settled on the swinging lantern. He nodded, as though his brain had caught up with current events. The captain reached over, tamped tobacco into his pipe, and lit it. "Then we're ready to jump to Earth?"

Roberts shook his head. "There *is* a problem." He hovered over to a chart table across the cabin and brought up an image of the galaxy. "I've scanned for five jump points and none are where they should be."

Firebrandt stood and joined Roberts by the galactic chart. He blinked and tried to recall long-unused navigation skills as he sucked on the pipe. After a moment, he removed the pipe from his mouth and slapped his forehead. "Of course. The Cluster is moving stars around at the galactic core. That'll muck with all the jump points."

Roberts nodded and a burning knot formed in the pit of his stomach. "I'm afraid we may have jumped into orbit for nothing."

Firebrandt returned the pipe to his mouth and stared at the chart. He commanded it to show both Earth and Sufiro's positions, then walked around, staring at the galaxy from several angles. After a moment, he looked at Roberts. "There are Clusters at the center of the galaxy and there are Clusters at Earth, right?"

"Right." Roberts narrowed his gaze, uncertain how this fact helped them.

"If the Clusters at the center of the galaxy are maintaining an open EQ channel to Earth, we can trace the signal and follow it right to our destination."

Roberts shook his head. "That would only do us good if we were at the galactic core."

The captain smiled around the pipe stem. "Precisely. The black hole at the galaxy's center is the single largest gravitational source. We can jump to it from anywhere."

"You've got to be kidding." Roberts sat back in the hover chair's seat. "No ship besides the Cluster has ever survived traveling to the galactic core."

"Why?" Firebrandt returned to his chair.

"You know why as well as I do, sir." Roberts turned to face the captain. "A ship that tried to jump to the galactic core would be ripped apart within minutes – not to mention the radiation surges we'd have to endure."

The captain turned on his heel. "How many minutes would a ship have?"

"I don't know." Roberts considered the hull's strength, the gravitational stresses, and the way radiation would affect electronics and personnel. "Maybe fifteen minutes. Twenty at the outside."

"You'd have that long to find the jump point and trace it," said Firebrandt.

Roberts looked down and sighed. "I don't know, sir. That's asking a lot."

Firebrandt stepped toward Roberts and knelt down beside him. "I know, but we've got to try. We've got to get to Earth to help Edmund."

Roberts looked up, meeting Firebrandt's gaze. "Do we, sir? Or, is this just an old man's attempt to regain lost glory?" He pointed to the door. "We have an inexperienced crew out there. There's a good chance we'll die in the center of the galaxy."

The captain ripped the pipe from his mouth. "According to the message Swan sent, if we do nothing we'll be dead – everyone on Sufiro will die. Like it or not, the people on Sufiro have always looked to me as a leader. Sitting around on Sufiro and continuing with my comfortable life while hoping someone somewhere will save my ass from the bad guys is not leadership. If there's any chance we can help stop the Cluster, we've got to do it." The captain stood and replaced the pipe, then strode over to a nail in the wall. He pointed to the nail. Roberts remembered that was where the captain's letter of marque once hung. "We may have been privateers, but when you signed aboard my vessel you took a vow to protect the Earth. Are you breaking that vow, Mr. Roberts?"

Roberts swallowed hard. "Sir, I thought you once said Earth abandoned you."

The captain removed the pipe and looked down at his feet. A moment later, he met Roberts' gaze again. "Yes, I did say that ... but I can't abandon Earth. Abandoning the Earth would mean abandoning our people on Sufiro." He stepped over and knelt down next to Roberts once again. "Now, can you make this jump happen, or can't you?"

"I can try, sir," said Roberts.

"How long will it take to set up?"

"Meet me on the command deck in half an hour. We'll either be ready to go then, or I'll be able to give you a revised estimate." Roberts turned his chair and floated from the cabin to the command deck, a worried frown etched into his features. He agreed with the captain's assessment, but that didn't ease the knot in his stomach, which came from taking inexperienced people into a dangerous situation. However, as he hovered into the command deck, he looked at Juan Raton at the gunner's rig. Juan had been kidnapped from his home and taken to work in Tejo's erdonium mines. Juan fought alongside Edmund Swan to free those New Granadans who had been taken captive. Roberts hovered alongside Anne McClintlock – a computer specialist. Although her father had helped to establish the New Granadan government, her brother had led Tejo's invasion of New Granada, which Edmund Swan and Juan Raton had helped to repel. The people aboard *Legacy* had been forged in battle, just the same as any crew before them.

Roberts detailed the captain's plan to Anne McClintlock. She nodded and frowned. "It's a dangerous plan, but it just might work."

He released a sigh and they began their calculations. They plotted several possible jump points, then looked at possible paths out of the galactic core. "If we jump here, I think we'll maximize our chances for finding the Cluster's EQ signal back to Earth." *Presuming the Cluster has a signal back to Earth*, he thought, but didn't say.

"I agree." Anne ran a calculation, then pointed to the results on the display. "We need to jump from these coordinates."

Roberts went over to the wheel console, raised the hover

chair so he could reach the controls, and entered the coordinates. Meanwhile Anne set up the scanners to search for the Cluster's EQ transmission to Earth, trace it, and enter the jump parameters into the computer.

Half an hour later, Ellison Firebrandt strode onto the command deck and looked around.

"We're en route to our best-estimated jump point," reported Roberts. "We'll be ready to jump in about two minutes."

"Excellent." The captain smiled, then faced Mary Seaton. "Start preparing the jump engines."

"We're all set to go when you give the word." Though Mary exuded calm, Roberts noticed the sweat on her forehead.

The first mate looked at his display. "We're at the jump point." He reached over, shut off the thrusters, and then drifted back over to the computer console next to Anne McClintlock. Once again, he lowered the chair to the grating and clamped it onto the deck.

"Sound the jump warning," called the captain.

"All decks are ready," reported Anne.

"Jumping," called Firebrandt as he pushed the button on the wheel console.

Once again, the floor seemed to fall out from beneath Roberts as the ship fell into the galactic core. He looked up. Colors swirled and drifted like psychedelic smoke drifting through the command deck. The captain dropped to his knees, gripping the handles on either side of the ship's wheel for dear life. Roberts thought he could hear the old man's determination to see the mission through right as the ship came out of jump.

Next to Roberts, Anne belched and then stood. She held her stomach for a moment, before running to the head. Roberts checked his displays. "Scanners came on line. They're searching for the EQ jump point."

"Gravitational stresses on the hull are off the scale," said Mary from the engineering console. "I have no way of estimating hull integrity." She stood up and approached the captain. "Even if we find that jump point, we may vaporize the minute we jump."

The captain gave a curt nod, then faced Roberts. "Turn on the display. While we're here, let's at least take a look."

The galactic core appeared in the holographic tank. Anne came out of the head, her hair disheveled, and gasped at the sight. Firebrandt stepped forward and stood next to Roberts. They both looked at light being warped around the black hole and the millions of stars around them, bathing the command deck in light. "This sight alone almost makes the trip worthwhile," mused the captain. He continued to gaze spellbound at the image. After a moment, he pointed at the hologram. "There!"

Roberts followed his gaze and noticed a silver glint. "I think it's a Cluster."

It fired a yellow beam at a star, which began to move. A loud groan from the ship's hull broke Roberts' reverie.

"Make sure everyone remains at jump positions," said Firebrandt. "We'll need to leave in a hurry."

"Sir, we've got a lock on the Cluster's signal," said Roberts. "I'm feeding coordinates to your station now."

As Firebrandt moved the ship toward the coordinates, a loud pop resounded through the command deck, like a gunshot. A second pop sounded, followed by a scream. Juan Raton knelt on the deck, his hand to his arm. A third pop sounded, and Roberts realized the command deck's walls were giving way.

Mary Seaton rushed to Juan's side and lifted his hand away to look. "It just grazed him, she said, "but I'm sure it hurts like hell." She untucked her blouse and tore off a corner, folded it, and handed it to Raton who put pressure on the wound. She then strapped him in and returned to her station just as another groan sounded throughout the ship. Roberts grimaced as he pictured structural supports twisting.

The first mate checked his display. "We're at the jump point. We better get out of here."

"I couldn't agree more," said Firebrandt and he activated the jump.

Eva Cooper double-checked the sensors attached to Samuel Coffin's all-but-lifeless body. She then activated the life support monitor on the nightstand next to Coffin's bed. His heartbeat and respiration seemed to be strong and steady. His kidney functions were nominal. She breathed a relieved sigh as she reached down and patted his hand. "Hang in there," she whispered.

She stepped from the room. Out in the hall, she discovered an open door, which she had assumed belonged to a closet. She poked her head inside and discovered daylight illuminating a stairway. She climbed the stairs and found herself on a platform atop John Mark Ellis's house. Kirsten Smart stood next to a railing and gazed out toward the ocean.

Eva cleared her throat.

Kirsten looked around. "They call these structures widow walks." Kirsten pointed out similar platforms on other houses. "They say sailors' wives used to come up to these and watch for their husbands' ships to return from the sea. There's a great view of the bay." She pointed. "I even think I see G'Liat and John Mark's boat."

Joining Kirsten at the rail, Eva thought she could make out a boat leaving the harbor. She then looked around and took in the island as a whole. Hundreds of similar gray houses surrounded her. Many had whitewashed platforms – widow walks – on their roofs much like the one she stood on, though she noticed many had fallen into disrepair. Crossing to the opposite side, she could make out the hospital where she and Kirsten had retrieved the life-support equipment. She shook her head, remembering the reception they'd received. The emergency room doctor had seemed less impressed with meeting the Gaean Alliance's surgeon general and more taken with her being a guest in John Mark Ellis's home. Even then, he had still been reluctant to release the life support equipment until she'd said she needed it for Samuel Coffin.

"Samuel Coffin *is* Nantucket," the doctor had said. "When he dies, this island will never be the same. It's possible the Earth itself will not be the same."

Kirsten crossed the platform to where Eva stood. The surgeon general followed her gaze to the green grass beyond the village.

"It's so quiet up here," said Kirsten, "and you can see so far.

You can almost believe Nantucket is the center of the universe."

Eva smiled and considered the doctor at the hospital along with some of Ellis's passing remarks. "Well Nantucketers certainly seem to believe it."

"Do you think there's any chance the Cluster can be stopped?" Kirsten turned around and leaned back against the rail.

Eva looked down at her own thin hands. "Why ask me? I'm just a doctor."

"You work for the president herself," said Kirsten. "You know the movers and shakers. You know the people who can work this out. Do we have a chance?"

Eva barked a cold, bitter laugh. "If we had to rely on people like Jenna Walker and Dick Richards, I'd say we're doomed." She shook her head, then stormed across the platform to look out over the bay once again. "I'll tell you who will save us. It's people like John Mark Ellis and his friends." She turned around and looked into Kirsten's eyes. "It's people like you." Her shoulders slumped and she closed her eyes. The energy seemed to leave her all at once. "The problem is, I don't know whether there are enough people like you." She turned around and inhaled the salt air. It seemed to revitalize her.

Kirsten didn't respond right away. After a few minutes, she said, "I don't think I can save the world."

"You can't," said Eva. "Not alone, anyway." She turned and stepped over to the hatch, which led back inside. "Just remember, you're not alone." She climbed down the stairs. Kirsten followed, closing the hatch behind.

As the two women passed Samuel Coffin's room, he moaned. Eva stopped short and Kirsten almost ran into her. The doctor spun on her heel and entered the room. They found Coffin awake and blinking. "Water," he gasped. "I'm thirsty."

Kirsten, who stood in the doorway, left and retrieved a glass of water from the bathroom. Eva helped Coffin sit up. When she returned, Kirsten handed him the glass and the old man gulped it down. He handed the glass back and Kirsten left to refill it. Eva focused on the monitors. The line that indicated heart function had turned ragged and she noticed other worrisome signs.

Kirsten handed the second glass of water to Coffin and pulled up a chair to sit beside the bed.

"What happened?" asked Kirsten.

"I was aboard a ship – a sailing ship…" The old man's voice trailed off.

"Yes, the *Pequod* at the center of the galaxy," said Kirsten. "John Mark told me all about it. He said he'd seen a fight on the ship's deck before he was pulled back. He tried to get back to you, but he couldn't." She looked up at Eva.

The doctor's chest tightened with guilt as she bent down to retrieve a medical bag.

Coffin nodded. "We were nothing but brain wave patterns stored within the Cluster." His eyes drifted shut. "The Cluster started moving stars around at the galactic core. We tried to stop it. The Cluster didn't need us anymore…" Once again, the old man's voice faded away.

Eva took a vial and attached it to hypodermic jet injector. She applied the hypo-jet to Coffin's upper arm and his eyes fluttered open. After a few minutes, his heartbeat resumed a more steady rhythm, though Eva didn't think the rhythm was as strong as it should be.

"What did the Cluster need you for in the first place?" Kirsten's brow knitted. "The Cluster can destroy starships. It can reason and observe the world around itself. Hell, it can move whole stars around. Why does an intelligence of that magnitude and ability need 'appendages' at all?"

Coffin closed his watery eyes for a moment before he looked up at Kirsten. "The first life forms on this planet were little more than conglomerations of organic chemicals that moved pointlessly from place to place," he said. "The Cluster is more akin to those chemicals than anything else I know." He once again became the old school teacher and the look in his eyes told Eva that he sought to pass on the most important lesson he would ever teach. "On Earth, those chemicals became more complex. They developed tools to survive in the world they had been born into. Those tools were appendages that allowed some to hunt others; allowed the hunted to flee. Exploring the universe required appendages."

Eva shook her head. "But intelligence was born as a way to better control appendages."

Coffin chuckled, then closed his eyes for a moment as a spasm shuddered through his body. "Who's to say that intelligence requires appendages? What about artificial intelligence? Does it have appendages?"

"Artificial intelligence experiments never achieved their full potential," said Kirsten. "Computers can store vast amounts of information. They can interpret meanings and take actions in response to input. They can even think and reason to a certain degree. For some reason, they've always lacked motive and imagination."

"They've never wanted for anything." A wracking cough kept Coffin from proceeding. Once it subsided, he continued. "Computers have never needed to hunt to survive. They've never been hunted. The Cluster is the same. It's not so much that they need appendages. It's that they need creatures *of* appendage to augment their intelligence – to give them direction."

Eva put her hand to her mouth. "We humans are obsessed with death. We're obsessed with building legacies to pass on to the next generation."

Kirsten frowned. "The art is the death. Isn't that what whales say about humans?"

"Precisely," said Coffin. "When the Cluster came to the galaxy looking for the Titans, they didn't know what they needed. They only knew they needed whatever motivates creatures of appendage. Rather than find the Titans, they found humans. The human drive to build something – to build a legacy to leave after death – was a very powerful idea to the Cluster."

"Now, the Cluster has a program," said Kirsten. "It doesn't need us anymore."

Coffin shook his head. "There's more than that. Humans also imagine an afterlife where things are better than in this world. It still has use for humans in that new world. What it doesn't need are the original programmers. We – the first ones to go to the Cluster – have done what we were expected to do. The Cluster will continue to use other humans."

"What happens to the humans it's done with?" Kirsten's eyes widened.

"The same thing that happened to the humans it couldn't use to begin with." Coffin closed his eyes. The pulsing line on the heart monitor flattened and a warning tone issued from the life support unit.

Eva began chest compressions, trying to get Coffin's heart to restart. Kirsten put her face in her hands and began to sob.

Manuel Raton, Suki Firebrandt, and Laura Peters had been led to the admiralty headquarters on Titan. On the way, Suki tried to ask Admiral Strauss what the Gaean Military planned to do about the Cluster around Earth. The admiral remained silent and when they reached the building, she went to an elevator while they continued downstairs into a basement level. Four military police officers escorted them to a room and told them to remove their wrist chronos and empty out their pockets into pouches. Manuel had to remove his belt and all three removed their shoes. A military police officer escorted each of them to a separate cell.

Laura studied the cell's bars. "Rather antique-looking jail."

Manuel appraised the bars, then tried to stick his finger between them. The shock spun Nuevo Santa Fe's sheriff 180 degrees. "I wouldn't recommend trying that," he said to Laura. "The bars are there just in case the power goes down for some reason."

Sanson's pilot chewed her lower lip. "How long do you suppose they'll keep us here?"

Fire and Manuel looked at each other. "I have no idea," said Fire. "One thing is clear. The admiralty is under the Cluster's influence."

"What about the ambassador?" Laura's eyes widened. "What about the Titans?"

Manuel moved over to the bunk and sat down. "The admirals have the power to keep signals from getting to the ambassador. However, I don't think they have to. I think the ambassador's under the Cluster's influence, too."

Fire reached out and almost put her hands around the bars in a reflexive move, but reconsidered. Instead, she put her arms behind her back. "The Titans may be powerful, but they're far from omniscient." She began to pace the cell. "I suspect they monitored our landing, but it's hard to say whether they ascribed any importance to our arrival. There's a good chance they don't know we're here or why."

"What can we do?" Laura dropped onto her bunk and scrubbed at her eyes, her voice thick.

Manuel twirled the end of his mustache and looked up at the pilot. "There's not much we can do, besides wait for dinner."

However, the expected dinner never materialized. Without windows or wrist chronos, they couldn't tell how much time had passed. All three experienced hunger pangs, rumbling stomachs, and finally the quiet, which settled in as they fasted. After a while, each of them drifted off to sleep, even though the lights had not been turned off in the cellblock.

When Fire awoke some time later, the lights were still on. Manuel snored in the next cell. In the cell across the way, Laura paced a few steps, turned and took a few more steps before turning again.

"Hey," called Fire. "How are you doing?"

Laura shook her head, her jaw clenched. Her neat and tidy uniform had grown disheveled.

"Laura, they'll get us some food, soon, I'm sure. I doubt they're used to having prisoners and they just forgot..."

Laura sighed and dropped to the bunk. "It's not that." Her voice sounded thick and raw. "It's just that I've tried so hard my whole life to stay out of trouble, to do the right thing. How could I wind up in a jail cell?" She threw up her hands.

"Listen to me," said Fire, keeping her voice firm but kind, "you didn't do anything wrong. We're being held unjustly. These people are under a hostile alien's control."

Laura looked up and ran her hands through her hair. "I keep telling myself that. The problem ... I keep thinking about their uniforms ... I'm in the reserves. These are people I've sworn my life to serve..."

Just then, the lights went out. Without windows, it became pitch dark. Fire listened for any shouts or calls. It seemed as though no guards occupied the nearby rooms – or perhaps there were guards and the power outage hadn't affected them. "Hey!" called Fire. "Did you know the lights went out? Can we get some food in here?"

"Keep it down over there," muttered Raton from the adjoining cell. "Hey," he said in a happier tone. "They finally turned off the damned lights."

Fire had been facing the door. She got down on her hands and knees and crawled toward the door, wary of the shock, but knowing somehow what she would find. As she touched the bars' cold steel, she nodded satisfaction when she could put her hand out into the corridor. "The power's off," she announced. "I can put my hand through the bars."

"Better pull it back." Panic tinged Manuel's words. "If the power comes back on, the forcefield could slice off your hand."

Boots tromped down the corridor. Soon, a space-suited figure stopped, facing Fire's cell. The figure peered down at her. The glare from the figure's helmet light prevented her from seeing the face within.

"Move back from the door," said a voice from a translator unit. The generic translated voice held no clues as to the person's identity. She scrambled back away from the door and the space-suited figure retrieved a hepler pistol from a holster and shot the lock. The person wrenched the cell open, then retrieved a miniature flashlight from a pocket and tossed it toward her. Their rescuer moved on, shot Manuel's lock, and then Laura's and gave them each flashlights.

"Who are you?" asked Fire, her eyes narrowed. She held up the flashlight and illuminated the side of the figure's mask. She gasped when she noticed the eye patch. "Arepno?" she asked.

"We must hurry," said the Rd'dyggian. He motioned for them to follow and led them further into the cellblock to an open hatch. He indicated they should go through.

Manuel went first and swore when he dropped ten feet and landed hip-deep in raw sewage. Fire landed next to him with a splash and Manuel raised his arms to try to stave off as much as possible. Then Laura landed next to them. Above them, the space-suited Rd'dyggian used magnetic clamps on his suit to grab onto the walls. He pulled the access hatch closed behind him and bolted it in place, then climbed down the wall to join them in the muck.

"As you have now surmised, we are in the human dome's septic system," said Arepno

"No shit!" said Manuel.

"Actually, quite a lot of shit." Fire giggled at her own bad joke.

Unfazed by the human's attempt at humor, Arepno pointed to a small circular airlock a few feet away in the wall. "Though the station is equipped with waste reclamation and recycling facilities, there is an emergency port in case there's a problem and the sewage must be removed."

"Oh." Laura seemed oblivious to the sewage around her hips. "In case all the toilets in the dome back up at once and they need to clean out the septic tank in a hurry."

"Precisely," said Arepno. "That door leads outside, where I have a rover waiting. We can then go to my ship and meet your vessel at Alpha Coma."

"That sounds like a great plan, Arepno." Fire held up her hands. "The only problem is ... isn't it cold enough outside the hatch for methane to become liquid?"

Arepno bent down and retrieved something from underneath the muck. As the brown slime dripped off, they realized he held a space suit built for humans.

Manuel's nose wrinkled and he shook his head. "I don't know if freedom's worth that."

"I can always carry you back to your cell," said Arepno. "There's still another hour before the program I installed on the prison block computers expires. By the time the power comes back on, they would see you safely ensconced in your cell. You do not have to go with me."

Manuel looked up toward the cellblock, then looked at the suit, his lip curled. "Okay, I'll go with you, but there better be showers on your ship!"

John Mark Ellis stood at the boat's wheel. The holo display on the console next to the wheel showed the place where his mother and Manuel had found Richard out in the open ocean. G'Liat stood rigid in the bow, his massive six-fingered hands to his side. Mark couldn't shake the image of those massive hands around Clyde McClintlock's body, literally squeezing the life from him. Despite those memories, Mark wondered what the warrior thought about while standing in the boat's bow, the wet salt air rushing past his hairless head. The Rd'dyggian warrior almost certainly welcomed the moisture. His planet was a good deal more humid than Earth. Though the air on the ocean was chill, it was not as cold as the warrior's own world. G'Liat didn't sweat, as far as Mark could tell. Mark pondered whether Rd'dyggians even had sweat glands when the boat's teleholo signal chirped.

He activated the unit. The hologram showed Kirsten in his home on Nantucket. She looked at him through red, swollen eyes. Mark's throat went dry and he somehow knew Samuel Coffin had died before she told him.

He struggled to ask a question. "How … How did it happen?"

Kirsten told him how Coffin had regained consciousness and what he'd said about the Cluster and the importance of evolved creatures. As she spoke, she gained composure. "I know how close you and he were," she said at last. "He struggled to stay alive long enough to give us that information. He knew you'd need it."

Mark's knees weakened and threatened to give way. Somehow, G'Liat was already beside him, supporting him with a hand under the elbow. Mark wondered how long the warrior had been there, listening. He hadn't seen G'Liat leave the bow nor had he heard him step up behind.

"I wish I could be there for you," said Kirsten after Mark was silent for a time.

"I'm glad you were there for him," said Mark. "We'll be back as soon as we can." He reached down to turn off the teleholo link, but stopped. "I love you," he said.

She blinked at him and her breath caught in her throat. "I love you, too." She terminated the call.

G'Liat stepped back and Mark took the wheel again. The warrior watched him for a time, but didn't say a word. At last, he returned to his place in the bow. Mark eased the boat's throttle forward, hoping to reach Richard's position as soon as possible. All at once, loneliness descended on Ellis. His father had died, his teacher had died, and his mother had gone to

Titan. Right then, he wanted advice and comfort from an old friend or a relative. He suspected his pirate grandfather, Ellison Firebrandt, might have especially useful advice for him.

After an hour spent in uncomfortable silence, they reached the place where Fire and Manuel had found Richard. Mark bent down and retrieved two translator headsets. He placed one on his head, then stepped into the bow and offered one to G'Liat. The warrior shook his head. "Thank you, no," he said. "I speak the language of the Sperm Whale as fluently as I speak your own."

Mark nodded. He retrieved a pair of binoculars from his belt and scanned the horizon for whale spouts. The boat tipped and Ellis had to grab onto G'Liat's arm to keep from being dropped over the side into the water. Richard's gray-black form rose near the boat and his spout washed over the deck, soaking both G'Liat and Mark.

"The cycle continues," said Richard.

Before Mark could speak, a series of clicks almost like static issued from G'Liat's mouth. The words were translated through Mark's translator unit. "The cycle continues."

Ellis echoed the statement, then said, "It is good to see you, though I'm surprised to find you right where my mother and Manuel Raton said they'd met with you."

"I have been waiting for you," said the whale. "Besides, there is good hunting here." The whale rolled toward one side so it looked up at G'Liat. "This Cluster the humans have described intrigues me. Over the last week, something has prickled at my consciousness. It is like the contentment of a full belly or the satisfaction that comes after mating, but it is there even when my belly is not full and I have not mated for many years."

"That sounds like the Cluster," said Mark, stepping a little closer to the boat's edge and kneeling down. "I've experienced similar sensations myself."

"The Cluster is a lifeform like me?" asked the whale. "It is a creature that hunts the dark of space, but does not build tools?"

G'Liat knelt down next to Ellis. "It is similar to whales, yes. It is large and it hunts. It is also dissimilar to whales. It is ancient life. It does not mate. It does not change unless it merges with other lifeforms."

"The only way any lifeform changes is by merging with others," mused the whale. "Whether they mate and create a life or they interact and exchange thoughts as we are now." The whale swam away from the boat a short distance and dove under the water, but surfaced a short time later.

"The Cluster is dying," said Mark. "It wants to leave a legacy so other life forms like itself can learn what it has learned." Just then, he better understood the full nature of Gibbs' work and Kirsten's report of Coffin's final words. "It wants to create a new world where it can continue in a new form, much like the human concept of an afterlife."

Richard swam close to the boat. "I, too, am dying," he said.

Mark grabbed onto the low rail surrounding the bow. "You can't die." His eyes grew moist.

"All creatures die," said the whale. "However, I do not understand the word, 'legacy.'"

"It is something humans leave for their children or for generations to come," explained Mark. He looked over at G'Liat who stared off at the horizon. "Sometimes it's a physical object such as this boat. My father left it for me. Sometimes it's a book or songs. I suppose you could say the humpbacks' songs are a legacy they leave for their children."

G'Liat said something in Rd'dyggian and then repeated it in Richard's language. Mark heard both translations: "The Cluster must learn to build a living legacy." He continued in the whale's language. "The humpbacks' legacy lives and evolves with time. Parents do pass on their songs, but the children change them. You, Richard, passed on your DNA to your children. Their mothers taught them how to hunt – how to live. Your children will live long after your death."

"I understand," said the whale. "The cycle resumes." With that, the whale dove below the water to resume hunting for a time. Ellis suspected the whale would ponder the recent conversation.

Mark stood, his thoughts divided. The revelation that his old friend Richard was dying, stunned him. He knew the time would come before long. After all, both Coffin and Richard had been friends of his father. Unless there was an accident, he would outlive them both. However, it seemed too soon. Mark also processed what the Rd'dyggian warrior had just told the whale. "What are you trying to do?" he asked at last.

G'Liat stood and looked down at Ellis with black, unblinking eyes. "You humans are so obsessed with physical things." He pointed to the boat. "Your father's legacy was this boat. Your ancestors' legacy to you was Nantucket Island and the houses upon it. You speak of books before you speak of living songs." The warrior let out a strange, warbling laugh and the sound chilled Ellis to the bone. "There is no reason the Cluster must die. The Cluster can be convinced to go on living in its current form. It can build a living legacy rather than some object at the galactic core."

"The whales are stagnant and so is the Cluster. However, the whales have evolved and can aid the Cluster. The Cluster can travel the stars and aid the whales."

A new chill ran down Mark's spine. "That means subjecting the whales to the same servitude humans are under now ... to the same servitude the Titans fought to escape. I can't condone that."

"Symbiosis is only servitude when one of the life forms is unwilling," said G'Liat. "This is out of your hands."

"Not if I can help it," said Mark.

Richard rose to the surface again. "The cycle continues."

"The cycle continues," repeated G'Liat.

"Tell me more about the Cluster," said the whale. "The more I hear, the more it fascinates me. I believe my kind have something to offer them."

Mark knelt down again. "Richard," he pleaded. "The Cluster is dangerous. It enslaves the beings it interacts with."

"Young one," chided Richard. "You do not want to see me die. Perhaps G'Liat gives me a reason to live just a little longer."

Ellis fell back into a sitting position, took a deep breath, and listened to the conversation between the whale and the Rd'dyggian warrior, trying to find a flaw in G'Liat's cold logic or the whale's desire to see the stars. Ellis couldn't find one and was forced to admit that G'Liat had perhaps found the solution they sought, though he didn't like it at all. He hoped his mother was having better luck on Titan.

Chapter Fourteen

ARMAGEDDON

Manuel Raton's nose still twitched as Arepno's ship came out of jump in the Alpha Coma Berenices system. "Will you give it a rest," said Fire. "You've been through the sanitizer three times. You don't smell like sewage any more."

Manuel rolled his eyes. "I didn't think I did, but then I kept seeing it – or did I hear it? – during the jump." He paced the small octagonal room. "Was it just me or did that jump take a long time?"

"Arepno's ship must be equipped to do mapping jumps, like the *Sanson* does," said Laura.

Manuel shook his head, not understanding.

Laura explained further. "The jump did take longer, because the ship took its time tracing the gravitational currents." She wrung her hands. "The Cluster's moving stars at the center of the galaxy. It must be playing havoc with jump points everywhere."

The door to the tiny cabin opened, and Arepno entered. Without a word, he waved his hand next to one wall and a hologram of Alpha Coma appeared. "We are in orbit," he explained. "It appears the *Nicholas Sanson* has already arrived."

"Why would they be here?" Laura's brow furrowed. "I thought they'd still be at Titan waiting for us."

"They're here because they took my advice and fled the Titan system," explained the warrior. "It is good to see them here. As we departed orbit without the Titans' permission, they fired upon us. I'm sure the *Sanson* must have been as well."

"But the Titans are peaceful." Laura sounded as though a paradigm had just shifted for her. "Why would they fire on our ships?"

"For the same reason an Earth admiral arrested us." Fire sighed. "Someone – or several someones – fears what will happen if the Cluster is confronted."

"But how did the Titans get missiles?" she persisted. "They've never armed themselves before."

"They didn't use them well," interjected Arepno. "*Sanson's* presence here demonstrates that. We also had an easy escape. I suspect the missiles are a recent acquisition." He turned toward Fire. "Your uncle has summoned us to the surface. Plans are being made to confront the Cluster."

"That's what I wanted to hear," sneered Manuel. "Let's go."

"Aren't you afraid you'll smell the place up?" asked Fire.

Arepno's prehensile mustache groped around as the warrior sniffed the air. After a moment, he made a gesture a little like a shrug. "We'll land in a few minutes." He left, closing the door behind him. However, he left the holo display on so they could watch the ship's progress toward the planet. Even though flames flashed around the ship as they entered the atmosphere, the ride was smooth. The ship dropped toward a large continent. Soon, grid-like patterns appeared on the ground below them as farms, cities and roads appeared. They continued to descend and soon, they could make out short structures – houses in the suburbs around a large urban area. Taller buildings stood in the distance. Though he had only been there once before, Manuel thought he recognized the city as Shangri La, Alpha Coma's capital.

The ship settled to the ground at a spaceport. Soon after, Arepno appeared in the doorway again and led the three through the craft's command center to a gangway that extended, almost like a living appendage, to the tarmac outside. The four stepped down through the gangway and met a contingent of armed personnel in Alpha Coma Berenices uniforms. A woman with a gold star on her collar stepped forward and saluted Arepno. "I'm General Honscheid. I've been ordered to escort you to Senator Firebrandt's office."

"A little better reception than we had on Titan," muttered Manuel.

"So it seems," said Fire.

Laura shushed them into silence.

The general led them to a hover bus, which carried them through the city. The buildings resembled fragile crystal palaces. Between them were vast, open areas with fountains or sculptures. Fluffy white clouds stood out in stark contrast to a deep azure sky. "It's no wonder they call this place Shangri La," mused Laura.

"Give me the Andes any day." Fire reached out and squeezed Manuel's hand. "Or, the Nuevo Rio Grande Valley back on Sufiro."

Laura pursed her lips and narrowed her gaze.

Fire chuckled. "Oh, this is a beautiful city, but I prefer natural beauty to offices, stores, and dwellings."

"It'd be a shame to see the Cluster destroy any of those," growled Manuel, bringing them back to the danger at hand.

At last, the hover bus arrived at the government complex. The soldiers escorted them out and led the way to Herbert Firebrandt's office. The general opened the door, stepped through, and then stepped sideways, executing a salute as Arepno, Fire, Manuel and Laura entered the office.

Simon Yermakov spoke to Herbert Firebrandt and two ship captains with his head bent down. After a moment, Firebrandt looked up and acknowledged the new arrivals. As he did, Simon followed his gaze and smiled. He ran around the desk and wrapped Laura in a hug. "I thought you were lost!"

"There was no reason to fear their loss," said Arepno. "I said we would meet you here."

Laura's arms hung at her sides until Simon released her and stepped back, a too-big smile on his face.

"It's good to see you, sir." She offered her hand.

Senator Firebrandt introduced Fire and Manuel to several captains and two admirals. "What's going on?" asked Fire.

"We're assembling a strike force," explained the senator. "From what Mr. Yermakov tells us, the galaxy is in jeopardy. We have to stop the Cluster now. I'm even more distressed the Titans fired upon the *Sanson* while they attempted to bring us this information. We can't count on them to help us."

"I don't think you can count on Earth ships either," said Fire. "The admiralty on Titan took us prisoner. I think they're all under the Cluster's influence."

The senator looked at his feet in a way that reminded Fire of her father. "I'm sure you're right and we can't count on any Alliance ships in the home system. However, Earth Alliance ships out on patrol haven't received any orders from Earth command. Several have responded to our call and will join the Colonial ships in the assault."

"How the hell are you going to attack the Cluster?" asked Manuel. "Every ship that's attacked one has been vaporized."

Senator Firebrandt nodded, his expression grave. "We know. Before, we never knew where to find the Cluster so we could never attack in force. So far, the Cluster has never faced more than one or two ships. We have over thirty ships ready to assault the Cluster and we know right where to find it."

"You may know it's at Earth," said Fire, "but the jump points are changing."

"True," said the senator. "That's where the *Sanson* comes in. Yermakov's crew has been working with staff here to realign the jump engines on the ship. By this evening, they should be calibrated well enough to lead the fleet back to Earth." He put his arms around Manuel and Fire. "Your service has been invaluable, but if you want to stay here on Alpha Coma, I'm sure we can find quarters."

"You can't keep me out of this fight," said Manuel. "If the *Sanson's* going back, then so am I."

Fire nodded and brushed a strand of her long hair over her shoulder. "I'm with Manuel," she said. "After all, my son's there. If I can help, I will."

The senator smiled. "There're a few hours before the ships will be ready. Let's go find some dinner." He looked into Fire's eyes. "I'd like some time to get to know my niece better before she gets herself shot at or thrown in jail again."

When the privateer *Legacy* came out of jump, Ellison Firebrandt fell to his knees and a cold sweat broke out on his forehead. He held up his hand when he noticed Roberts' concerned frown. The captain looked back at Mary Seaton. "Get me a vessel status. Are we still in one piece?"

Mary looked as though she fought to keep her breakfast down, but nodded and turned toward her station. She brought up displays as she made calls on the intercom.

Firebrandt pulled himself upright and looked over at the gunner's rig. Juan Raton had released his arm and fresh blood seeped through his shirt. "Juan, get down to the medic and get your arm tended to. We'll need you ready to work soon."

"Yes, sir," breathed Juan through clenched teeth. His eyes looked forward, a bit unfocused from the pain. He struggled to his feet and left to see the medic.

"Captain," called Roberts. "We're right on target, near Earth orbit." The first officer activated the holo tank and the blue-green Earth materialized. Behind and below the planet hung the Moon's bright gray form. Though numerous human colonies had been established on planets that resembled Earth, the combination of Earth and Moon was unmistakable.

Firebrandt's breath caught and he stepped forward, toward the image. He put his hand on Roberts' shoulder and squeezed. An unexpected tear ran down his cheek. "I never thought to see Earth again." He looked down at the deck grating below his feet and the walls on either side. "I never thought I'd see Earth from this ship again." His voice hitched. He cleared his throat and stepped closer to the display. "Can you show me where the Clusters are located?"

"As far as I can tell, there's just one Cluster in orbit around the Earth." Anne typed a command into the computer console and a red orb appeared over Australia. "The other three must be at the galactic core."

"Does that help or hinder us?" asked Roberts as he un-clamped the hover chair from the deck and drifted next to Fire-brandt, raising himself to the captain's eye-level.

"Captain," called Mary Seaton from the command deck's stern. "I've just received reports from all crew chiefs. We suf-fered a minor hull breach amidships on deck three. The section is sealed off. Junior doesn't think we should attempt another jump until it's repaired. He also doesn't think we can repair the damage ourselves. We'll need time at a dockyard."

"But, it can be repaired," reflected Firebrandt. "That's good. How about injuries?"

"Juan Raton and two others suffered minor injuries. Doc Krishnamurty says she'll have them patched up in no time."

"How are we for combat readiness?"

Mary took a deep breath, then blew it out. "As good as we were when we left Sufiro. We have functional weapons and once Juan is back at his station, people that can fire them. The engine crew is ready to go." She pursed her lips as though she wanted to say more, but the captain interrupted.

"That's about as good as can be expected." The captain knew she shared his concern for the small crew. He retrieved the pipe from his pocket and lit it, projecting calm. After staring at the image of Earth for a few moments, a self-satisfied grin appeared and he looked at Roberts, who approached. "I think it's time to contact Edmund Swan and see if we can form a strategy."

Roberts nodded and pressed several buttons on the hover chair. He had slaved certain ship functions, including communications, to a control panel on the chair. A moment later, Earth faded, replaced by Edmund Swan standing in a dim room with four people grouped behind him.

"You're here? At Earth?" Swan's eyes widened. "When I sent the message with the *Sanson* I expected you to get Arepno or someone to come and help us out."

"You said it yourself. The Cluster endangers all human life in the galaxy – including Sufiro." The captain spoke around the pipe stem. "I've never run from a fight," he added, almost as an afterthought.

"No, you haven't," said Swan with a genuine smile. "Especially one where your people's safety is concerned." The deputy sheriff turned and spoke to a woman behind him, then turned back. "Can you meet us at the Southern Arizona space port? We have a plan, but I'd rather not discuss it over the link."

"Understood," said Firebrandt. "We'll see you soon." Roberts shut off the comm channel. Together, they left the command deck and went to the launch bay. Firebrandt disconnected the safety and fuel lines while Roberts drifted into the launch and prepared it for the excursion to the surface. After a moment, Firebrandt entered the launch, closing the door behind him. Once the captain had strapped in, Roberts opened the bay door. Firebrandt took the controls and eased the launch forward, out of the bay.

Ellison Firebrandt's head swam as he gaped at Earth through the launch's windows. Forty-nine years earlier, he had told Roberts and Suki that he hadn't wanted to return to Earth humiliated and defeated in a broken-down star cruiser. He corrected the launch's flight path and looked back at the *Legacy* against a backdrop of stars, and a lump formed in his throat. He had not realized before how much he had wanted to return to Earth. Aware that he and his ship might prove necessary to save the planet, Ellison Firebrandt's heart raced. At long last he had defeated his mother's plans to strand him on Sufiro for life. As the launch descended through the atmosphere, the captain realized his mother still had achieved her own victory. He had not returned to Earth as a pirate, but on a mission to save all of Earth's colonies – including his mother's adopted world, Alpha Coma Berenices. He snorted a laugh as he homed in on the Southern Arizona spaceport.

"Are you feeling okay, sir?" Roberts looked at the captain in concern.

"Never felt better." Firebrandt activated the thrusters and settled the launch into a docking bay.

Firebrandt unstrapped from the seat and opened the door. As he stepped down the ramp, Edmund Swan and two other people entered through an archway at one end of the bay. Firebrandt shook the deputy sheriff's hand. "Tell us about your plan."

Swan gritted his teeth and closed his eyes. After a moment, he opened them and looked at the captain. "I wish I was asking someone else to do this. There's no way to predict how the Cluster will respond. The *Legacy* may well be destroyed."

"If the *Legacy* had remained on Sufiro, and the Cluster succeeded, she would be destroyed just the same. What do we need to do?"

Swan began pacing back and forth, as he outlined the plan he had formed with the resistance.

On the way back to Nantucket, G'Liat returned to the boat's bow while Ellis steered. Above them, dark clouds began to form and the water churned. Mark applied a little more throttle hoping to get back to port before the storm broke out in force. A storm also seemed to brew in his thoughts. It distressed him to hear Richard announce his imminent demise, but it didn't surprise him. Mark knew sperm whales typically lived around seventy years. He didn't know Richard's actual age, but he knew the whale had been an adult when his father first met him.

He looked up at the Rd'dyggian warrior in the bow and frowned. On one hand, he couldn't help but be grateful G'Liat had given the whale a reason to hold onto life a little longer. On the other hand, G'Liat had suggested that whales should subjugate themselves to the Cluster. Ellis tried to argue the point to Richard – tried to suggest that whales not be so willing to give up the oceans' freedom. However, the whale rebuffed him. "How dare you laud the freedom of the oceans? You not only have their freedom, but you can travel to other worlds and the stars beyond."

Mark didn't know how to answer the whale. He needed to find an alternative way to stop the Cluster, before G'Liat found a way to suggest whales would be better symbionts for the Cluster than humans. Mark consoled himself by realizing the Cluster might not even consider such a proposal. He didn't know whether the whales offered enough to attract the Cluster. After all, why did the Cluster choose humans over say, the Rd'dyggians, the Alpha Centaurans, or the Zahari?

A rumble built over the ocean and, at first, Mark thought thunder rolled over the waves from the brewing storm. However, the more he listened, the more he realized it was not thunder, but an approaching craft. Just then, a silver egg-shaped craft dropped through the low, dark clouds and descended toward the water. Mark pulled back on the throttle and turned to keep from running into it. The boat sent up a wall of spray. He looked up into the boat's bow, certain he must have dumped G'Liat into the water. Instead, the warrior had hooked his foot into the low railing and followed the boat's roll with the grace of a surfer riding a wave. When the boat stopped, Ellis looked over his shoulder. The egg-shaped craft settled with its bottom in the water and the narrow-part pointed skyward.

Despite the rolling waves and the slick deck, G'Liat strolled to the boat's stern. He glanced at Mark. "Thank you for the opportunity to speak to Richard once again. After so much time among humans, I found our conversation refreshing."

"Where are you going?" asked Mark.

Without answering, G'Liat dove over the boat's rail into the churning waves. A light drizzle started coming down. Mark ran to the stern and looked. G'Liat swam for the egg-shaped craft. "Where are you going?" called Mark again, even though he knew G'Liat would not answer. A door appeared in the craft's side and another Rd'dyggian appeared – Rizonex. G'Liat reached the craft and Rizonex pulled him inside. The door closed and soon after, the ship lifted back into the sky.

The rain came down harder and soaked Ellis. He didn't bother to go inside to get rain gear. Instead, he returned to the wheel, set course for Nantucket and pushed the throttle to full.

After meeting with Ellison Firebrandt, Edmund Swan returned to Tim Gibbs' apartment. He stepped over to the armchair opposite Gibbs and sat down. His friend sat, immobile. Swan found himself thinking back to high school and remembered Gibbs as he had been – not too different in the past than he was in the present. He remembered Gibbs tinkering with electronics and computer equipment and describing the perfect computer, which he then learned required a black hole.

"Did you ever dream that such a device would mean humanity's end?" he asked, even though he knew Gibbs couldn't hear him. "Oh, I know what you're thinking. Some humans will go on, including you. But, will you retain the fundamental spark that makes you human?"

Swan sighed and rubbed the bridge of his nose. After a moment, he stood and looked in the refrigerator. He rummaged around for a few minutes and threw out some cheese covered in green fuzz along with an entire carton containing something that almost made him throw up when he cracked the lid. At the back, he found a bottle of beer. The deputy sheriff pulled it out and examined it. After a moment, he unscrewed the top, took a swallow, and then made a face. He looked over at Gibbs' limp form and held up the bottle as if asking for an explanation for the poor quality beer.

When he received no response, he took another swallow. Maria Gonzalez would be there soon, with a hypo-jet of Proxom. The resistance planned to inject Proxom into as many people in the Cluster trance as they could. At the same time, the *Legacy* would fire at the Cluster in orbit around the Earth, in an attempt to knock out the EQ signal connecting that Cluster to the ones at the galactic core. They hoped it would throw the Clusters into confusion. By pulling as many human architects responsible for the memory core away from the Cluster as possible, they hoped they might stop the Cluster. However, as Roberts and others pointed out, the Cluster had probably already stored all the data it needed. At best, this action would delay the Cluster a short time. Still, as Jerry Lawrence pointed out, any time they bought would be more time for help to arrive.

Swan took another swallow of beer and then prayed for such help. He feared that they would pull Tim Gibbs away from the Cluster, the *Legacy* would fire, and the Cluster would retaliate, killing Ellison Firebrandt and Carter Roberts.

The door chime sounded. Swan swallowed more beer, then set the bottle down on the counter. He opened the door for Maria Gonzalez, who carried a hypo-jet and wore a headset, which put her in contact with other resistance leaders around the planet. She looked over at the counter. "Have you got another beer? I think I need it."

"I'll go look," said Swan.

Soaked from the storm, Mark Ellis reached his front door. Out of habit, he wiped his feet on the sopping wet mat and entered the house. Kirsten jumped up from the kitchen table, ran to him and threw her arms around him. She backed off a moment later when she realized how cold and wet he was. "You better get upstairs and change into something dry."

"Would you mind putting on some coffee, or tea?" asked Mark as he sloshed toward the stairs. "Anything hot would be good now."

Eva started a pot of coffee as Mark went upstairs. He returned a few minutes later, wearing dry clothes and he dropped onto the couch. Kirsten sat down next to him and pulled him close. "How did the talk with Richard go?" she asked.

"Not well." Mark shook his head. "I feel like such a fool." He stood up and began pacing. "G'Liat had his own agenda all along. I need to find a way back to the Cluster as soon as possible."

Kirsten stood and put her hand on Mark's arm. "Mark, Coffin's gone," she reminded him. "You can't help him anymore."

"I know, but we have a new problem." Mark looked down at the floor. Eva stepped up and handed him a cup of coffee. He drank it down in two gulps and handed the cup back to Eva. "G'Liat's convinced Richard that whales should replace humans as Cluster symbionts."

Kirsten looked up at him wide-eyed. "Would the Cluster consider such a thing?"

"What the devil would it mean for whales and the Cluster to form a symbiosis?" Eva returned to the coffee pot and refilled the cup.

"I don't know – to either question." Mark returned to the couch and sat down. He opened a wooden box on the coffee table and retrieved a cigar from within. Biting off the end, he thrust the cigar in his mouth and lit it. "After talking to Richard, I'm guessing the Cluster fears death as much as we do. If we can't destroy the Cluster, we must convince it to go on living in the real universe."

Eva sat down in the armchair next to the couch and set the coffee cup on the table for Mark. "Wouldn't it be better to destroy the Cluster?"

Mark nodded. "If we knew we could, sure." He knocked some ash into an ashtray. "The problem is we don't know whether the Cluster can be destroyed or not. G'Liat thinks the answer is to find a new symbiont for the Cluster. I think the answer is to convince the Cluster to continue without symbiotic appendages. If it does want to create a virtual world, it can do it without destroying life in the galaxy."

Kirsten sat down in a chair at the kitchen table, avoiding Mark's cigar smoke. "Where's G'Liat gone?"

Mark shook his head. "His henchman – Rizonex – picked him up out at sea and took him somewhere. I think it's now a race. Which of us will get to the Cluster first."

"Well, I think I might be able to help." Eva leaned forward. "This afternoon, we took Samuel Coffin's body to the hospital morgue. On the way, I thought about how emotions seem to attract the Cluster. Proxom suppresses emotions, and makes people less susceptible to the Cluster's influence. Thinking along those lines, I realized that if I could suppress the amygdala, it would free up emotions." She sat back and folded her arms.

"What's the amygdala?" asked Mark as he returned the cigar to his mouth.

"It's a pair of nucleic clusters in the brain linked to the limbic system," explained Eva. "It helps you push fear to the back of your mind. It helps you repress sexual desire at inappropriate times. In short, it keeps your emotions in check – keeps them from overwhelming your day-to-day activities."

"Aren't there dangers to suppressing the amy … the amig … the part of the brain that suppresses emotion?" asked Kirsten, with a somewhat frustrated look.

Eva nodded. "A malfunctioning amygdala can lead to disorders such as schizophrenia, anxiety or depression…"

"Disorders where people suffer from an overload of emotion," said Mark around the cigar.

"That's right." Eva stood. "However, I can give you a controlled dosage of drugs to suppress the amygdala without leading to those disorders." She retrieved her medical bag and pulled out some small vials. "I obtained some from the hospital today."

Mark laid the cigar butt in the ashtray to allow it to burn out. "I've got to see if I can get to the Cluster before G'Liat does. If you think this might work to get the Cluster's attention, I think we need to try."

"You've already shown a certain tendency to get the Cluster's attention," said Eva. "Let's hope this enhances it."

Kirsten stood up. "Mark, don't you think we should talk about this a little more?"

He started rolling up his sleeve. "I'm afraid it's a race. It's a race to get there before the Cluster finishes its project at the galaxy's core and it's a race to see if I can talk to the Cluster before G'Liat finds a way."

Kirsten stepped over, took Mark's right hand and kissed him as Eva applied the hypo-jet to his left arm.

Maria Gonzalez paced back and forth in Tim Gibbs' apartment, talking to other resistance leaders around Earth. She worried that their numbers were shrinking fast and she worried about what the Proxom injections would do to those people who received them. Some speculated it would revive them. Others speculated it would kill the bodies while leaving their minds trapped in the Cluster. Either way, she hoped the resulting confusion would do more good than harm.

She raised her finger to the earpiece as the signal came in and pointed to Swan. "Get ready," she told him. "All teams are in position." She signaled the *Legacy* and told them to stand by.

Just then, the door flew open and two Rd'dyggian warriors entered the room. The shorter one, in more traditional Rd'dyggian robes, leveled a weapon at Swan.

"Drop the hypo-jet," called the tall one, dressed more like a human – wearing a black turtleneck shirt and slacks, but no translator unit. Swan looked from Maria to the two Rd'dyggians, evaluating them for a moment. At last, he dropped the hypo-jet. It seemed he had decided he couldn't take action without the Rd'dyggians shooting one or both of them.

"*Legacy* fire in five," called Maria.

She raised her hands as the tall Rd'dyggian crossed the room in five steps. He patted her down, found one hepler pistol, dropped it to the ground and stepped on it, crushing it under his weight. He examined the headset with his pitch-black eyes, but let her keep it. The tall Rd'dyggian spoke to the other in their native language just as he left the room.

The other Rd'dyggian gestured with his weapon. "On the couch, both of you."

"Gonzalez just signaled, 'fire in five,'" reported Anne McClintlock from the computer console, her hand to her own headset.

"Set five minute countdown," ordered Ellison Firebrandt. "Roberts, do we have a targeting solution yet?"

Roberts adjusted the hologram and zoomed in on the Cluster. "Since the Cluster doesn't have a radio per se, their transmission isn't a tight beam. Also, we don't want to scan them since active scans have been known to trigger attacks." Roberts floated into the holographic tank and changed the light frequency displayed. Most of the Cluster shone a dull red, but one orb stood out in bright green. "This orb," he said, pointing, "seems to be emitting in radio frequency. I'd focus the attack there."

"Very good." Firebrandt stood at the wheel console and checked the readouts. They had almost reached weapon's range.

"Three minutes," said Anne McClintlock.

"Give me a forward view – real projection," ordered the captain. In the holo tank, the Earth replaced the magnified view of the Cluster. In the distance, ahead and below the ship the Cluster orbited the planet. Firebrandt adjusted his course, then looked over at the gunners' rigs. Juan Raton, his shirt torn, sat at one rig studying the display. Roberts floated forward to the modified rig and activated the guns.

"Mark the target orb on the display," ordered the captain.

Anne typed in a command on the computer console. An orb on the Cluster's side glowed green. Firebrandt brought the ship around to face the target orb.

"One minute to firing time," reported Anne.

"Acquiring target," said Roberts.

"I'm getting it, too," said Juan.

The target orb was now centered in the display. Firebrandt applied a gentle thrust and brought the ship closer. Anne started a ten-second countdown. Roberts and Juan reported they were both ready. When Anne reached the end of the count-down, the captain growled, "Fire."

Every gun on the *Legacy* opened fire. The Cluster absorbed all the energy from the hepler guns. However, the false-color overlay that indicated the radio frequencies faded away. "Cease fire," called the captain.

"I'm not reading any EQ or radio emanations from the Cluster," said Anne.

Firebrandt brought the lateral thrusters on-line and turned the *Legacy* to starboard, getting her away from the Cluster as fast as possible while praying for deliverance and cursing the powers that kept his ship from jumping away from danger.

Ellis said he didn't feel anything right after the injection, other than a little annoyance at the pain in his arm.

"It'll take a few minutes to take effect," explained the doctor. "Maybe you'd better sit down."

Mark nodded and Kirsten led him over to the big armchair and he sat. As he looked around the room, his eyes fell on the kitchen area and he grew annoyed at the clutter in the sink. "Why hasn't anyone cleaned that up?"

"We haven't had time." Kirsten's eyes narrowed. "A lot has been going on. Samuel Coffin died this morning, for God's sake."

When Kirsten mentioned Samuel Coffin, Mark's eyes grew wide. "I failed him. I wasn't here to say good-bye to my teacher and my father's best friend. What kind of friend am I?"

"You're a good friend." Kirsten knelt down next to the armchair. She took Mark's hand and began patting it. "Coffin would have wanted you to talk to Richard – it was what you needed to do. Without the information you gained, the Earth had no hope."

"Does it have any hope, now?" Mark appeared to wilt. He waved Kirsten away from him and the corners of his mouth turned down. "What hope does the human race have if we can't even take time to say good-bye to our friends? Coffin taught me so much … so much…" Mark put his face in his hands and unrestrained tears began to flow.

Eva knelt down next to Kirsten and helped her to stand. Kirsten's eyes glistened with the moisture of unshed tears. "It's the drug," whispered Eva. "Mark can't control his emotions. They'll be a constant flood until it wears off and his amygdala takes control again." Eva led Kirsten away.

Feeling otherwise helpless, Kirsten nodded and went to the kitchen where she gathered plates and glasses, then placed them into the cleansing unit. She then turned her attention to the living room and dining area, looking for neglected plates. As she did, she chewed her lower lip and wondered whether they'd chosen the wisest way to attract the Cluster.

When Mark hadn't raised his head in five minutes, Eva knelt down and checked his pulse. She lifted his head with her finger and looked into his eyes. His breath caught for a moment as he noticed her, then his respiration increased. Eva stood to get her medical kit. Mark reached out, grabbed her wrist and pulled her close. Wrapping her in a bear-like embrace, he drove his lips into hers, forcing his tongue into her mouth.

Kirsten turned and gasped. She dropped the plate she carried and it shattered on the hardwood floor.

G'Liat returned to Tim Gibbs' apartment a few minutes later, carrying a case. Swan recognized it as the same traveling bag the warrior had brought to the apartment before. He opened the bag and revealed a smooth machine, shimmering like mother-of-pearl. Without looking at the humans, he started making adjustments.

"What's going on here?" Maria looked from one Rd'dyggian to the other. "We're trying to stop the Cluster. If we don't, a shock wave will destroy all life in the galaxy – Rd'dyggians included. You should be helping us, not stopping us."

G'Liat spun on his heel. "Our aims are the same, young woman."

Swan noticed that his Rd'dyggian accent was more pronounced than before. He took a step toward the couch, his hands clasped behind his back. "However, your plan will, at most, delay the Cluster for a short time – and I suspect will have rather devastating consequences. If successful, my plan will rid us of the Cluster for good, and no one will have to be harmed."

"What do you plan to do?" asked Swan. He looked from one warrior to the other, trying to find an opening – some way he could attack the one without the other blind-siding him.

"You shall see soon enough," said G'Liat.

Maria inclined her head as she started receiving reports from other resistance cells. She put her hand to her mouth and shook her head. "What's the matter?" asked Swan.

"They're dying," she said. "All those people we've injected with Proxom – they seem to stir into consciousness for a short time and then they die. It's as though they have no will to live any longer."

G'Liat sneered. "Then there's a good chance I saved your friend's life." He gestured to Gibbs' unconscious form. "Let's just hope his mind is still alive inside the Cluster." The warrior turned and began to make more adjustments to the brain scan device.

Captain Ellison Firebrandt held onto the *Legacy's* wheel console and watched a set of numbers floating in the holo tank as they increased. They were putting distance between themselves and the Cluster, but not as fast as he wanted. "Mary, can Junior give me any more power at all?"

"Any more, and he says she'll blow apart given the hull rupture," said the technician.

"Captain, we may have a problem," called Roberts. He changed the view in the holo tank so it displayed the Cluster in ultra-violet light. Several orbs glowed a bright purple at that wavelength. "They're either getting ready to pursue or fire. I don't know which."

"Any suggestions," called the captain. "We're running from them as fast as we can and I don't think evasive maneuvers will do us any good."

Roberts put a plot up on the viewer. "There's an old satellite debris field twenty-two degrees from our present course."

An arc appeared, connecting the *Legacy* to the debris field's position. "If we get in there and shut off our engines, they may lose us."

"You don't sound too certain." The captain made the course adjustment.

"I'm not." Roberts sighed. "But, it's the best option we've got."

The numbers that showed the *Legacy*'s distance from the Cluster continued to increase while a second set of numbers that showed their distance to the debris field appeared and began decreasing. "I'm shutting down the engines," said Firebrandt. "We should drift right into the debris at this point. We'll just need a slight reverse nudge to stop."

"Oh my God," said Anne. "They've fired."

Firebrandt looked up in time to see a red beam emerge from the Cluster. At the same time, something slammed into the ship's stern and threw him headfirst over the wheel console. The last thing he remembered were all the lights going out and the screams from around the command deck.

As soon as the *Nicholas Sanson* jumped into Earth's solar system, Simon ordered Natalie to activate the holo viewer. The Earth appeared in the distance. Laura activated thrusters and accelerated to full speed. Right behind the *Sanson*, dozens of black, cylindrical war ships jumped into normal space and activated their own thrusters. Almost unnoticed in the pack was Arepno's silver egg-shaped craft.

"Simon." Natalie turned to face him. "I'm detecting one Cluster in orbit and ... I think there's an Earth ship running away from it."

"Let's see it." As Simon stood, Manuel Raton emerged from the captain's office and joined Suki Ellis beside the command chair.

"I'm picking this up on a satellite relay." Natalie touched a control and the view snapped onto a close-up of Earth. A black ship, silhouetted against a white cloudbank, moved away from a Cluster.

Simon stepped closer to the tank and pointed to a fuzzy patch he couldn't identify. "What's that?"

Laura squinted at the tank from her station. "I think it's a satellite debris field."

Fire joined Simon at the holo viewer, her head inclined. As she studied the ship, her eyes grew wide. "That ship's called the *Legacy*." She pointed to the name on the hull. "That's the name of my father's old privateer vessel."

Manuel moved up next to Fire, and studied the image. "I think it *is* your father's old privateer vessel." He entered the tank and pointed to patterns of light and shadow on the hull's surface. "You can see where the adobe additions discolored the erdonium hull."

"It can't be," said Fire.

Just then, a bright, red flash caused Manuel to throw his arm up over his eyes and he staggered backward out of the tank. The beam came from the Cluster, caught the *Legacy* on its EQ generator, and sent the ship into an end-over-end spiral.

"Oh my God!" Fire reached out toward the tumbling hologram, as though she could stop the ship by stopping its holographic image.

"I've got a fleet-wide signal," said Natalie. "I'm putting it on speakers."

"This is Commodore MacPhearson of the *Astrolus*," came a sonorous voice from the intercom. "We have a ship in trouble near the Cluster. I want the *Bismarck* and *Yamato* to get in there between the Cluster and the damaged ship right away. *Sanson*, you're the third fastest ship, do you have medical personnel?"

Simon nodded to Natalie who responded, "We don't have any doctors, but we have two emergency medical techs."

"That'll do," said MacPhearson. "Get in there, get that ship stabilized and help out anyone who's injured. All other ships, prepare for attack plan delta…"

Simon made a cutting motion across his neck and Natalie turned off the speakers. He nodded to Laura who adjusted course for the spiraling *Legacy*. He stepped back to the command seat and Fire followed on his heels. As he sat, he ordered the EMTs to the launch.

"May I go over there with them?" asked Fire.

Simon rubbed his hands together and looked at his console, avoiding Fire's gaze. "We don't know what we'll find over there."

Fire knelt down beside Simon. "I have a pretty good idea my father's over there – alive or dead. Either way, I've got to go over."

"Well someone's alive over there," said Laura.

Grateful to break away from Fire's intense gaze, Simon looked up at the holo tank. Fire turned and stood to watch as well. The *Legacy* fired thrusters, slowing her spin. As the ship straightened, two star cruisers shot past the wounded ship and positioned themselves in front of the Cluster. Fire sighed.

"We'll be in range to send out the launch in two minutes," said Laura.

Simon ground his teeth, then looked up at Fire. "You and Mr. Raton get down to the launch bay and see what you can do to help."

"Thank you." Fire turned and sprinted toward the elevator with Manuel hurrying to catch up.

"Tell the launch crew to wait for Dr. Ellis and Mr. Raton – but have them launch as soon as they're aboard and secure," ordered Simon.

Natalie carried out the orders as the Cluster fired again. This time the beam hit one of the two ships that had positioned themselves between the Cluster and the *Legacy*. Fog-like atmosphere burst from the ship's hull, indicating a breach, but the military crew locked down the breach almost as fast as it appeared.

"The launch says Suki and Manuel are aboard. They can depart any time," said Natalie.

Laura nodded ascent. "We're in good position. They can go across to the *Legacy* when they're ready."

"Tell them to launch." Simon put his hand on the back of Laura's chair and continued to watch the holo tank.

More ships began to form up between the Cluster and the *Legacy*. The Cluster fired again at the first ship it had hit. The ship spun away from the others and exploded. Two ships moved in and filled the gap made by the lost vessel.

The *Sanson's* launch could be seen on the screen, making its way to the *Legacy*.

The Cluster fired again at two other ships. Simon stepped closer to the tank. He suspected those ships had sustained damage also. The Cluster continued to fire as more Alliance and Colonial ships formed up. Another Earth ship exploded in a blinding flash.

"The launch reports it's docked on to *Legacy*. Someone opened the airlock for them," said Natalie with a faint smile.

Simon nodded, not taking his eyes from the holo tank. "Let's hear the fleet signals again."

"All ships in position," came one voice from the speakers.

The Cluster fired at another ship.

"This is the *Witch of Endor*, we've sustained heavy casualties and may have to withdraw."

"Stick with us for a few more minutes."

"All ships report target lock."

"This is Commodore MacPhearson. All ships … Fire!"

Natalie dimmed the holo tank's intensity as every ship in the fleet opened fire on the Cluster. The Cluster fired another shot and the ship that had identified itself as the *Witch of Endor* vanished in a flash. The Cluster fired again and destroyed another ship.

"Maintain firing solution," called MacPhearson.

Simon reached out and gripped Laura's console near the pilot's own white knuckles.

She focused on the display. "The *Legacy* has moved into the satellite debris field."

"I think we better take cover there as well." Simon's voice cracked.

Laura set the course and began moving the *Sanson* closer to the *Legacy*.

Within the tank, a blinding flash overwhelmed the dampers Natalie had set up. Simon looked away and found himself blinking at spots before his eyes. When he faced the tank again, he noticed it was empty. "Where's the signal?" he asked.

"Our sensors have been overloaded," reported Natalie. "We're blind."

"We got it," came a voice from the speaker. "The Cluster's been destroyed!"

Within moments, the speakers buzzed with cheers and

congratulations. Commodore MacPhearson's authoritative voice tried to gain control and calm the chatter. Laura rose to her feet. Simon turned and the two embraced. Natalie sat trembling at the communication's station, a lone tear running down her cheek.

Timothy Gibbs' eyes flew open. He looked around his apartment, confused. A Rd'dyggian held two people on his couch at gunpoint. A second Rd'dyggian approached him wielding a strange machine. "I'm back," he said, startled.

The Rd'dyggian with the machine lowered the device and studied him for a moment.

Swan jumped toward the other Rd'dyggian, but the warrior pushed him back onto the couch with his free hand.

"Oh," said Gibbs. "Guess this was a short break." He slumped back into his chair and heard a question just as he returned to the lab.

"What the hell just happened?" asked the woman.

Part IV: The New Clusters

And another angel came out from the altar, which had power over fire; and cried with a loud cry to him that had the sharp sickle saying, Thrust in thy sharp sickle, and gather the clusters of the vine of the earth; for her grapes are fully ripe.

Revelation 14:18

Chapter Fifteen

SUPPLICATION

Fire gasped when the airlock door opened and she found herself face-to-face with Junior Kimura, the best hover tractor and laser plow repairman from New Des Moines on Sufiro. She restrained the urge to ask what he was doing there when she looked beyond him and discovered that the ship she faced was, in fact, the house where she had grown up. She couldn't imagine how her father had managed to get the ship into space again.

"Sir, are there injured?" The question from *Sanson's* EMT brought Fire back to the present.

Fire stepped across to the *Legacy* and out of the EMTs' way. "Yes, we have quite a few – Doc Krishnamurty could use the help, thanks," said Junior.

"You brought Parvati Krishnamurty out here?" Fire remembered the gray-haired, wiry doctor from her childhood.

Junior nodded. He pointed along the hallway. "The doc's up in the command deck with your father and Roberts. I haven't been able to get the lights on yet, do you have flashlights?" When Fire held hers aloft, Junior nodded, satisfied. He looked at the two EMTs. "Can you two come aft with me? I've got injured in engineering."

The two EMTs grabbed their gear from the launch and made their way aft with Junior, leaving Manuel and Fire alone. "Come on." She turned on her flashlight.

The walk through the darkened corridor was eerie – especially as the flashlight touched on familiar door and hatch markings. Although she worried about her father, Fire wondered what was happening outside. As they'd crossed from the *Sanson*, ships had barreled past them to form up between the *Legacy* and the Cluster. She had strained her neck to get a better

view through the windows to see the action. There had been
some red flashes and one ship had spun away from the battle
group.

As they approached the command deck, they heard quiet
but agitated voices. Fire stepped up her pace. Manuel hurried to
keep up and nearly tripped over some debris. They reached the
command deck and found it bathed in red emergency lighting.
The holo tank at the front of the deck had died. Twisted metal
and wire tendrils sat smoking where the engineering console
had once been. A sheet covered something on the deck near
the ruined console. Roberts hovered next to the wheel console,
typing in commands. Fire scanned the deck until she found her
father. He sat on the floor beside the console opposite engineering. Doc Krishnamurty shined a flashlight into his eyes. Fire
ran past Roberts and knelt down next to her father.

He looked up with watery eyes. "Fire, what the devil are
you doing here?" He croaked the words out. He wore a ban-
dage on his forehead and a sling around his arm.

"Save your strength." The doctor looked up at Fire. "He has
a concussion and a broken arm; damned lucky for an eighty-
one year-old man who took a tumble over the wheel console
and slammed into the forward wall. More lucky than Mary Seaton." She cast a meaningful glance at the sheet-covered mound
at the engineering station.

"Can you try it again?" asked Roberts in a gentle voice
from the wheel.

Fire looked up and recognized Anne McClintlock at the
console where she knelt. Anne seemed to be having difficulty
getting her fingers to work the controls. Fire stood and helped
Anne out of the seat. "I think you better have the doc check you
out." She looked up at Roberts. "What are you trying to do?"

"Fire!" he exclaimed, with a genuine smile. "I'm trying to
get the holo tank working, see if we can find out what's going on outside. I'm also trying to get engine control working
through this station."

"I might be able to help with that," said Manuel. He had
joined his brother at the front of the command deck.

"So can I," volunteered Juan, who rose unsteadily to his
feet.

"I think you'd better sit there for a few minutes." Manuel patted his brother on the shoulder. He stepped over to Roberts and the two talked for a moment. Roberts pointed to the ruined engineering console and explained what he needed. Manuel nodded, went over to the console and aimed his flashlight into the smoky mess.

"I think I have hologram control." Fire pushed a button and the holo tank flickered to life. The ships in the fleet unloaded everything they had on the Cluster. Light flashed through the deck and the holo tank went dead again. "Damn." Fire blinked back spots as she checked the readings. "That blast overloaded the sensors. It's going to take me a few minutes to get it back on line."

"What happened?" asked the captain, as he stood. "Did they destroy it?"

As though in answer, a shock wave shuddered through the ship. The captain stumbled, but steadied himself on the wall. Anne caught her breath and Manuel swore as he shocked himself on a bare wire. Roberts floated over, took Manuel's flashlight, and examined his finger. Manuel waved him off. "Just bit me a little," he said. "Do you have any wire clippers?"

Roberts produced a pair from the hover chair and then held the flashlight while Manuel returned to work. A few minutes later, the white lights came back on and fresh air blew from a nearby vent.

The EMTs from the *Sanson* appeared in the command deck's doorway and took in the scene. The doctor stepped over to them and they conferred with one another in hushed tones – heads close together. The doctor pointed to Anne and Juan. "Those two are our priority patients here." She then left the command deck to tend to more seriously wounded elsewhere on the ship.

One EMT helped Anne to her feet and led her from the deck. The other talked to Juan for a moment, gave him a pill from his kit, then followed the other EMT.

"How are the sensors doing?" Firebrandt knelt down next to his daughter.

"Just about got it." She typed a command into the computer and the holo tank flickered to life once again. The fleet dispersed from the formation.

"They're leaving in a hurry." Firebrandt's brow furrowed. "What's going on?"

Fire shifted to another sensor bank. The holo tank now displayed a view over the Earth's North Pole. Sunlight glinted off something reflective. Fire zoomed in. Three Clusters had arrived and the fleet repositioned itself to intercept the new arrivals.

Firebrandt approached the tank and began tallying ships. "I count twenty-one Colonial and Alliance ships moving in."

Manuel looked up from the engineering console. "That means over a third of the ships are disabled."

"Can we help them out?" asked Firebrandt.

Roberts shook his head. "We've managed to restore some basic thruster control, but we can't get there in time." He looked down at Mary Seaton's body on the deck. "Besides, I think we've already done our share for this cause."

Firebrandt looked at the sheet, as though seeing it for the first time, then turned away. "Perhaps you're right." His voice caught and a tear ran down his cheek.

Mark Ellis blinked in confusion as Eva Cooper backed away and joined Kirsten. "I'm okay. This isn't Mark's fault. We can't expect him to control his impulses. Maybe you'd better take him upstairs."

"Is that a good idea?" Kirsten's voice shuddered as she knelt down and picked up the broken plate, sitting the pieces on the table one by one.

"The emotions he's expressing are largely positive," said the doctor. "I think it would be best if he keeps expressing positive emotions. Try not to let him descend into depression and he should be okay."

"What if he does descend into depression?"

"Come get me. It would be safe to give him one more dose of Proxom, but..."

"He might not reestablish contact with the Cluster." Kirsten stood and took a step toward Mark.

"This all presumes the Cluster will have me back," he said. Both Eva and Kirsten started when he spoke. "Just because I'm having a hard time controlling my emotions – just because I'm horny as all get out – doesn't mean I can't think. The problem is that I'm acting before I think."

Kirsten's lip curled up and she took Mark's hand and led him up the stairs.

"I'm sorry – about Eva," he muttered once they reached the hallway at the top of the stairs. "All I could see was a beautiful female face. It didn't seem to matter who it belonged to."

"Don't worry about it." Kirsten's words were flat. She led him into the bedroom and closed the door behind them. "It's the drugs the doctor gave you." She removed her blazer and unfastened her blouse's top button. "I think you can make it up to me." She stepped over to Mark and put her arms around him.

He returned the embrace and his hands roved down and fondled her buttocks for a moment then moved up and began untucking her blouse. She pushed him onto the bed then sat on his lap and unbuttoned his shirt, letting her hands run through the hairs on his chest while he nuzzled her neck. With one hand, he undid another button on her blouse and his hand wandered over her skin. Her nipple responded to his thumb's gentle pressure. His mouth moved up to her earlobe as he cupped her fleshy breast.

As he explored her body, he began to register a subtle change. Though the weight on his lap hadn't changed, the fleshy, warm breast became unyielding and marble-chill. His other hand no longer grasped a soft, cloth-covered backside. Instead, it seemed as though he grasped polished stone. He pulled back and found himself gazing into a black-haired woman's piercing green eyes. He knew this woman – had met her before. He must have returned to the Cluster. This woman was the manifestation of the Cluster's persona.

"Why do you pull away?" asked the green-eyed woman. "I need you. I need your kind to help me build my legacy." She reached down and gave Mark an intimate caress. "Once we've built our new home at the galactic core, you can join me. You can imagine me with the soft flesh you long for so much."

He let out a low moan but shook his head. "Why do you have to end your physical existence?" He allowed his hand to remain on the marble-like breast. As he caressed it, it grew warmer – whether from his own hand's heat, his imagination, or some rising heat within the Cluster itself, he didn't know.

"We are ancient in your eyes. We have traveled as far as it is possible for us to travel. We have seen stars born. We have seen them live and die. We have seen their matter recycled into new stars. We have seen galaxies collide and move apart, becoming whole but taking on new forms." As she spoke, she began to age. Her hair grayed and her skin wrinkled. The breast in Mark's hand grew languid and he released it. "We have seen many life forms come and go and we fear we shall never achieve any more than we already have." She stood up and walked a short distance away.

"What about other galaxies? Couldn't you travel to other parts of the universe?" he asked.

"We cannot." When she turned, her hair was black again. Her features, as before, were sculpted perfection. "The gravity waves are too weak for us to travel from our home cluster to other clusters orbiting the Milky Way. We cannot ride those waves that connect one galaxy to another. Even your people do not see a way to accomplish such a feat."

"Just because we don't see the solution now, doesn't mean we won't see it in the future," said Mark. "That's the beauty of evolution. We learn and we change through the generations."

She took another step closer. Her green eyes turned dull and glistened with unshed tears. "We cannot evolve and your people do not want to stay with us forever. Even now, they withdraw from us. There are people on Earth who are helping them leave. You are the only one who has sought to come back." She shook her head. "In the quantum computer we build, we will no longer be limited to a physical form. We can explore a world limited only by our imagination and the imagination of others who wish to join us. We gain more as others discover our beacon, respond, and join us in the perfect world we'll build."

Mark frowned. "The tachyon burst unleashed when the beacon and quantum computer are activated will destroy most life in the galaxy. There's no guarantee anyone else will ever arrive." Mark stood and took her hand. "What if we worked together? Why must you absorb us into your being? Couldn't we find a way to cooperate?"

She pulled her hand away from his. As he reached out to take it back, it shrank from him and changed. Her arms transformed into spheres, as did her legs. Soon, she had morphed into a floating, cluster of spheres. "Cooperate? With this?" Four of the spheres unrolled tentacle-like and became arms and legs once again. Another sphere became her head and she resumed her human appearance. "In this world, your mind must be inside me to converse with me. There can be no other cooperation unless we meet within the quantum computer's reality."

"There must be another way." Ellis pursed his lips and tried to think.

"Perhaps there is." The woman looked over her shoulder and Ellis noticed a door he had not seen before. The door opened and Tim Gibbs entered.

In Southern Arizona, G'Liat balanced his brain scan device on Timothy Gibbs' head. The warrior closed his own eyes and found himself looking out at a darkened human laboratory. He realized he must have been seeing the view as a human would see it with their light-insensitive eyes. Computers lined one wall and a table with charts and graphs stood in the room's center.

"It's changed," said a booming voice from all around him.

"What's changed?" asked G'Liat.

The view through the warrior's eyes shifted from side to side and he realized Gibbs must have shaken his head back and forth. "The room. I had returned to my apartment for a moment, then I came back to the lab and it changed. It's like it had been two days ago."

"That's because you're in a different Cluster now," said the warrior. "Two days ago, the Cluster must have copied the lab to another Cluster – like a backup."

"Why would I be in the backed-up version?" came the booming voice.

G'Liat thought Gibbs asked a good question and he had suspicions about the subject but he didn't voice them aloud, afraid he would upset Gibbs. Instead, he had a mission to accomplish. "Perhaps you should talk to your supervisor," suggested the warrior.

"That does seem like a good idea."

G'Liat watched through Gibbs' eyes as he stood, turned, and moved toward a door. Gibbs entered a room filled with artifacts and antiquities, not unlike G'Liat's house on Rd'dyggia. An image of Earth filled the sky overhead. G'Liat sensed the view could be changed to reflect any place the Cluster had visited, much like the view in a holo tank. As Gibbs faced straight ahead, G'Liat saw Mark Ellis looking disheveled, talking to a woman with long dark hair and striking, green eyes. The woman's features were indistinct. She seemed more like an idealized sculpture of a human woman rather than a real woman. She lacked the myriad little flaws that human skin developed due to aging and damage.

With a force of will, G'Liat separated himself from Gibbs. His feet touched the hardwood floor and he clasped his hands behind his back.

Somehow, Mark Ellis was not surprised when G'Liat materialized next to Tim Gibbs.

"My name is G'Liat," said the warrior. "I represent the planet Rd'dyggia. We object to your actions, which will destroy life in this galaxy."

"What manner of creature are you?" The woman's eyebrows came together as she approached G'Liat. She put her hands on his shoulders and morphed into a Rd'dyggian female – a little larger than G'Liat with the same bald head and prehensile purple mustache. "Ah, yes, you call yourselves Rd'dyggians, which means 'the chosen' in your language. We encountered you on our travels." She looked at the ceiling above, which displayed a Rd'dyggian star cruiser. A green beam shot toward the craft and then the view shifted again. This time space vessels filled the sky, taking positions and firing on one another. Some were egg-shaped Rd'dyggian star cruisers. Others resembled flying wedges. Ellis recognized the wedges as Tzrn ships. They watched a thousand-year old scene from the Rd'dyggian-Tzrn war.

The scene shifted again. A mist-filled, lush swamp teaming with purple vegetation appeared. For a moment, Ellis thought he could smell ammonia and sulfur, characteristic of Rd'dyggia's surface. Great war machines pushed through the swamp, firing at other war machines. Rd'dyggian soldiers poured from the first war machines with hand weapons and fired at spider-like beings from the other machines.

The view returned to the Earth. The woman morphed back into her idealized human form, but didn't take her hands from G'Liat. "Your kind is obsessed with conquest," she said. "Perhaps even more so than the humans. We deemed you inadequate to our needs since you would no doubt try to conquer us and we would have to destroy you." She looked into G'Liat's eyes. "I admire your ingenuity getting here, but we cannot merge with your kind."

"You show great intuition, my lady. I do not believe humans are the best species for you to merge with," said G'Liat, "but I don't presume to suggest Rd'dyggians as an alternative. I had another option in mind."

"We do not wish another option. With humanity's help, we have found a compelling future." She stepped toward Tim Gibbs and put her hands on his shoulders. "We will build a legacy, much as humans do. We will end our physical form and continue in a world without limits."

"Do you have any guarantee that you *will* continue?" G'Liat held his hands out. "You could die and your consciousness would be reduced to algorithms. There is no guarantee you will awaken in the afterlife Gibbs is building. Something that approximates you may wake up and it may remember being you, but it may not be you at all. Your experience might end. What's more, Mr. Gibbs indicated his laboratory has changed. From what I observed in his apartment and from what I know about the human resistance, I suspect they have destroyed one of your kind already and are massing to attack again."

"What!" Ellis looked up at the ceiling just as the view shifted again. Several ships approached. His old ship, the *Astrolus*, led the battle group. The *Nicholas Sanson* brought up the rear.

"They can injure us," admitted the woman. "They cannot destroy us."

"Why be injured at all?" Ellis thought he recognized an opportunity. "Retreat today. Come back and negotiate."

"You were right to seek Earth," interjected G'Liat.

The woman looked at him with building interest.

G'Liat took a step closer. "It is a planet where evolution has happened rapidly. This world's creatures grow and change in mere millennia while many other beings are much more stagnant. I submit, you picked the wrong species to be your appendages." He flourished his hand and a sperm whale's image appeared. Ellis grunted. He couldn't help but admire how G'Liat had already learned to manipulate the Cluster reality.

"These creatures have the largest brains on the planet," said the Rd'dyggian. "They are as eager to see the sights you can show them as you are to have input from evolving creatures. They are less obsessed with death and more with the hunt. You and the whales would make formidable allies."

"Wait," interjected Ellis, "I thought you said the Rd'dyggians could not be trusted."

"No." The woman spoke in an undertone, as though she forced herself to tolerate a petulant child. "We said the Rd'dyggians were inadequate to our needs. Often times their motives are far more transparent than humans', making them far more trustworthy than you."

A woman with golden eyes appeared next to the first woman. Other than her eyes, she was identical in all respects to the first woman. The green-eyed woman took the whale image from G'Liat and handed it to the golden-eyed woman. "The Rd'dyggian has proposed an interesting alternative to the humans. Perhaps we can avoid the end of our physical existence – of our kind and theirs – of the ... uncertainties inherent in ending physical existence."

The golden-eyed woman vanished.

"What does all this mean for my memory core?" asked Tim Gibbs.

Richard – or T'Li'Ch'D, as he was known in his own language – had found a large school of squid. He swam through them, scooping them up in his massive mouth and crushing their shells between his lower teeth and upper jaw. *The hunt is the art*, he thought with joy as the tasty morsels went down his throat. He looked out over the ocean and remembered all the sights he'd seen in his long life, ranging from the Caribbean's coral reefs and the clear blue waters to glaciers near Iceland. In those northern waters, he'd battled a ferocious giant squid. He still carried the battle's scars with pride and it had made a tasty meal.

The ocean carried other dangers as well. Orcas and sharks had attacked and tried to carry him into the depths to drown him. Richard had survived by his cunning, speed, and sheer power. He gulped down another mouthful of squid and realized he should return to the surface for air.

"The cycle continues," he said as he broke the water's surface. Night had fallen while he had been under water. The recent storm had broken and stars filled the sky above. He rolled over onto his side so he could get a better look at the stars. Again, he considered all the places he'd seen, but he found himself wondering what it would be like to travel among those stars. What a grand hunt that would be!

As those thoughts occurred to him, he began to float upward, out of the water and toward the stars themselves. The waters receded below him. The horizon was no longer a flat line, but an arc that fell away from him. He began to discern landmasses and then the clouds themselves fell away below him. He looked out to each side and the stars were clearer than he had ever seen them before.

He swam upward and then swam downward again. In a panic, he began to wonder where this wonderful new ocean's surface was. As he sought the surface, the most beautiful female whale he'd ever seen approached him. She had captivating golden eyes and she rubbed herself against him, making him feel stirrings he had not experienced in many years.

"Breathe," she commanded him. "I have created a medium for you that is both water and atmosphere. You can breathe."

Though he could feel water all around his body, he took a tentative breath and air filled his lungs. He exhaled and then took another breath. He then swam around in a great vertical circle, excited to be able to breathe as he swam.

Aboard the *Sanson*, Simon stared slack jawed at the view in the holo tank. Just as the fleet regrouped to attack the three Clusters over Earth's North Pole, one Cluster broke formation and made a giant loop-the-loop. "What the devil is it doing?" he asked.

Laura stood up next to Simon and stared at the image wide-eyed. "Is it getting ready to attack?"

"The Cluster has lost interest in humans," said Natalie. "They've found someone else, someone more suitable to their needs."

Both Simon and Laura turned and looked at her.

"What does it mean?" asked Laura.

"Life in the galaxy won't be destroyed in a big tachyon burst," answered Natalie.

Simon let out a relieved sigh despite his skepticism at Natalie's words. "Then we're safe."

"No." Natalie shook her head. "We're not safe at all."

The golden-eyed woman materialized next to the green-eyed woman and a broad smile appeared on her face. John Mark Ellis shuddered as a violet-eyed woman also materialized. "I like the way these whales make me feel," said the golden-eyed woman. "I feel alive. I want to explore. There is no end to the universe."

"What about our future and our legacy?" asked the violet-eyed woman.

"Our legacy will be our children," said the golden-eyed woman. "We have always had the ability to reproduce. It's the desire we lacked. I want to make more of my kind. I want them to see the universe as I see it. There can be no greater legacy. It is far better than living within a machine."

"I feel your joy." The green-eyed woman turned and looked at Timothy Gibbs with something like contempt. "There is a joy in the machine you want to build, but it is fleeting. Once it is built, the joy will be gone and you will, once again, worry about your future and endings yet to come." The green-eyed woman looked at her two sisters. "The humans are not grateful for what we have given them. The Titans were not grateful. The whale is grateful. I say we join with the whales. They shall be our new appendages."

The violet-eyed woman looked worried. "Is that wise? Should we discard one appendage in favor of another on a whim?"

The green-eyed woman smiled. "There are many kinds of legacies. A legacy of continued life seems better than a legacy of death."

"Indeed," echoed the golden-eyed woman.

Without warning, Gibbs and G'Liat vanished. Ellis thought he'd seen a self-satisfied smirk on the warrior's face right before he disappeared. The antiquities in the room also vanished and Ellis found himself floating in water. The green-eyed woman swam up to him and before his eyes, her legs merged together into a tail and her arms became fins. Her still-human face smiled and she said, "Your kind must learn to seek joy." As her head transformed into a sperm whale's, he realized he faced his bedroom's ceiling on Nantucket.

Kirsten dropped onto the bed next to him. "You're back!" She scooped him up in her arms and kissed him. "When you went slack in my arms, I was afraid we'd lost you for good, like Coffin."

Ellis pulled Kirsten close. "I think the Cluster has found a new ally. To be honest, I'm terrified of what the future will bring."

Richard noticed a group of cylindrical objects gathering nearby. They resembled a school of squid. Like squid, they seemed somewhat menacing. Also like squid, he somehow knew they

were to be hunted. He vocalized his stunning sound – the loud
gong that sperm whales make – and swam toward the cylindrical objects. He then made another sound – a sound like laughter.

Aboard the *Legacy*, the repairs to the command deck proceeded.
White light bathed the consoles and fresh air circulated. Mary
Seaton's body had been carried down to the infirmary and the
EMTs had returned to the *Sanson*. Fire and Manuel decided to
remain aboard *Legacy* to help where they could.

Captain Ellison Firebrandt watched the scene unfold in
the holo tank with growing confusion. As the battle group had
formed to challenge the Clusters, one Cluster broke formation
and performed a loop. Now that same Cluster broke away from
the rest. A golden beam issued from it, vaporizing an Alpha
Coman battleship. As the Cluster plowed through the line of
ships, it destroyed two more. After which, the Cluster jumped
away.

The human fleet tried to regroup. As they did, the other
two Clusters retreated a short distance and also jumped.

"Dad," said Fire from the computer console. "EQ frequencies to the outside galaxy have just cleared. I can reach Alpha
Coma, Sufiro, anywhere."

Manuel and Juan joined Firebrandt and his daughter at the
front of the command deck. "Does this mean we won?"

Roberts looked around at the destroyed engineering console, at the missing rivets in the wall, and at the bloodstained
deck. "I don't think 'won' is the right word. Somehow, I think
the Cluster has found a new legacy."

Firebrandt nodded and looked back toward Roberts and
around at the damaged command deck. "And we must rebuild
ours." The captain turned to Fire. "Let's see if we can find someone who can help us get this ship rebuilt. I think it may be time
to return home and attend to the harvest."

"Aye aye, Captain." Fire winked at her father.

"I dare say your work is done, young man." G'Liat spoke to Swan as he packed the brain scan device into the case. "I would recommend that you find transport to Sufiro."

Edmund Swan stood up from the couch, casting a wary glance at Rizonex who had lowered his weapon. "What do you mean?"

"The Cluster has relinquished its hold on humankind," said the warrior. "They have found another species more to their liking. As a result, they have abandoned their project at the galactic core."

"That's right," said Timothy Gibbs. Tears ran down his face. "They're gone. There will be no quantum computer."

Maria Gonzalez stood up and slapped Swan on the back. "We won!"

Tim Gibbs fell from the chair into a broken heap, crying.

"No," said Swan. He helped his friend stand, took him in his arms, and gave him a hug, then helped him lie down on the couch. "We've still got a lot of work to do."

G'Liat closed the clasps on his case, and hefted it over his shoulder. "As do I. If you'll excuse me." G'Liat joined Rizonex at the door.

"Wait a minute," said Swan. "You still haven't told us what you did."

"You'll find out soon enough," said the warrior. "Talk to Ellis. I'm sure it'll be a whale of a good tale." With a brief nod, the Rd'dyggian left the apartment, with Rizonex on his heels.

Chapter Sixteen

THE NEW GALAXY

Three days after the Cluster left Earth, Mark Ellis and Kirsten Smart invited their friends and family to Nantucket for dinner. Ellison Firebrandt, Roberts, Manuel, and Fire came down from the *Legacy*. Firebrandt had secured a space dock for repairs.

Mark greeted them at the door. He hugged his mother. "You made good time."

Fire sighed. "We were able to land at the Nantucket spaceport. It's close by..."

"But it reminds us how many people have died here on Earth." A lump formed in Mark's throat.

Firebrandt grasped his grandson's shoulder.

Manuel and Roberts brought in an antigrav unit loaded with food. They took it to the kitchen and set to work. Mark peeked in and smiled as Roberts chopped vegetables. Manuel brought out a mix of chile peppers and sprinkled them into a pot he'd placed on the stovetop.

A short time later, Edmund Swan arrived. He held up a bottle containing an electric-red liquid. "It's saguaro wine," he explained to Mark and Kirsten. "Carlos, a plumber and resistance fighter back in Southern Arizona gave it to me."

"How's Tim Gibbs doing?" Kirsten led Mark and Edmund to a table where glasses waited.

"Improving." Edmund removed a stopper from the bottle and poured a glass. "He's suffering a hefty dose of guilt for helping the Cluster and a hefty dose of depression because the quantum computer he dreamed about will never be built. His old supervisor, Jerry Lawrence, checked him into the psychiatric ward at St. Mary's Hospital down in the Bisbee Sector. It's quiet and peaceful down in that part of Southern Arizona. He's

236

got a tough road ahead, but I think he'll recover." He handed the first glass to Kirsten and poured a second.

"It's a good thing he has you as a friend," said Kirsten, lifting the glass of electric-red wine.

Mark took the second glass of wine and sat down on the couch. He took a sip. His eyes widened and he pursed his lips. He gave an appreciative nod, then set the glass on the table next to him and looked at the floor.

A weight settled next to him. He looked up and met his mother's gaze. "What's the matter?" she asked.

"I suppose I'm feeling a little like Timothy Gibbs," he said. "After all, I led the Cluster to Earth in the first place."

"You can't blame yourself, Mark." Ellison Firebrandt stood beside the fireplace, his arms crossed. "The Cluster was attracted to humans." He strode over, tugged on his pant legs and knelt down next to Mark's chair. "Feeling guilty because the Cluster found your thoughts and emotions interesting is like saying you're feeling guilty because you're human." The old privateer captain smiled. "And you know something? You might be the most human person I know."

Mark snorted. "Once I brought the Cluster here, I couldn't get rid of them."

Firebrandt looked up into his grandson's eyes. "What counts is that you tried. No one person – or ship for that matter – could do it alone."

Ellis's jaw tightened. "G'Liat did."

"G'Liat did not solve the problem." Fire clasped her son's hand. "He just changed it. Who knows what the Cluster's up to now."

Kirsten sat down next to Fire and sipped her wine. "I shudder any time I think about it. The Cluster is now a symbiont with a creature whose mantra is 'the hunt is the art.'"

"Why do you suppose he did it?" Mark's curiosity overrode his frustration. "Why did he introduce the whales and the Cluster? Somehow, I think he had a motive besides stopping the galaxy's destruction."

"No doubt," came a singsong voice from the door. Mark looked up. Arepno stood in the doorway holding a bowl of something that resembled purple gruel. He set the bowl down on the coffee table. Mark looked around at other confused expressions. "It's a Rd'dyggian specialty called ruas'ordah." Mark looked at Kirsten, who shrugged. He turned to his grandfather who shook his head. Arepno moved to the kitchen table, retrieved a tortilla chip and dipped it in, then popped it into his mouth.

Manuel picked up a tortilla chip. He hesitated a moment, then stepped over and dipped it into the ruas'ordah, then nodded. "Not bad," he said. "It even has a little spice to it."

Firebrandt stood and bowed to his old friend. "Arepno, what do you think G'Liat was up to?"

"G'Liat has connections on my world and beyond." Arepno stuck a finger into the purple gruel. "He, like many of my people, fears one thing above all – the eventual human domination of the galaxy." The Rd'dyggian lifted his hand to his mouth and the purple mustache-like growth began shoveling the gruel in.

Mark's brow furrowed. "There's one thing I don't understand then. If you knew G'Liat was so dangerous, why did you take me to him when I first arrived on your world?"

"Because I thought he could help you with your quest." Arepno scooped up more of the purple dip. "I believed you already understood him to be dangerous. In the end, he did help you make contact with the Cluster as you desired."

Firebrandt turned and looked at the pipes on the mantel. After a moment, he looked down at Mark. "Do you have any tobacco for those pipes?"

"I do indeed." Mark brightened for a moment before he remembered who had given him the tobacco. "Old Man Coffin gave me some."

"That seems fitting." Firebrandt selected a pipe. "We shall smoke to his memory."

Kirsten rose to her feet, wobbled a moment and sloshed just a little wine. "If you're going to smoke to his memory, do it outside. The food in here smells too good."

Mark selected a pipe from the rack, then led his grandfather to the door. Before they went outside, he looked over his shoulder. Eva Cooper came down the stairs. She smiled. Kirsten went to her, took her by the elbow and introduced her to Swan, Arepno, and Roberts.

Out in front of the house, Mark and Firebrandt packed their pipes with the tobacco Ellis kept in a pouch in his trousers pocket. They smoked in companionable silence for a time. Mark's thoughts drifted to Coffin and sailing the galactic core aboard the *Pequod*. He would miss his teacher and his friend, but his grandfather's presence comforted him. He thought he should say something to Firebrandt about Coffin, but every time words started to form, his throat tightened. He looked up the street and noticed three people approaching. He soon recognized Simon, Laura, and Natalie from the *Sanson*. He stood and greeted them. He tamped down his pipe and led the guests inside.

Kirsten approached and smiled at her crewmates. She narrowed her gaze at Ellis. "I thought you went outside to pollute the clean island air with your pipe."

Mark smiled. "My grandfather's doing a fine job all by himself." He went to the kitchen, grabbed two bowls, filled one with chips and scooped up some of Arepno's purple ruas'ordah into the other. "I'm not about to let everyone else hoard the food, though."

Before Mark could go back outside, Firebrandt stepped through the door. "It turns out we have a surprise guest tonight." He stepped aside and Senator Herbert Firebrandt entered.

The senator looked around at the crowded room open-mouthed, then looked down at his own somber, gray trousers and jacket. "If I'd known that I was coming to a party, I would have dressed for the occasion." He looked up and his eyes met his half brother's. "What you did…" He shook his head. "That will go down in the history books."

"I think our mother would have been rather astonished," said Ellison.

"She would have also been proud." Herbert clasped his brother's hand. He leaned in and Mark could just make out his words. "I believe she loved you more than she ever said."

Ellison pursed his lips. "It's not what she said. It's the actions she took." He shook his head. "It's all in the past and I look forward to getting to know you after all this time."

Mark took a step closer to the half brothers. "So, Senator, what brings you to Nantucket?"

Herbert looked up and searched the room. Mark followed his gaze and noticed Eva Cooper. "As it turns out, I came to speak to the surgeon general of the Gaean Alliance." He looked down at his feet for a moment. "The Earth – hell, the whole galaxy – is in an upheaval. People are calling for Jenna Walker's resignation after she helped the Cluster. The problem is that the Cluster affected almost everyone. There are real questions about whether she was responsible for her actions or not."

Mark looked to his mother, who looked to Manuel.

"To be honest," said Fire, who had just poured herself a glass of Edmund Swan's Saguaro wine, "she seems far less responsible than the Titans who sat on their furry asses all through this. What's going to happen to them?"

"The Alpha Centaurans, Zahari, and Tzrn are calling for a change of leadership," explained the senator. "As for the humans – I think we need to get our own affairs back in order. Perhaps we should even discuss reuniting Earth and her colonies." He looked over at Eva. "I'd like you to help me. Rebuilding Earth's government is going to be a tough job."

Eva nodded. "Yes, sir. I'll do whatever I can."

The senator then turned to Mark. "I also came to offer you something." He reached in his pocket and pulled out a silver star. "I think you've earned this."

Mark Ellis took the star from the senator and held it in his palm. It was an Alpha Coma captain's star. He closed his fingers around it and a lump formed in his throat. He met Kirsten's gaze, then showed her the star.

She gasped. "It's what you've always wanted."

Simon approached from behind Kirsten, looked at the star, and smiled. "Congratulations, sir."

"I don't..." Mark shook his head. "I don't know if I deserve this," he stammered at last.

The senator grasped Mark's shoulder. "There's no question you deserve it. Also, we need your expertise. You know the whales better than most. We need someone who can speak to them as well as the Clusters who have joined with them."

John Mark looked down at the star in his hand, his brow furrowed. He'd looked for Richard the day after the Cluster departed Earth. He'd found no sign of the bull, and other whales had gone missing as well. Unlike humans, their bodies couldn't be found. Their utter disappearance was a mystery. "I'd like to help, if I can," said Mark.

"At least consider a reserve appointment," urged the senator. "You don't have to give me your answer tonight."

"That's a good thing," said Roberts from the kitchen, "because dinner is ready."

"Unless you'd rather stand around talking all night," added Manuel.

Laughter erupted from around the room and people shuffled toward the kitchen to fill their plates from the pots on the stove and the bowls on the kitchen counter.

As the dinner drew to a close, Senator Herbert Firebrandt stepped up to his brother and shook his hand. "I'm glad we met at last."

"Likewise," said Ellison. "When you get some time, my invitation to visit Sufiro is still open."

"I may take you up on that," said the senator. "I have a feeling I'll need to rest a while once we've sorted everything out." After saying the rest of their good-byes, the senator and Eva Cooper left together for Washington, D.C. to find lodgings and make plans for the coming week.

"We should get going, too," said Simon to Kirsten and Mark. "I need to see how repairs to the ship are coming."

"Sounds good." Kirsten nodded. She still had a lopsided grin after drinking the Saguaro wine, but she held her head as though a headache loomed. "I'll be up tomorrow and we'll check in with TransGalactic – see if anyone's still there." Her grin dissolved into a frown.

Simon held out his hand. "Captain, can we expect you back on the ship tomorrow?"

Mark took Simon's hand and shook it. "I'm not sure." He reached into his pocket and took out the silver star. "I need to sleep on this decision." He looked at Kirsten, who narrowed her gaze. "I think we need to spend some time talking."

Simon pursed his lips. "I don't envy you the decision." He

joined Natalie and Laura who waited by the door.

Ellison turned around. Roberts sat next to the couch in his hover chair, dozing. Edmund Swan sat next to him, hands folded over his chest, staring at the ceiling. Fire and Manuel stood together at the sink, washing dishes and speaking to one another in hushed tones. Ellison faced Mark and Kirsten again. Mark continued to gaze at the silver star. He looked up and met Kirsten's gaze. Ellison remembered decisions he had made. At one time, he'd considered giving up life as a privateer captain and buying a trading vessel. Just Suki, Roberts, and him. How different might his life have been?

He cleared his throat. "I think it's time we got back to the ship ourselves."

"We've almost got the dishes cleaned," protested Fire, but Ellison inclined his head toward Mark. She gave a curt nod and picked up a dishtowel, dried her hands, and passed the towel to Manuel.

Firebrandt looked down at Swan, "Care for a ride back to Sufiro?"

Swan sat up and smiled. "If you've got room for one more passenger."

"Passenger?" asked Roberts, startling awake. "No passengers on the *Legacy*. You'll have to work for your passage."

"I was afraid you'd say that." Swan struggled to his feet.

Mark hugged his mother and shook Manuel's hand. Ellison took his grandson aside. "My mother stranded me on Sufiro almost fifty years ago," he whispered. "At the time, I hated her for it because I thought it meant my career as a privateer captain had ended. However, as I stand here and look over my family – not just you and Fire, but Edmund, Manuel, Kirsten, Arepno and so many more – I realize she gave me a far better life than I'd ever dreamed possible."

"Are you saying I should stay with the *Sanson?* That I should stay with Kirsten?" asked Mark.

Ellison smiled at his grandson. "All I'm saying is make sure you consider all your options before you decide. Dreams are tricky things, as you learned when your mind was in the Cluster. You can get caught up in them and lose track of where reality is taking you."

"What are you two conspiring about over there?" called Fire. "Our ride's here."

"Keep your options open, son, and you'll do fine." Ellison patted Mark on the shoulder. He stepped out the door and into a foggy night with Manuel, Fire, Roberts, and Swan. They all piled into Charlie Rogers' hover van.

They rode to the spaceport in silence and listened to the foghorn's mournful bellowing through the dark night. Ellison imagined being a lost soul, called home – called to rest.

The captain piloted the launch back up to *Legacy* while most everyone slumbered in the back. Fire crept up into the co-pilot's chair, next to her father.

"I thought you would stay behind, on Nantucket," he said to her. "By coming back to Sufiro, you're giving up your career … your home…"

"It's Mark's home, now," she said. "The Earth has changed and I'm not sure I belong anymore. I guess I fit in more with the pirates of Sufiro than the heirs of this new Earth."

"The whole galaxy has changed." Ellison looked out at the stars. "I don't think anything is ever going to be the same."

Fire looked at the *Legacy* and noticed the new landing rockets that Junior Kimura had installed, folded up against the ship's body. "Not even the *Legacy* is the same. I gather the homestead needs repair."

Ellison nodded. "You know, two old men like Roberts and I don't need such a large house … I don't know if I'd rebuild at all if it were just the two of us. We could get on just fine in the ship."

"I don't know if I'd trust you two in a ship that can take off and land. You got into enough trouble as it is." She looked back at the men, sleeping in the back. "Manuel and I could always move in with you … help you with the homestead."

"I'd like that." Ellison flashed a wicked smile. "The real reason you're doing this is because the ship functions again, aren't you?"

"Why be stuck on an island when I can go on adventures in the galaxy?" Fire stood, hugged her father around the shoulders, and then joined the others in the back of the shuttle.

The next morning, Simon Yermakov turned around when the elevator doors opened. He frowned for a moment when John Mark Ellis entered with Kirsten Smart, but he stood up and offered him the captain's chair. Mark placed his hand on the back of the chair.

"Welcome aboard, sir," said the first officer.

"Thank you," said Mark. "What's our status?"

"Mr. Mahuk says the mapping engines will be fully operational within the next forty-eight hours."

"Good." Mark looked at Kirsten. "That should give me time to sell the house on Nantucket."

"I still can't believe you're giving up that property." She took his hand. "In a way, though, I'm glad. You belong to the stars, not tied to one small island."

Mark nodded and gave Kirsten's hand a squeeze. Natalie looked up from the communication's console. "We're getting a signal from TransGalactic. It's Ms. Meiji."

Kirsten and Mark looked at each other. "She's all right!" Kirsten flashed a smile. "What are our orders?"

"As soon as the ship is repaired, we're to start mapping the Epsilon Eridani and Gamma Eridani sectors. More orders to follow as ships are contacted and assigned," she said.

"I guess we'll be getting in some overtime," said Laura.

"The Cluster played havoc with the jump points." Kirsten sighed. "I'd better start getting the mapping instrumentation on line."

"Lots to do." Mark bent down and kissed Kirsten, then both turned to go into their offices. Before the door closed, Mark turned around and faced Simon. "Oh, Simon, you should know that I've accepted an appointment in the Alpha Coma reserves. So, one week out of every month, I'll need to be away from the ship. Kirsten has already approved the schedule. Do you think you can fill in as captain during my absences?"

Simon's heart raced and his thoughts scattered. After a moment, he collected his thoughts. "Yes, sir, I think I can." He looked down at his feet, grinned, then faced Ellis again. "Thank you, sir."

"Let's get back to work, people. Lots to do." With that, Mark stepped into his office. Simon strode over to the command chair and put his hand on the headrest for a moment. He reflected on the last few weeks and months as he glanced around the command deck. He'd always wanted to command a mapping vessel. He began to think it might happen after all. With a contented sigh, he tucked in his flannel shirt and then sat in the chair.

G'Liat entered the conference room in the government building inside the Rd'dyggian dome on Titan. He savored the moist, cool air, but he still longed to return to his home on Rd'dyggia. He reached out and touched a potted, purple plant, then closed the door and checked the seals. He then pulled out a scanner and checked the air and surfaces for cameras and microphones. Once certain everything was secure, he pushed a button on the table.

A door opened and Teklar, matron of the Titans, stepped through. At first glance, she seemed unprotected against the room's atmosphere, but G'Liat caught a faint shimmer, which indicated a personal force field surrounded her.

G'Liat bowed. "I have done as you asked, M'Lady."

"Very good," she growled. "You found an excellent solution. You not only stopped the Cluster but you have put them in a position to keep the humans occupied indefinitely." She ambled over to a large couch that could accommodate her bulky frame and dropped onto it. "In fact, I think the Cluster will keep everyone busy for a long time. You have assured the Titans of continued dominance. We are most grateful."

G'Liat sat down at the table, steepled his fingers and looked at the matriarch over them. "You say I've assured your dominance, yet your position in the galaxy is weaker than ever. You did nothing overt to stop the Cluster. People wonder why."

She opened her mouth to speak, but G'Liat held his hand up to silence her. "I think you knew that if you did nothing, the Cluster would keep this solar system safe so that humans would always be available to provide data for their quantum computer. If the Cluster succeeded, the humans would be slaves, all your rivals would be eliminated and you would be the dominant creatures in the galaxy. If I succeeded, the Cluster would be transformed, keeping all the galaxy's races occupied. The principal barrier to maintaining your dominance of the galaxy would be political in nature."

Teklar inclined her shaggy head. "Political problems are trivial to us." She pulled herself off the couch, lumbered over to G'Liat and gazed down into the warrior's black eyes with her own. "We will double your payment if you keep this knowledge to yourself."

G'Liat's mustache twitched. "We Rd'dyggians are a pragmatic people. I would be foolish to refuse such a generous offer."

"Very good." She turned to leave.

"I would not underestimate these humans, though," said G'Liat. "Given more time, Ellis would have come up with his own solution to the Cluster problem. Also, the human fleet could have destroyed another Cluster. With time, reinforcements would have arrived. The humans could have won. If they had won that way, they would have been in a position to topple your dominance of the Confederation." He paused and stepped next to the Titan's ear. "They still could."

"Our probes indicate that two Clusters have already reproduced. There are now five. There will soon be more." She turned to face G'Liat. "Thank you for your help, but I think the time has come for you to see to your people's safety." With that, she loped through the door.

G'Liat watched as it closed behind her then turned. She was right. It was time to go home.

About the Author

David Lee Summers lives in Southern New Mexico at the cusp of the western and final frontiers. He's written novels about space pirates, vampire mercenaries, mad scientists in the old west, and astronomer ghosts. He's edited thrilling anthologies of space adventure that imagine what worlds discovered by NASA's Kepler mission might be like. When he's not writing or editing, David explores the universe for real at Kitt Peak National Observatory. To learn more about David or his books visit his website at http://www.davidleesummers.com